Bone Idle

Also by Suzette A. Hill

A Load of Old Bones
Bones in the Belfry

Bone Idle

The Case of the Vicar and the Prancing Pig

Suzette A. Hill

Constable • London

Constable & Robinson Ltd
3 The Lanchesters
162 Fulham Palace Road
London W6 9ER
www.constablerobinson.com

First published in the UK by Constable,
an imprint of Constable & Robinson, 2009

First US edition published by SohoConstable,
an imprint of Soho Press, 2009

Soho Press, Inc.
853 Broadway
New York, NY 10003
www.sohopress.com

A copy of the British Library Cataloguing in Publication
Data is available from the British Library

UK ISBN: 978-1-84529-937-8

US ISBN: 978-1-56947-591-1
US Library of Congress number: 2009007854

Mixed Sources
Product group from well-managed
forests and other controlled sources
www.fsc.org Cert no. SA-COC-1565
© 1996 Forest Stewardship Council

FSC

Printed and bound in the EU

1 3 5 7 9 10 8 6 4 2

To the happy memory of
Sheila Vera Llewellyn

1

The Vicar's Version

When Detective Sergeant Sidney Samson appeared on my doorstep to announce the reopening of the Elizabeth Fotherington murder enquiry I thought at first that I was hallucinating. And then as he stood there thin and expressionless I began to wonder whether it was not I, but he who was delirious: one of us had to be out of our mind.

But as I stood transfixed on the threshold of my modest vicarage it became quickly apparent that each was seeing and hearing perfectly well. This was no figment, but a stark reality. The worst had at last occurred: they were going to resurrect the whole ghastly business, and this time I really would be for the high jump . . . What you might describe as beginner's luck had surely come to its murky end!

Perhaps the term 'beginner' is a trifle misleading, for it must be said in my own defence that when I dispatched Mrs Fotherington almost eighteen months previously* I had no intention that the deed should be the forerunner of similar events – and nor fortunately has it been. One mistake of that kind is as much as anyone can cope with – or at any rate, as much as the Reverend Francis Oughterard, Canon of Molehill, Surrey, can. The dreadful business (not to mention its aftermath, the picture theft affair**) had put

* See *A Load of Old Bones*
** See *Bones in the Belfry*

me under a considerable strain; and to have it now suddenly disinterred – the enquiry not the corpse – was a blow I felt I could barely survive.

However, the survival instinct being the force that it is, I pushed the dog out of the way, took a deep breath, and smiling bravely invited the wretched Samson in for a cup of tea.

I must explain that Samson is the junior and surlier half of Detective Inspector Gilbert March, a man known less for his perspicacity than for his plodding and genial obstinacy. His sidekick is less plodding, more obstinate, and largely uncongenial. The pinched features, thin frame and pale darting eyes give him the air of a peevish whippet, and while normally in the shadow of March, his watchful presence is invariably an irritant – and at times a fear.

Such a time was this – as I ushered him in, settled him on the sofa, and with frozen marrow waited in the kitchen for the kettle to boil. I stood there trying to work out what on earth had gone *wrong*. What had happened to rekindle their interest? What matters had been overlooked, found, said, to resurrect the whole thing again? *Why* were they not content to leave the blame with dead Robert Willy, the flasher in the woods? He had been a most fortunate scapegoat, and at the time I had marvelled at how just occasionally fate deals a winning card. But then, as I might have known, such luck is invariably treacherous . . .

Thus, armed with chocolate cake and a blank mind, I returned to the study to face The Whippet. With March absent he had taken the liberty of rolling one of his own scraggy cigarettes – but, seeing the cake, seemed to have second thoughts; and putting the weed back in the tin helped himself to the larger of the proffered slices. Typical.

I watched irritably as he busied himself with what was to have been my after-supper treat; and then, clearing my throat, said in mild tones, 'So what makes the police think the case should be reinvestigated? I was rather under the impression that it was all cut and dried.'

'Impressions mislead,' he said woodenly, scooping up the globules of chocolate icing and licking his fingers, 'and things are rarely cut and dried.'

He was right there, I acknowledged bitterly, and recalled my sister Primrose's voice saying: 'Of course, they'll never drop that case, you know. They never do, not fully . . . You mark my words, it won't be the end of it.' Evidently not.

'No . . . no, I suppose they aren't,' I agreed vaguely. 'But, er, has there been anything in particular that's started things up? Fresh evidence or something?' I held my breath and tried to look unconcerned.

'Slowcome.'

'What?'

'Slowcome,' he repeated, 'of the Yard. The new super-intendent, he's on our tail. Thinks we're too sleepy down here. *Complacent* was the word he used.' And whippet-like he twitched his nose in distaste.

'Ah, one of those new brooms,' I said sympathetically, lighting a cigarette. 'They can be a bit of a pain!'

'Yes,' he replied slowly, 'they can.' And then as a seeming afterthought he added, 'Though in this particular case I think he's got something.'

'But surely you were satisfied it was that flashing tramp, Willy!' I exclaimed.

'Mr March was,' he said, 'but *I* never thought things quite added up. Not quite . . . if you get my meaning.' And he shot a sideways look at me, almost smiling.

I was so used to Samson's sneers that a smile, even an incipient one, immediately struck terror and I almost upset the teapot. However, as a diversionary tactic I produced my cigarette case, and with cringing grace offered him a Craven 'A'. He was about to take it, when Maurice made one of his sudden sorties through the open window, and with flying leap settled himself neatly at Samson's feet.

'Cor! Not that cat again!' the detective exclaimed, getting up hastily and shoving the cigarette behind his ear. 'Bloomin' hazard!'

3

I could understand his response, for a year earlier when he and March were visiting the vicarage pursuing their 'routine enquiries', Samson had become embroiled in one of the more blood-curdling disputes between the cat and my dog Bouncer – a skirmish which had left us all (except the contestants) in a state of quivering shock. Evidently the memory still lingered.

'He's all right really,' I lied, 'just gets a little testy now and again.'

'Should think he does!' muttered Samson, edging towards the door.

I was relieved that he was going, but at the same time avid to know more about the fresh development. 'So, uhm, you'll be restarting things again, will you? Of course, if I can be of any use . . .'

'Oh yes,' he replied quickly, 'you'll be of use, sir. We shall have to interview all those we saw before – to see if anything else emerges. It's just that, since I was passing, I thought you might like to hear about it first – she being one of your parishioners and you having been a close friend of hers. Sort of put you in the picture.'

'Most thoughtful,' I said warmly (inwardly recoiling at the use of the term 'close'), 'and, er, give my regards to Inspector March.'

'Will do that, sir. I daresay he'll be glad to see you again – and quite soon too, I shouldn't wonder.' And taking the cigarette from behind his ear and fumbling for a match, he sloped off down the path.

I returned to the study, consumed the last crumbs of the cake, and stared bleakly out of the window. So much for my holiday plans!

Readers having access to the previous jottings will recall that, exhausted by the rigours of dealing with my aide and bane Nicholas Ingaza (on whose behalf I had been forced to store a couple of stolen paintings), I had been about to arrange a brief visit to the island of Lindisfarne. This little jaunt was intended to restore lost energies – easily mislaid, I fear – and fortify me against further calamity. Unfortunately, it would seem the calamity had anticipated this hope and I was now back at square one, terrified and tense.

I say of Nicholas that he was my aide because, although wholly ignorant of the exact nature of my crime, he had been helpful in corroborating a yarn I had spun the police about a pair of incriminating binoculars. But Nicholas is one of those people who, however useful, will always remain a natural irritant. Favours that he may be minded to confer will require payment in full – if not excess. Forcing me into the role of receiver for his ill-gotten plunder had been in his view a fair exchange for, as he put it, 'keeping an old chum out of hot water'. In fact I had never been his chum, merely his contemporary at St Bede's theological college (from which, for soliciting in a London Turkish bath, he had been booted out), but fate and my ghastly blunder had somehow thrown us once more together. At a time of maximum danger Nicholas Ingaza's support had been vital, but in terms of subsequent angst and trouble it had certainly cost me. Thus just when I was beginning to feel moderately free from his anarchic presence, and hopeful that the ghost of Elizabeth Fotherington was all but laid, the arrival of police officer Sidney Samson on my doorstep once more frustrated that long-sought peace and quiet.

Indeed, it was the need for peace and quiet which had necessitated Elizabeth's disposal in the first place. Had she been less insistent in her garrulous and arch pursuit I assume she would be alive today, and Foxford Wood no longer the place of dread it has come to be. But as it is, I can rarely go near its precincts without hearing the gush of those interminable tones and their febrile inanities. Nor do I forget the fluttering of the wood pigeons, the bluebells, the far-off rasp of the roebuck, and the soporific drone of the aircraft as it circled high in the sky above the tall and innocent trees ... while far below, down in that dense wood, my nerve finally and fatally snapped.

I continued to sit in the study for a good hour after Samson's departure – fretting, brooding, reliving the past and dreading the future. The cat, having conveniently unsettled my visitor, had disappeared again. But Bouncer wandered in, burped loudly, and proceeded to dance around in preparation for his evening walk. At least that stirred me. So collecting ball and lead, and banishing other thoughts, we set off briskly to check the church and sniff the evening air.

2

The Cat's Memoir

The moment I saw that specimen coming up the garden path I knew that something was amiss – or at any rate, more amiss than usual. (Life with the vicar, or *canon* as we are now obliged to call him, is rarely free from disturbance.) Our master has long had an aversion to Samson, which I am inclined to share; and of the two 'rozzers' – to use Bouncer's term – the emaciated one is certainly the more dangerous. Thus curious to know what was afoot, I established myself on the ledge outside the study window and gave ear to the conversation within.

Much of this seemed to be taken up with the consumption of chocolate cake, but to my dismay there was also talk about the reopening of the Fotherington murder case. I could see that the vicar was in agitated mode, and felt it appropriate that I should make my presence felt. So, with a well-judged leap, I projected myself through the open window and landed within inches of the visitor's feet. This had the desired effect: the weedy one jumped from the chair and announced his imminent departure. F.O. (as it is convenient to call the vicar) affected disappointment, but it was apparent to all and sundry – well, to me actually – that he was only too glad to be rid of his guest; and alone once more, he sank white-faced into the usual haze of smoke and lethargy.

I returned to the garden to cogitate beneath the holly bush. As I crouched there Bouncer ambled by, and I called him over and described what I had heard.

'And so how is he going to get out of this one?' I asked.

'God knows,' the dog replied.

Returning from my afternoon stroll a few hours later, I was just passing the tool shed below F.O.'s bedroom window, when my pawsteps were arrested by the most unsavoury noise coming from within: what you might call a mélange of prolonged belches and strangulated wails. A distasteful sound but not without interest, and for half a minute or so I listened intently. Eventually it ceased, and the perpetrator – Bouncer naturally – emerged into the sunlight wagging his tail.

'How do you do that?' I enquired. 'And why?'

'Oh, it's something we dogs do from time to time,' he replied airily. 'Cats don't have the skill for it.'

'I should hope not,' I retorted, 'it is far from pleasant!'

'Oh well, *shark cat arse on glue* – that's Frog-speak, you know, for "each to his own".'

Ignoring both ignorance and insult, I stared at him coldly, pointing out that there was nevertheless a hierarchy in such matters and that my *goût* was considerably better than his.

'If you say so,' he said, grinning amiably.

I paused, and then asked again what had prompted the performance.

He became earnest, solemn even, and replied in lowered tones: 'Mark of respect. Sort of fellow feeling for the vicar – just to show him that we're on his side in this new mess he's got himself into.'

'Hardly a *new* mess,' I exclaimed. 'It's the same one come back with a vengeance and we are all in dire jeopardy!' And not wishing to be outdone by Bouncer, I too braced my lungs and embarked on a series of exquisite caterwaulings. The dog joined in and together we produced a fine and harmonious lamentation in support of our master. Unfortunately this was cut short by the subject of our commiseration throwing open the window and hurling down abuse and a bucket of water. It just goes to show that humans, particularly the clerical sort, have even less good taste than their canine companions.

An hour passed, and I was just carefully monitoring the movements of a fat spider in the grass when Bouncer reappeared, snuffled about aimlessly and then started to scratch. He was obviously at a loose end and eager to talk. But, reluctant to leave the spider, I pretended not to notice . . .

'Oh rapture!' the dog suddenly barked.

I recoiled, startled. '*What* did you say?'

'Rapture . . . Oh,' he repeated.

'What's that supposed to mean?'

'Don't you know, Maurice? I thought you knew *thousands* of words!'

'Of course I do,' I replied irritably. 'Thousands. But why are *you* saying it?'

'Just thinking out loud. It's what she used to say.'

'Who used to say?'

'Her – your dead mistress, old Fotherington.'

'I don't recall her saying that – certainly not to me.'

'Well, no. I mean, she wouldn't say it to you, would she, Maurice?'

'I can't think why not!'

'I can,' he replied darkly.

I twitched my tail impatiently. 'You're talking nonsense as usual. And in any case, you don't really know what the word means.'

'Oh yes I do,' he said doggedly. 'It's what I feel when I've got a marrow bone all to myself and you and F.O. are out of the house and there's no one there to interfere!'

I said nothing but thought the more. Obviously it was the Irish setter's influence again: all that Hibernian blague was making Bouncer get even more above himself than usual. I was about to begin one of my sulks, when there was a sudden explosion of mirth and he roared, 'Anyway, Maurice, bet she didn't say "rapture" in Foxford Wood when F.O. was up to his tricks – not with that scarf round her gullet!'

For a moment I watched the ensuing antics as he rolled about helplessly, waving those outlandish paws in the air. And then, unable to retain my normal sangfroid, I too lapsed into unseemly jollity, and the garden was rent with barks and yowls.

An ineffectual oath of protest came from the study window followed by a carpet slipper, but we side-stepped it neatly, and I set off with sprightly foot to the graveyard refreshed and invigorated. The dog does have his occasional use.

3

The Dog's Diary

Phew! It's all blowing up again. And the vicar is in a right palaver with himself! Been effing and blinding and crunching those humbugs all day long. Jaws must have started to ache, I shouldn't wonder. I know about that from my bones: if you go on gnawing too long they seize up and it can take a bit of time to get them working again. So he'd better watch out! Mind you, I knew something was in the wind when he started singing 'All Things Bright and Beautiful' during our walk round the church the other night. He always picks that one when he's in one of his stews – calms him down, I suppose.

But I like it best when he plays the piano, that's really good – though Maurice doesn't like it. But then there are a lot of things the cat doesn't like: water, church bells (says they mangle his nerves), my bones, my basket, my blanket, the Veasey sisters up the road (ever since they gave him a seeing-to for putting the frighteners on their goldfish), loud bangs, horses, bicycles (says they're useless for sitting on to get warm, unlike car bonnets), my friend O'Shaughnessy the setter (thinks he's uncouth), most other cats – especially tabbies (common), sour milk, cat food – refuses anything out of a tin, the newspaper boy, the newspaper girl, my biscuit Bonios . . . oh and hundreds of other things which I can't remember. He's what you might call picky. But I suppose that's what cats are; they can't help it and you get used to it – though *some* are pickier than others! But I don't mind really, and sometimes he can be quite fun – in a cattish sort of way of course – and most of the time we get on pretty well. And when we don't I either go down to my crypt for a snooze and a listen to the ghosts, or we have a nice noisy scrap which we both like. So that's all right.

Still, what isn't all right is poor old F.O. The policeman Samson, the puny one, has really messed things up again and I'm worried that this time the vicar's luck will run out – and then we shall all be in the cart. And apart from anything else, I shan't get my GRUB! I'll be skinny like Maurice and waste away. Maybe I should start stocking up in case of a siege – perhaps make a midnight raid on Mavis Briggs's dustbin . . . or on second thoughts, perhaps not. She's got a mind like a hamster and eats like one too: the last time I had a nose round there were only mangy lettuce leaves – no good for a growing fellow like me. Have to think of somewhere else. I'll ask Maurice, he's bound to have an opinion.

But I'm feeling sleepy now. Could do with a lie-down in my basket next to the boiler in the kitchen, but F.O.'s in there cooking . . . well, if you call hammering away at tins and throwing soup and jelly all over the shop 'cooking'. So maybe I'll just slip down to the crypt instead and give the spiders a nasty turn. They won't like that but I will. Can't let them have it all their own way!

4

The Vicar's Version

The day after Samson's visit I had to go into Guildford to negotiate terms with the parish magazine's new printer. I am not very good at negotiating, and although I think I managed a fair deal, I had found the whole process wearying. The Angel and its cream cakes beckoned, and I spent a restful hour ensconced on one of the capacious leather sofas with newspapers and coffee éclairs. However, all good things come to an end, and reluctantly I paid the bill and made a move.

Emerging from the hotel, I encountered Theodore Pick, rector of St Hilda's in the neighbouring parish. He was meandering along draped in his usual pall of gloom, but greeted me cheerfully enough and offered congratulations on my recent appointment as canon.

'Well, yes, it did come as rather a surprise,' I acknowledged, 'and of course it's non-stipendiary so it doesn't exactly swell the coffers. Still, at least that means they won't foist further jobs on me. Bit of a sinecure really: modest status without responsibility!' And I gave a jovial laugh.

'Huh,' he observed darkly, 'they'll find something for you. They always do.' (Typical of Pick, I thought, casts a cloud over everything!) 'Besides,' he added, 'you'll still be required to deliver the annual Canonical Address at the cathedral in front of the Lord Lieutenant and his satellites, and there's bound to be the usual three-line whip for us all to attend.'

'Oh, that!' I exclaimed blithely. 'That's months away yet . . .'

'Ah,' he replied, 'but it will hang over you, you'll see: finding a theme, researching the stuff, polishing your delivery. It's a big occasion – not just a common or garden sermon, you know. Nearly drove Dewlap to a breakdown the first time he did his. But daresay you'll survive . . . Still, must be on my way now. Nice talking to you, Oughterard. Always a tonic!' And so saying, he loped off in the direction of the undertakers.

I stared after him irritably. Trust Pick to enliven things! And then I thought bitterly that if surviving the lecture were the only thing I had to worry about I should be a happy man. There were other matters pending of a rather more crucial nature . . . A police car glided by and I scuttled into a shop doorway like a startled rabbit.

Back in the refuge of the vicarage, I first sought solace at the piano and then ease with a gin on the sofa. Maurice and Bouncer were together in front of the fire, the one toying with his woollen mouse, the other sprawled on the carpet, chin resting on the beloved rubber ring. He seemed unusually still and I wondered what was going on behind the fronds of fringe and between those shaggy ears.

However, the cerebral processes of my dog were soon displaced by other thoughts. How, for example, should I prepare myself for the inevitable visit from March and Samson? Their previous investigations had been irksome enough: this time it would be far worse and I quailed at the prospect. How would they proceed? What line would they take? Which aspects of my story would they require 'clarifying'? I brooded.

Eventually I reluctantly concluded that I should have to contact Nicholas Ingaza. The police were bound to rake up the matter of the binoculars, and it was imperative that my corroborator stuck to his story: any deviation in that area would be pounced upon immediately. But Nicholas's reliability was problematic and he would need to be primed and courted. Gloomily I went to the telephone and dialled.

On the few occasions that I had previously rung Nicholas I had been greeted by the rasping tones of his cockney companion Eric, and in preparation for the blast I positioned the receiver accordingly, i.e. a few inches away from my ear. But rather to my surprise it was Nicholas himself who answered, and I adjusted the phone to catch the faint tones of his nasal drawl.

'What brings you to the blower, dear boy? Changed your mind about coming down to Brighton? Lindisfarne lost its charm to the lure of the bright lights?'

'Er, no, not really,' I muttered. 'It's to do with that little matter of last year . . . the, er, binoculars . . .'

There was a pause. 'Oh yes?'

'Yes. You see, for some peculiar reason the police are raking things up again about that unfortunate murder case, and there's a remote possibility that they might want to interview me again – along with everyone else of course,' I added hastily.

'Of course.'

'So I thought I'd just, uhm . . .'

'Get me to go over my story with you? To ensure no loose ends are hanging about, that sort of thing?' He sounded smoothly affable, but long experience of Ingaza told me that this was not necessarily a comfort.

'Yes, that's it . . . well, more or less. I mean, you know how obsessive the police can get about things and then go off at absurd tangents. Ridiculous really!'

'I remember,' he said drily.

Yes, he would remember. Doing time for the Jermyn Street Turkish bath episode would have honed his memory to perfection – just as my unfortunate incident in Foxford Wood had filed mine . . .

15

I cleared my throat. 'So perhaps it might be an idea if you were to come up here again – stay the night of course, like last time – and we could sort of go over things. I'll get some drink in,' I added enticingly.

'Fine by me, old chap. But I take it this time your Mavis friend won't be paying us a visit – don't think my nerves could stand a second performance!'

I winced at the recollection. Mavis Briggs – every parish's genteel nightmare – had indeed paid us a visit; and under the impression that Ingaza was a passing archdeacon (as recounted in my previous volume), and despite assuring us that she was a stranger to the grape, had proceeded to imbibe the greater part of Nicholas's best brandy at the rate of knots. In their sedate way the results had been spectacular, and clearly still rankled with the owner of the lost cognac.

Thus I assured him that no such interruption was likely, and that in any case the said lady was currently laid up with a bad leg. (Mavis is frequently laid up with something or other, but the leg business seemed more protracted than usual and I could thus speak with confidence.)

There was a gap in the parish diary; and grasping this lull in my schedule, I hastily pencilled in his arrival for two days hence. This was a relief, for although Ingaza's proximity is a dubious pleasure, it at least meant that I could fully rehearse him for the inevitable enquiries. Second time around, precision was vital!

He arrived a little before six o'clock, his svelte frame clad in its usual passé chalk-stripe, and right hand sporting an even flashier signet ring than usual. I was glad to note that this time the vintage Citroën was parked neatly at the kerb and not, as on the previous visit, spreadeagled halfway across the pavement impeding everyone – not least Mavis Briggs whose ineffectual efforts to get round it had lent additional woe to an already fraught evening.

The preliminaries over and his things deposited in the spare room, my guest returned downstairs and I offered him whisky. At first neither of us said a word about the purpose of his visit, and we talked in generalities – his journey up from Brighton, runners for the National, the weather and the price of coal. Gradually, however, as the whisky did its work, the mood relaxed and Nicholas embarked on a series of anecdotes involving what I took to be the more legitimate end of his art-dealing business. He tactfully made no mention of the recent Spendler fiasco from which I was still smarting,* and I was soothed and amused by some of his more bizarre (and probably embroidered) tales. He had always been a diverting raconteur, and glancing at the clock I was surprised to see how late it was getting.

'Goodness, past supper time and I haven't even opened the wine!'

I went into the kitchen, hastily heated up the stew and tried to draw the cork from the Fleurie. It was not what you would call a deft movement, but after much wrenching and gouging I finally managed to pull it out, and put the bottle on the table. Preoccupied with the cork I hadn't noticed Nicholas enter, and when I looked up he was lounging in the doorway, whisky in hand and grinning sardonically.

'Cack-handed as ever, Francis! Don't know how you manage to play the piano so well. One of life's little mysteries, I suppose . . . And talking of which, when are you going to tell me more about this police business? It all strikes me as pretty fishy – in fact it's been fishy right from the start when you asked me to perjure myself over those field glasses. Never could really grasp what was going on.' And taking a chair at the table he reached for the bottle and poured himself a liberal glass.

'Nothing fishy at all,' I protested, doling out the stew and mash. 'I told you at the time it was all just a stupid misunderstanding. And besides, I did *not* ask you to

* See *Bones in the Belfry*

17

perjure yourself, merely to support me when the police started their absurd snoopings.'

'And now they're at it again and you're shit scared.'

'I am *not* sh . . . I am not scared! Merely anxious to avoid further involvement in this ridiculous affair. I have a parish to run and it wouldn't look good should it ever be thought that the newly promoted canon was among the key witnesses in a murder case, let alone on the list of possible suspects! Unfair to the Church, you know.'

'Oh, absolutely,' he agreed solemnly.

I poured us both some more wine, heaped up his plate, and began to recapitulate the details of the binoculars and his particular part in the tale.

When I had finished, he said, 'Oh, don't you worry, dear boy, I shan't mess up *my* version. Went very smoothly last time, wouldn't you say? You can always rely on Old Nick!'

I was not exactly reassured, but those in tight corners must perforce trust what is on offer. So after a final run-through of the 'script', we finished supper, and at Nicholas's behest opened another bottle (which I had been foolishly hoping to keep for a later occasion). We took it with us into the sitting room where we smoked his Sobranies and reminisced a little about St Bede's. And then feeling suddenly expansive, I treated him to a brief display of my *un*cack-handed piano playing: a bit of Ellington, some blues, a dash of Ivor Novello – and remembering his particular penchant at St Bede's, concluded with Coward's 'Mad About the Boy'.

'Just occasionally, Francis, you can deliver the goods,' he murmured appreciatively. And sleeking his hair in that characteristic way, he gave what I can only describe as a wistful smirk.

And then it happened: the drink, I suppose – we had consumed quantities – and of course I had been under a dreadful strain for months, and in the end it must have taken its toll.

18

Anyway, I told him. The whole damn lot. I sat there smoking my head off and staring at the ceiling while the words just came pouring out. I didn't seem able to stop them . . . funny really. On and on I went, every detail and mannerism: her voice, her absurdities, that awful ruthless sweetness, the deluge of invitations and coy innuendoes, the gurgling laugh and simpering affectation – and above all the remorseless, inescapable intrusion of privacy. I told him about my walk in the woods and the blissful solitude, the sense of sanctuary and blessed repose . . . the silence, the rabbits hopping among the bluebells, the soft cooing of the wood pigeon, and the scent of moss. And then *her* – suddenly rearing up out of God knows where, clutching my arm, giggling, jabbering, braying; putting the doves to flight, scattering the rabbits . . . And then I told him everything else.

The moment the words ceased I was paralysed with shock, aghast at what had been said. The drink, which must have prompted my outburst, had entirely evaporated and I was suddenly appallingly sober.

There was a long silence, while I continued to stare fixedly at the ceiling. And then he said thoughtfully, 'Bit rash of you, if you don't mind my saying. I mean, a pretty wild gamble, if you ask me. Didn't think, I suppose.' He sighed.

'No,' I agreed faintly, 'I don't suppose I did – '

'That's your trouble,' he cut in severely, 'always was. I remember watching you play chess at St Bede's. Hadn't a clue how to cope! Painful to behold!' And he winced as if in recollection. 'No forward planning, that's your problem. Far too easily rattled. It was just the same with those paintings – a right pig's ear you made of it all!'

'I'm sorry,' I said meekly, still too stunned by what had been revealed to think of anything more pertinent.

'Oh, don't apologize!' he exclaimed magnanimously. 'Daresay you've got rather more on your mind than the paintings fiasco – especially now that they've reopened the case. Quite a little facer, that one!'

'Yes, quite,' I replied, beginning to feel very tired.

19

'Still, shouldn't worry too much. It'll probably be all right in the end – you never know what's round the corner!'

'I know exactly what is round the corner,' I cried, the numbness fading, 'Albert Pierrepoint and his noose!'

'Shouldn't bank on it, old cock. Many a slip 'twixt rope and neck etc., etc.'

'For Christ's sake, Nicholas, stop being so sodding cheerful! I'm in one hell of a mess and all you can do is spout gross platitudes. Why are you taking it so lightly!'

'*Because*, Francis,' he enunciated slowly, 'one of us needs to keep a cool head and it clearly won't be you. Really, dear boy – haven't heard such language since I last took Aunt Lil to the dog track at Kemp Town. Raised the roof, she did, and now you're at it as well. *Most* unseemly for a parson!' And he gave one of his nasal titters.

'So's murder,' I muttered.

He was silent for a moment, and then pouring himself the dregs of the wine said musingly, 'Yes, you do rather surprise me there. Would never have thought you had it in you . . . after all, anyone less like an assassin it would be hard to imagine. Better watch my back, hadn't I!' And he gave a crack of laughter.

I was hardly able to share his mirth; and in any case, thought the remark in rather poor taste but didn't like to say so, being relieved that he hadn't made a drama of it all. There was enough drama as it was without Ingaza adding his pennyworth.

'Anyway,' he continued blandly, 'I'm for bed. It's been a most interesting day, Francis, *most* interesting. In fact,' he added, 'I haven't had such an interesting day for a long, long time.' With a mocking grin he got up from the chair and moved towards the door where he paused and, giving a slow wink, drawled, 'Well, well, what d'you know! What *do* you know!' And so saying he disappeared up the stairs.

It was a dreadful night. I slept for perhaps twenty minutes, and for the rest of the time tossed from back to front and left to right, trying vainly to achieve some repose, some oblivion. Neither was forthcoming and I replayed endlessly the words of that incontinent confession. What on earth had possessed me to pour it out like that, babbling into Ingaza's sharp and predatory ears? For eighteen months I had nursed the secret: kept it safe and hidden, hugged to my chest, securely zipped and fastened. And now, unprompted, uncued, in a matter of a mere ten minutes, I had divulged the whole damn lot. And of all people, to Nicholas Ingaza! What idiocy, what ineptitude! And echoing down the years I could hear my father's scathing tones as yet again I missed a trick at the family card table – 'Buffoon, boy, buffoon!'

The buffoon got out of bed, lit a cigarette, and standing at the open window gazed across at the churchyard's dark and looming trees. One thing was a blessing at any rate: at least she wasn't buried out there! St Elspeth's at Guildford had had that privilege; and for a brief moment I gave thanks for the ghastly daughter, Violet Pond, who, having a rooted dislike of Molehill, had been so insistent that her mother's remains be interred in the adjacent parish.

The next morning breakfast began neutrally. It ended less so. Surprisingly, given the previous night's intake of alcohol, neither of us had a hangover; and my guest talked fulsomely of how well he had slept (unlike the host), the comfort of the bed, and the pleasures of waking to the sound of birdsong. I was a little sceptical of that last comment, feeling that Ingaza's sensibilities, such as they were, were unlikely to be stirred by the fluting of birds. Presumably he was trying to be tactful after my intemperate revelation. I was grateful for that, and thus relieved busied myself with boiling the eggs while he parleyed with the cat and then applied himself to the coffee and newspapers.

Eventually, however, he said mildly, 'I've been giving some thought to your little problem. I sympathize – must be quite tricky for you.'

'You can say that again,' I replied woodenly.

'Yes, quite tricky . . . but then of course, given the circumstances, it *could* be quite tricky for me too. Not really sure what the penalty is for supplying a false alibi, or at least, misleading Her Majesty's law enforcers . . . and of course, I'm not *mad* about having those charmers sniffing at my door again. Not good for business, you might say!' He spoke lightly but pointedly, and I felt sick at heart.

'No, no, of course not,' I mumbled. 'Must have been crazy to try to involve you, very thoughtless. Panic, I suppose. Forget all about it – and if they come back to you about those binoculars, just tell them that I had told you a pack of lies and you were confused.'

'Oh, good Lord, no!' he replied. 'I'm not trying to pull out if that's what you're thinking. Not at all – always eager to help an old mate, even one as woolly as you . . . it's just that it could be rather *complex*, not entirely easy, you know. A mite troublesome, if you see what I mean.' And he tapped with delicate precision on the shell of his egg.

I somehow doubted the professed eagerness to help and was irritated by the term 'old mate' (we had never been close at St Bede's, he being two years ahead of me and moving in realms far different from my humdrum sphere). I was also somewhat stung by his reference to my 'woolliness'. Still, it was certainly a relief to hear that he hadn't changed his mind about the corroboration; and expressing awkward thanks I also – but with rather less dexterity – attended to my egg.

There was silence as we reabsorbed ourselves in the newspapers – or at least he did, my own mind being far too tense to do other than merely gaze at the print. The night's insomnia coupled with the shock of my confession was already taking its toll, and glad though I was to have Ingaza's assurance of help, I was beginning to feel more than tired and wished that he would go. But he showed no signs of wanting to, being fully engrossed in his reading and evidently intent on a lengthy breakfast . . .

'Ever heard of the Pontoon Idol?' he suddenly asked. I shook my head.

'No, thought you probably hadn't. Things artistic not up your street really, are they?'

'If you mean that I hadn't heard of those crass Spendler paintings that you tried to palm off on me, you're quite right. A load of rubbish they were!'

'Ah, but *not* this Pontoon Idol – different class of goods altogether, the real McCoy you might say.'

'Well, what about it?' I asked wearily. 'And anyway, what is it?'

'The Pontoon Idol is one of the world's most sought-after *objets curieux* and there are a number of fakes and copies. However, I happen to know who has got the original . . . except that *he* doesn't.'

'You mean doesn't know that he has the genuine article, thinks it's some sort of imitation?'

'Exactly, Francis. The speed of your deduction delights me!'

I scowled, and asked him what was so special about the thing.

'Comes from Poona. It's a bone effigy of a rampant pig sporting emerald eyes and a bejewelled tail.'

'A rampant pig!' I exclaimed. 'Who on earth would want that sort of thing? Sounds hideous!'

'That's as may be, but there are those who would give their eye-teeth to get their hands on it. The gems themselves aren't all that important – it's the origin and history which collectors find fascinating.'

'Oh yes?' I replied drily.

'Yes. You see, at the end of the eighteenth century, 1797 to be exact, it fell into the hands of Sir Royston Beano –'

'The explorer, you mean?'

23

'That's it. He was being entertained at cards in the Viceregal Lodge in Delhi – some sort of house party with a number of distinguished guests, European largely, but also a number of high-ranking Indians including an irksome chap called Hyder Ali, a dabbler in rare tribal artefacts. His wife was with him, a rather beautiful girl by all accounts. Apparently Beano was very smitten with the lady but found Ali less entrancing – in fact according to the unpublished diaries he was a "boor of the first water", and I seem to recall that the term "tiresome toad" was also used . . . Anyway, in the course of the evening a number of the guests, including the begum, were mad keen to play a few rounds of pontoon, and as Beano had a passion for both the game and the girl he was only too keen to participate. Ali wasn't good at cards – wasn't good at anything according to Beano, except getting in the way – and he elected to leave early, directing the wife to be escorted home by coach and chaperones once the gaming had finished.

'After he left a good time was had by all – except that in the course of it the beautiful wife lost very heavily to Beano, and unbeknown to her husband was already up to her neck in gambling debts. So she found herself in the embarrassing position of having to offer yet another IOU – and one which she could not possibly honour.'

He paused for a moment, smiled, and then went on: 'Now, you might think that there was an obvious solution to her problem and that the debt could have been settled in the age-old way. But although Beano was a philanderer he was not a cad, and apparently it was always a point of honour with him never to press home an unfair advantage on the opposite sex. So instead of requesting the lady's presence in his bed, he said he would cancel the debt if she were to give him some little memento of the evening's events – a memento whose charm should be enhanced by being both rare and obtained at some small risk to herself.

'The begum, evidently a gal of sporting spirit, rose to the challenge; and two days later sent Beano the most prized object of her husband's special curio collection, i.e. the prancing pig from Poona. It was carved from a tiger's femur by some obscure early tribe, and the only one of its kind. Beano was delighted, and it's said that in an access of further gallantry he paid the donor a nice little packet to cover the rest of her gambling dues. But according to several accounts it was less the pig itself that pleased Beano, than the fact that it had been lifted from under Hyder Ali's self-satisfied nose by his own wife: a sort of substitute for cuckoldry without the attendant risk.' Nicholas stretched out his arm for the marmalade, buttered more toast, and giggled.

'But surely,' I said, 'if it was such a primitive piece of carving it wouldn't be decorated with jewels.'

'Of course not. It was Beano who had those added, and then back in England gave it to his own good lady as some sort of anniversary present.'

'So what happened to it? And in any case, what made it look so different from the later fakes?'

'They had a row and she threw it at him.'

'Well, that doesn't tell me anything!'

'Oh, yes it does. You see, he ducked and it hit the fender. When they picked it up one of the emeralds had fallen out and they found the tiniest nick on its underside, the merest blemish but it's there all right, and he mentions it briefly in one of the diaries – something to the effect of: "Gadzooks! Thanks to Lucinda's temper I've had to have the creature's right eye reset, but otherwise none the worse except for a snip under the stern. No matter, I'll have Beeston put that right. What a harpy the girl is!"'

'Who's Beeston?'

'Beeston & Littlejohn. They were a firm of silversmiths in the City; but as a sideline the senior partner used to do all sorts of renovation work and was much in demand. Beano obviously had him smooth the mark out, but if you look really hard and run your thumbnail over the surface you can still detect the merest trace.'

'So I take it that you've seen this thing recently?'

'About a year ago, give or take.'

'And you think the owner has no idea what he's got?'

'From what he was saying, hasn't a clue. He's obviously very attached to the thing but seems to assume it's just a pleasing Victorian copy.'

'Why didn't you enlighten him?'

Nicholas gazed at me in wonder. '*Enlighten* him, dear boy? Whatever for?'

'Well . . . might have made his day I suppose – learning that he'd got the real thing which everyone else is clamouring for.'

'My dear Francis, it is not exactly *his* day that I am interested in.' And he slowly raised his eyes to the ceiling and sighed.

I cleared my throat and lit a cigarette, not quite grasping the implication but sensing something dubious. However, he made no further comment and went on munching his toast.

After a while I said curiously, 'So, where did you see it then? I mean . . . who exactly is this lucky owner?'

He crumpled his napkin, and then pushing back his chair replied casually, 'Blenkinsop's brother.'

I gaped. 'You don't mean *Archdeacon* Blenkinsop, here in Guildford – surely not! Didn't even know he'd got a brother, certainly never mentions him!'

'From what I remember of the archdeacon, he never mentions anyone except himself. Besides, I doubt whether they've much in common: brother far too arty-farty for old Vernon's prosaic liking.' And he smiled wryly, adding, 'But they share one thing all right – both windbags. I met a sister years ago – crashing bore she was too! Runs in the family, I imagine.'

'So where does he live, this other Blenkinsop? Your neck of the woods, Brighton?'

'No, London. Behind Wigmore Street – just off Manchester Square. *Very* salubrious. Wouldn't mind having a little pad there myself one day, a handy pied-à-terre tucked away in some secluded nook and far from the hurly-burly of the south coast . . . just the job.' He looked thoughtful. And then leaning across the table, he said quietly, 'In fact, Francis, that's where you come in.'

'Me!' I exclaimed. 'What do you mean? How on earth do I "come in"? Don't know what you're talking about!'

'Well, you're a colleague of the archdeacon, you know him. As did I once, of course – Oxford before the war. He was on the periphery of Clinker's mob. But that was ages ago, and in any case, ever since that little contretemps at St Bede's I've never been exactly *persona grata* with our clerical brethren.' He gave a mocking smile.

I said nothing. And then with tightening throat, I asked slowly, 'But how does my being a colleague of Vernon Blenkinsop have anything to do with your aspirations to owning a pied-à-terre in Manchester Square?'

'Possibly quite a lot, old chum – if things go right, that is.'

'What things?' I asked suspiciously.

'To do with the pig.'

I splashed the dregs of the now very cold coffee into my cup, took a gulp, and said as distantly as I could: 'Nicholas, I do not know what you have in mind, but whatever it is I can assure you that in no respect do I intend becoming involved with your domestic arrangements, let alone with that rampant pig! So please put any such ideas out of your head.'

Ignoring both my tone and words, he went on: 'What is in my *mind*, Francis, is that you should persuade Archdeacon Blenkinsop to give you an introduction to his brother – under some pretext or other which we can work out later; gain access to the flat, and whilst there engaging in gay social chit-chat, liberate the pig and substitute a copy. Blenkinsop the younger will continue in blissful ignorance, I can flog said article for a whopping packet, you'll get a neat cut (never let it be said that Old Nick isn't fair) – and we shall all be as happy as sandboys!'

'Like hell we will!' I cried. 'Have you lost your scheming wits? This is preposterous!'

27

'Oh no,' he said smoothly. 'Not preposterous at all – perfectly feasible. Should be quite a simple little operation. Needs attention to the finer details of course, but actually the whole thing could be done in a trice and nobody would be any the wiser – least of all Blenkinsop Minor.'

'It's hardly the logistics that concern me,' I exclaimed angrily. 'It's the principle ... the whole suggestion is disgraceful!'

'Perhaps,' he said sweetly, 'but not quite as disgraceful as murder ...'

I stared helplessly, dumb with fear and outrage. Eventually I muttered something to the effect that I thought it a bit much being subjected to that kind of manipulative blackmail and that I had expected better of him. (I hadn't really, but it sounded suitably pained.)

He was quite unruffled, and observed suavely that in view of the delicacy of my situation and the perilous nature of his own involvement in it, I could hardly begrudge him a little favour. Deep down I acknowledged that he had a point, but instinctually I was furious. However, there was little that I could do, and, having nothing else to say, I weakly offered him some more cold coffee. He accepted.

5

The Cat's Memoir

It was quite obvious that something of moment was afoot. Not long after Samson's visit the vicar made a frantic telephone call to Brighton; the result being that two days later the questionable friend arrived – the Gaza fellow – replete with suitcase and unctuous goodwill. At first F.O. seemed pleased to see him, but by the end of the evening it was apparent that he was working himself up into 'a right lather', as the dog would say. In fact I rather got the impression that the vicar had foolishly divulged details of the murder business – a typical blunder, though I suppose it was only a matter of time!

Thus the following morning, curious to learn what had transpired from the night before, I settled myself discreetly under the kitchen table and lent ear to the proceedings above. At one point the visitor had the grace to address a few words to me. I responded cordially and kept my ears primed. He then embarked on some elaborate tale involving, of all things, a bone pig. Since I have an aversion to both pigs and bones I did not find this especially edifying; but in the interests of intelligence-gathering remained at my post, where listening carefully I was able to grasp the gist of his discourse – and its purpose.

As feared, the Gaza person was intent on persuading F.O. to participate in some madcap scheme which would inevitably line his own pockets but do little for the vicar.

This worried me somewhat as our master is not noted for keeping a cool head in times of crisis – and being under pressure both from the Molehill police and from his visitor could well be regarded as such.

Thus I summoned Bouncer and told him I had been listening in on their breakfast conversation and there was something he ought to know. 'From what I could ascertain,' I said, 'the type from Brighton was launching a plan which would involve F.O. raiding a flat in London and stealing some bone ornament.'

'Likes bones, does he?' asked the dog with interest.

I sighed. 'No, but he likes money, and this bone thing costs a lot, and the Brighton type wants to get his paws on it. Thinks he can use the vicar to do his dirty work.'

'And will he?'

'If he's desperate enough. At the moment there is much huffing and puffing and crunching of humbugs, but I think he is snared so he'll probably have to in the end.'

'Just as long as we're all right.'

'Yes, Bouncer, but that is the whole point – we may not be all right! It is bound to be more than F.O. can cope with, and coming on top of this latest development in the Fotherington affair it could make him crack under the strain.'

'Shall I savage the Brighton type?'

'Certainly not! That would do untold harm to all of us.'

'Just a thought . . . Anyway, whereabouts in London? Any place I know?' he asked with a casual air.

'Of course not,' I laughed, 'you are hardly familiar with the Great Metropolis!' I rather like the sound of that phrase and can trip it neatly off my tongue, but it was wasted on Bouncer.

'The great what?'

'*London*! You do not know it!'

'Yes I do,' he barked truculently.

'All right, name me one place that you know.'

There was a long silence while he chewed his paw. And then bounding to his feet and rushing manically around the room, 'H . . . H . . . HARRODS!' he exploded.

The sound was deafening and it was as well that F.O. was out taking a service. But the dog was right: he did indeed know of that emporium (as detailed in my first memoir), and for some reason it has remained deeply embedded in his memory whence periodically he will pronounce its name with pride and thunder.

'So *now* you can tell me,' he said smugly.

'Manchester Square.'

'Never heard of it!'

I mewed irritably. 'Exactly, that is what –'

'But,' he went on, 'I did know a Manchester terrier once, called Marlene. A bit of all right, she was, if you get my meaning!' And he clicked his tongue – an unpleasant sound that I have heard humans make when they wish to accelerate the speed of their horses.

I regarded him bleakly. 'Trust you to consort with a terrier called Marlene. And in any case, your unsavoury liaisons are hardly the matter in question. What *is* in question is the vicar's sanity and our survival. Kindly stick to the point and listen to what I am saying.'

He lay down and began to snore.

6

The Vicar's Version

Having assured me that he would be in touch before too long to 'discuss strategy', Nicholas departed with a cheery wave and a spluttering exhaust. I stood on the pavement watching as the vintage Citroën wound its way out of sight. The car had always had a faintly sinister air, and now, despite the brightness of the morning, its Reichstag image struck me more forcefully than ever.

I was about to return to the house, but instead sat down on the garden roller (never used and fast rusting), and lighting a cigarette pondered who would destroy me first – the police or Ingaza.

But such speculations were suddenly interrupted by an ear-splitting screech: Mrs Carruthers, Bishop Clinker's tiddlywinks partner. She stood at the front gate wearing her customary grin, hat jauntily angled, and sporting a pair of hoop earrings of even more outlandish proportion than usual. In my current state I was hardly in the mood for visitors, or indeed passers-by. But it could have been worse: Mavis Briggs for example.

The first time I had encountered Mrs Carruthers was when I had been detailed by Clinker to request that she be discreet about his attendance at her weekly tiddlywinks parties. It was, he had explained, a vice to be kept secret at all costs; and it had fallen to me to persuade the lady to secrecy. Apart from having to endure the nightmarish sight of her array of garden gnomes, the visit to her house had been quite diverting – not least for what I had learnt of the bishop's skills on the carpet amidst the plastic counters. It was, however, an episcopal pastime never to be spoken of.

'Hello, dear!' she hooted, opening the gate. 'Long time, no see!'

'Well, actually,' I said, getting up from the roller and moving forward to greet her, 'I did see you in the distance at the bishop's annual tea party but you were rather hemmed in at the time, and there was such a crowd that –'

'Wasn't there just!' she exclaimed. 'Never been to one of those smart church dos before – far too high and mighty for me! But His Nibs wanted me there for some reason – he can be ever so sweet, you know.' (I did not know.) 'Still, it wasn't bad really – quite fun in its way. What my Alfie used to call a good posh and nosh!' And she crowed merrily.

In fact, from what I recalled of the event, the sole source of fun had been the lady herself – hugely enlivening a group of admiring curates, while Clinker's wife, Gladys, cast venomous looks from the other end of the room.

I asked her how she was and if she had won any tiddly-winks contests lately.

'Well, dear, that's just what I was going to tell you! You'll never guess . . . you remember I told you that we thought our Mr Clinker might win the Penge Championship for us?'

I nodded.

'Well, he has! No doubt about it, without him we'd have lost the last two matches and there would have been a draw. But you should have seen him! Saved our bacon, he did, and more!' Further gusts of parrot-like mirth.

'Good gracious!' I exclaimed. 'Didn't know he had it in him. But – er, tell me, when he goes to these things is he incognito?'

'In what, dear?'

33

'For instance, does he wear a false moustache or anything?'

'Well, he doesn't wear his mitre, if that's what you mean. But he does generally arrive in a dark raincoat.'

'Ah yes, that's bound to disguise him,' I observed drily. She looked thoughtful for a moment, and then added, 'And of course he always goes under an *assumed* name.'

'Oh really?' I asked with interest. 'What is it?'

'Canon Oughterard.'

I stared incredulously. '*What!* You mean to say he actually . . . He can't do!'

'Oh yes,' she said firmly. 'Always Oughterard.'

I went on staring, open-mouthed and furious.

She gazed back wide-eyed. And then, if you please, took a compact from her handbag and started to powder her nose!

I was enraged, and just about to expostulate further when I noticed the merest twitch at the corner of her mouth, and the next moment the garden was rent with the calls of joyful cockatoos.

When the laughter finally subsided, she cried, 'Got you there, dear, didn't I? Got you there. Walked straight into it, you did!'

I conceded that indeed I had. And despite the residue of shock, I couldn't help smiling at the sheer audacity of the woman . . . Yes, she was definitely better company than Mavis Briggs.

Comparisons being odious, it was perhaps a suitable penance that later that morning I had the misfortune to bump into Mavis in the High Street. She was drooping along wearing one of her innumerable dirndls and toting an outsize string shopping bag. It dangled limply from her wrist.

'Ah, *Canon*,' she quavered, 'I have been wanting to speak to you for some time – it's about the pipes in the vestry.'

'Oh yes? What about them?'

'Well, Vicar – Canon, I mean –' and she simpered, 'you see, they are gurgling!'

'Yes, well, pipes tend to do that, Mavis.'

She paused. 'But not when the heating is *off.*'

I wasn't sure what to say about that but suggested vaguely that perhaps sometimes it was only partially off.

She looked puzzled. 'But surely, Canon, the heating can only be on *or* off. There's a little switch, you know, just behind the door.' (I did know, it was one of my evening tasks to check it.)

I sighed but said reassuringly, 'I am sure there is some simple explanation, probably won't take a moment to fix.'

'I hope so – you see, it has been going on for some time, Friday mornings mostly. I hear it when I'm doing the flowers. I did mention it to Edith but she didn't seem very interested.' Bully for Edith.

'As a matter of fact,' she continued, 'it's not really gurgling, rather a sort of knocking and grinding sound, quite loud sometimes!'

'I expect it's a poltergeist – a lot of them about these days.'

She looked startled. 'Oh dear! Do you really think so?'

'No, not really, Mavis. But don't worry, I'm sure something can be done.' And tiring of the pipes, I asked brightly why she was carrying such a large shopping bag. 'It's big enough to buy up the whole of Molehill!' I exclaimed jocularly. A mistake.

'Ah, I was coming to that,' she replied earnestly. 'You see, I am collecting items for the Cubs' tombola – jars of pickled onions or Brylcreem, chocolate, bars of soap, packets of junket, that sort of thing . . . I was wondering if you have any to spare?' (Oh yes, I thought, pantry stocked to the gills with junket and Brylcreem!)

'Well, I'm not sure – but I expect I can find something.'

She beamed. 'Oh, that would be nice! I'll come round this afternoon to collect –'

'No!' I said hastily. 'Couldn't possibly trouble you. I'll leave them in the vestry on the side table.' Another mistake. Reference to the vestry brought her back to the pipes.

'So you *will* look into those noises, won't you, Canon? It's really rather worrying.'

I assured her I would put it at the top of my Urgent Agenda list. And raising my hat and donning a busy expression, I side-stepped her neatly and scurried on my way.

7

The Vicar's Version

As promised, I put a collection of tombola articles on the vestry table; but in so doing was irritated to find a note propped up against one of the candlesticks. It was from Mavis: 'Just a little reminder, Canon, about the noise in the pipes. I heard it again this morning. Most disturbing! The sound seems to be coming from the cupboard under the basins. If it's not too much trouble perhaps you would be kind enough to investigate.'

Of course it was too much trouble! As if there wasn't enough to think about without the confounded pipes. However, I knew that if I didn't pursue the matter, the matter via Mavis would certainly pursue me.

So taking off my jacket and getting down on hands and knees, I started to grovel about in the recesses of the glory-hole. It was slightly damp and distinctly smelly, and I hit my head on one of the pipes, and then my knuckles on some ancient cleaning bucket. The small space was far too dark to see anything clearly, and I was about to reverse out to fetch matches from my jacket when my hand closed on something round and hard but also slightly rubbery.

Back in the light I examined my find, which appeared to be a child's dummy or teething toy. I stared at it curiously. It consisted of a pink plastic ring to which was attached a half-chewed effigy of Donald Duck. What an extraordinary place for such a thing! Had it been abandoned by an errant toddler escaping from its minder? Unlikely. Besides, on closer examination it struck me as being rather large for the average child's mouth – though of course I was no expert in such matters.

I was about to put it to one side, but must have pressed the duck part, for it emitted a tired whimper. Then of course memory and recognition suddenly dawned: one of Bouncer's early playthings! When he had first appeared in the vicarage it had been something which he had toted around with dedicated devotion, and it was only when I had bought him a smart rubber throwing-ring that the item finally lost its appeal and the plaintive squeaks had been silenced. So this was where it had ended up!

I fetched the matches from my coat pocket, lit an altar candle from the pile on the table and crawled back in to rootle further. There was something else there: the tattered remnants of a small plaid blanket. No mistaking *that* for a toddler's comfort rag: another of Bouncer's worn-out accoutrements. I had put it out by the dustbin months ago! The dog must have dragged it all the way to the vestry. What on earth had he been doing – making some kind of lair? ... And then I saw them: wedged neatly under one of the pipes – two large ham bones, one clearly ancient, the other still with the marks of meat upon it.

I scrambled out and lit a cigarette. What had Mavis said? 'Not so much gurgling as knocking and grinding.' The dog attacking one of its bones was noise enough, but in a small space against the backing of metal pipes it could well be the sort of sound she had described. There was something else she had said, 'Friday mornings mostly.' Yes, that was the day when more often than not I took the dog on my parish rounds. On the way back we would generally stop off at the church where I would unleash him to potter around on his own while I gossiped with the sexton or bandied words with Tapsell. Sometimes he would disappear but always turned up at the vicarage in time for his lunchtime Bonio. So that was where the little blighter went in the interim – into the vestry sink cupboard to gnaw his bones and scare the wits out of Mavis Briggs!

It had its comic side but also put me in a dilemma. It seemed a shame to deprive the dog of his secret sanctuary if that's what he liked. On the other hand, to allow things to continue would only generate more mournful complaints from Mavis, something to be avoided at all costs. And in any case, if I did nothing she would doubtless prevail upon Tapsell to play the bloodhound, and the last thing I intended was that he and the smitten Edith should exploit my embarrassment in the matter. As they surely would! Neither liked Bouncer, and since I had twice encountered them in flagrante – once in the woods and once in the organ loft – both were hostile to me.

So there was nothing to be done except clear the cupboard of the dog's comforts and firmly lock the door. He would just have to find an alternative place. That was his problem. Mine was considerably greater: how to cope with Nicholas and the matter of Blenkinsop's pig.

Three days after returning to Brighton the former had telephoned me with his proposals as to how I should 'acquire the merchandise'. I was to approach the archdeacon with the request that he introduce me to his brother who I had heard was in the fortunate position of owning a distinguished reproduction of the Pontoon Pig. This apparently was of great interest to me as I was currently engaged in some amateur researches into the life of Sir Royston Beano and hoped eventually to publish a modest paper on the subject. The story of how the bone idol had passed into Beano's hands was a popular anecdote and one to which I should naturally have to refer. However, since my reputation as amateur historian was at stake, second-hand references were not enough, and to give substance and additional interest to my account I would really need to see the thing for myself, or at least as authentic a copy as possible. Did the archdeacon think he might prevail upon his brother to . . . etc?

'That's all very well, Nicholas,' I protested, 'but I know nothing about Beano's life other than that he was an eccentric explorer. How can I possibly convince the Blenkinsops that I'm writing a paper?'

'Well, dear boy, *you* may not know much, but I do. There's been only one proper biography written, produced in the 1920s and now out of print, but which I happen to have read; and more to the point, I'm also one of the few people to have had access to the unpublished diaries. I'll send you a potted history along with some key references which you must memorize thoroughly – *and* of course a fake artefact as replacement for the original. Expect a registered parcel within the next few days.'

'I suppose you imagine I've got all the time in the world to mug up this stuff. Let me remind you that –'

'Yes, yes, Francis, I know. You've got a busy parish to maintain. Run off your feet etc. . . . Absolute nonsense. You're bone idle, old chap, always have been really. Anything for a quiet life, that's you!' And he laughed good-humouredly.

I felt less good-humoured. 'Chance would be a fine thing,' I snapped.

'Should have thought of that at a certain sylvan moment eighteen months ago,' he countered. 'Anything less likely to induce a quiet life it would be hard to imagine. Still, as I've observed before, calculation is not your forte!'

I was about to retort that it was precisely because of my desperate need for a quiet life that I had committed the act I had, and that at the time it had seemed a pressing necessity and calculation not an option! But it was pointless to wrangle: neither Nicholas, nor anyone else, would ever understand . . . And so I resigned myself to absorbing and falling in with his instructions.

The younger Blenkinsop's first name was Claude. And his abode on the edge of Manchester Square was a chic third-floor apartment overlooking the trees of the central garden and within spitting distance of the Wallace Collection. My brief was to make an appointment via the archdeacon, drive up to London, lift and replace the pig, and then drive speedily down to Brighton where it would be delivered into the hands of my ringmaster. 'Not risking it going back to Molehill, old cock,' Nicholas had said when I had protested that such driving would make a very long day. 'No fear! Not after last time's little charade. An idol in hand is worth two in your damn belfry!' He alluded of course to the business of the paintings. I said nothing but inwardly admitted he was probably right.

As it turned out, persuading the older Blenkinsop to ingratiate me with his brother was an easier task than I had imagined. He was on the verge of retirement, and I was currently in favour for having helped to foil the Reverend Basil Rummage from stepping into his shoes.* Blenkinsop disapproved of Rummage (as well he might) and he had been hell-bent on blocking his promotion, and for some reason had got it into his head that I was the person to lead the opposition to the appointment. I was not exactly a natural candidate for the role, but Blenkinsop had leant heavily upon me, and after some rather crude manoeuvrings Rummage's name had been dropped from the shortlist. The archdeacon was well satisfied and evidently regarded me as some kind of moral saviour to the diocese. (Indeed, I think it was due to his discreet and grateful string-pulling that I had achieved my canonical status – an accolade as much a shock to me as it had been an irritant to Bishop Clinker.)

Thus when I rather diffidently approached the archdeacon about his brother he was moderately receptive to the idea ... or at any rate, as receptive as Vernon Blenkinsop was to anything.

* See *Bones in the Belfry*

41

'Didn't know you were interested in that sort of thing, Oughterard. Kept it very dark, I must say! Not my line of country at all – historical research. Far too many contemporary matters to attend to. And from what little I know about that Beano fellow he sounds to have been a rather questionable type . . . women, and all that sort of thing. Still, if you think Claude can be useful I'll give him a ring. Don't see much of him these days. Better things to do with my time than listen to my brother pontificating about *nescioquid nugarum* – as our Roman friend would say – but he's bound to see you if he thinks you're interested in one of his bits and pieces. Nothing he likes better than to blah on about "my precious collection"!' And so saying, he picked up the telephone and dialled the number – while I sat wondering who our Roman friend was.

The line was evidently engaged and Blenkinsop replaced the receiver with a sigh of irritation. 'Typical: always gassing. But then it's not as if he has anything else to *do* – nothing useful at any rate. Polishes his ornaments and gives talks on bits of china to old ladies. I ask you! Fortunately some of us are rather more seriously employed, there's quite enough trivia around as it is . . . And talking of trivia, Oughterard, I take it you haven't heard from the Reverend Rummage lately?'

I said that I hadn't and believed him still to be in Swaziland.

'Hmm,' he muttered darkly, 'and let us hope he remains there. Best place for him! A good piece of work you did in that little matter. As I said at the time, it is just as well there remains a modicum of sobriety in the diocese . . .' He had mounted upon his favourite hobby horse, church discipline and the perils of laxity, and I hastily tried to steer him back to the matter in hand, i.e. me getting into Claude's flat.

'No need to worry, dear fellow. I'll have another go at him later this evening. Rest assured: no one can accuse Vernon Blenkinsop of not being persistent.' No, I thought wryly, no one could ever do that.

Thus I drove home secure in the knowledge that the first hurdle of the dreadful project was all but over; yet oppressed by the prospect of others still to come, higher and more arduous.

8

The Vicar's Version

The next day the registered package arrived and I opened it with reluctance. It contained a closely (and badly) typed résumé of Beano's life and exploits, plus a five-inch bone model of a pig with rearing trotters. Just as Nicholas had described, its eyes were represented by tiny flashing emeralds – or so they appeared – and the tail too was studded with some sort of sparkling gemstones, presumably paste. It was, I suppose, an amusing little trinket but not something that I would personally get excited about. However, there was no accounting for taste, and if this was what Ingaza thought would 'bring home the bacon' then far be it from me to strike a dissonant note. Just as with the paintings, I was now its guardian, and guard it I must if I were to achieve any respite, let alone release, from my master's diktats! Thus I wrapped it carefully in tissue paper, took it to the garage and deposited it in the glove box of the Singer. There it could wait in readiness for the invitation to London from Blenkinsop Minor.

A week passed, and I was just beginning to think that the archdeacon had overestimated his brother's interest in my 'researches', when I received the awaited call. The voice was similar to his elder brother's, but feline rather than brusque and a good octave higher. It shared, however, the same self-absorbed earnestness and note of tart rectitude. But fortunately he seemed well disposed to the idea of my visit, apologized for the delay in contact ('so many little talks to prepare, you know') and cordially issued an invitation for lunch the following Tuesday.

Thus, engagements cancelled and Bouncer's meals taken care of by a neighbour, I set off for London encumbered only by nerves and annoyance, and arrived in the vicinity of Manchester Square shortly before the prescribed time. This was as well for I get flustered parking in unfamiliar areas, and the square and the adjacent streets proved more congested than I had thought. However, after some circling about I was able to shunt into a vacant spot beneath a plane tree and conveniently just around the corner from Claude's flat.

Walking towards the tall Georgian building I thought of Nicholas, and for once wished I shared some of his brass neck. A little of that might have made the project less daunting! As it was, I climbed the three flights of stairs to my host's front door in a state of furtive and panting agitation, convinced that all would fail and I should be exposed for what I assuredly was – a bumbling thief and conman. Then, trying to convince myself that exchange was no real robbery, I squared my shoulders and with a sudden spurt of confidence rang the bell.

It was answered almost immediately by a miniature Blenkinsop: Claude was about half the size of his brother, but in every other respect looked depressingly similar – though, as suggested from the telephone, the voice that greeted me was mild and silken (unlike Vernon's rasping tones) and there was something distinctly mannered in his movements.

'Ah, the Reverend Canon Oughterard, I presume. Welcome to my little eyrie 'midst the tree-tops!' He bowed theatrically and ushered me into a neat hallway and thence into an elegant and high-ceilinged drawing room decorated in delicate shades of cream and grey. The furniture was largely French Empire, with scrolled and gilded mirrors adorning the walls. The rosy tones of a faded Aubusson covered the floor, and on a marble console-table groups of porcelain harlequins and cherubs besported themselves among lavish peonies. Defying the looped silk curtains, light poured in from the long windows. It would be hard to imagine anything more distant from the archdeacon's stern and fusty study – or indeed from my own workaday domain!

For a couple of minutes he chatted inconsequentially, enquiring about my journey and the vagaries of the weather; and then rather to my surprise commented on features of St Botolph's church with which he was apparently quite familiar: 'Some very pleasing touches, but of course the Lady Chapel is entirely ruined by that monstrous Victorian reredos. Such a blot! Can't you do something about it?' He peered up at me with that intent and querulous gaze which I had seen many times on the face of his brother. (What on earth did he expect me to do – repaint the thing? Or was I expected to stash it out of sight in the belfry as I had once had to do with certain other artistic embarrassments?) I explained that it was in the hands of the Church authorities and not something over which I had much control.

'Ah yes ... the *Church authorities*,' he replied bleakly, 'a fat lot they know about matters of taste – least of all my venerable brother!' He gave a biting laugh and offered me sherry from a sparkling decanter. 'Now, come and enjoy the view. My visitors always love staring down at the pavements – gives them a sense of detached superiority, I suppose.' He took me over to one of the large windows with its tiny French balcony. And as we gazed down admiring the quiet square with its trees and discreet architecture, a woman emerged from a side street. She was about forty, nondescript, with a limp perm and flat sandals.

Claude gave a pained sigh and then murmured quietly, 'Have you ever noticed that ladies who wear those Roman sandals with thick leather ankle straps are invariably of a certain ilk and bore the pants off one?' I was startled by that – both the observation and its metaphor – and mumbled something to the effect that it had never really occurred to me. 'Oh yes,' he continued confidently, 'and what's more, it is always those with the thickest ankles who wear the thickest straps!'

I digested that piece of information and said that I would start to look more closely in future.

'Won't have to look far: should think Molehill abounds in them!' He chuckled thinly.

'Well, now that you mention it . . .' I began.

'Exactly! . . . Oh look – now that's what I call a decent shoe, good ankle too!' And gripping me by the elbow, he gestured towards the corner of the square. I could just make out another woman briskly exercising a wire-haired fox terrier. Dog and owner pranced along with nonchalant skip, and as she drew closer I could indeed discern a neat pair of ankles encased in tiny high-heeled shoes. The dog's grey and white markings matched the check of her shapely suit, and I was struck by the pert slant of the pill-box hat.

He beamed. 'One of the pleasures of London life. One sees so little of that sort of thing in the provinces . . . But still,' he added archly, 'we can't stay here all day ogling the girls! Luncheon beckons, I fancy.' And he ushered me into a small but exquisitely furnished dining room.

The fare was cold, concise, and meticulous: iced consommé and melba toast, poached salmon and asparagus, and a half-bottle of delicious '55 Montrachet. Of the last I had not enjoyed such a treat since my father's demise three years previously. We talked of this and that, of porcelain, curios, and cabbages and kings. Or rather he did, while I listened politely, abstracted with thoughts of the pig and how to get my hands on it.

Nicholas Ingaza had been right about Blenkinsop Minor being a windbag. The prattle was unceasing but not without humour, and now and again I was pulled from my cogitations by a sly witticism or barbed aside. At one point I enquired, perhaps mischievously, if he saw much of his brother.

'Not if I can help it,' was the acid reply. 'He's a dreadful bore, you know. Takes himself too seriously. Were he a woman he too would wear thick ankle straps!' And he laughed scornfully. I began to wonder if my host was a foot fetishist. I had read of such people.

Lunch over, we returned to the drawing room for coffee; and snapping open a sleek cigarette case he offered me a Turkish Abdullah. I remembered my mother smoking these before the war; and their flat shape and distinctive smell took me back down the years to hushed afternoons in our ramshackle house on the East Sussex coast, when our parent would be 'resting' – it was never clear from what – on the rose sofa in the morning room. The ritual invariably involved several Abdullahs and a steady stream of jet black coffee in the tiniest of green cups. And at such times my sister and I would be firmly directed to 'leave Mother in peace' – although I do remember as a small boy, on occasions and on sufferance, being allowed to play with my toy elephant with the proviso, of course, that I was to be 'very good'. As with Proust's madeleine, the smell of that oriental tobacco triggered a sudden spate of such memories, and I savoured the novelty, enjoying the contrast with my own workaday Virginians.

The reverie was interrupted by Claude's reedy voice saying, 'Now tell me more about this little paper you are engaged upon . . .'

I duly reproduced the spiel about my researches into the life of Sir Royston Beano – in which at Nicholas's behest I had so laboriously immersed myself – saying how eager I was to view even a reproduction of the original idol, recognizing of course that my host's was one of the earliest copies and thus of particular note. 'There are so many base imitations,' I declared earnestly, 'and it is a privilege to encounter one made within the lifetime of Beano himself!'

'Ah yes,' he acknowledged with preening modesty, 'I am indeed fortunate to have it in my possession, and while I fear the original has been lost in the mists of time, I like to feel that in some strange way fate has picked me to be the custodian of its most worthy successor. Naturally, being a copy it is not valuable in the vulgar commercial sense, but nevertheless *highly* regarded by those of a discerning sensibility.'

'Indeed,' I murmured, trying my best to look discerning.

We talked a little longer about my 'researches' and the difficulties of doing justice to private passions when so pre-occupied with the exigencies of professional duty.

'But at least you *have* private interests,' he exclaimed, 'unlike my brother, who seems to spend his entire life chairing diocesan meetings and writing officious letters to Canterbury. As you probably know, he is due to retire at any moment, so goodness knows what he'll do then – but at least it will let the archbishop off the hook!' He gave a caustic snigger, adding with patronizing relish, 'Poor Vernon, so dull! You'll never believe it, but the last time I tried to interest him in my precious little collection he actually said that he had far better things to do than drool over piddling gewgaws! So sad . . .'

I was about to say that talking of piddling gewgaws, how about showing me the pig – when we were interrupted by the discreet chimes of the doorbell.

Claude tutted. 'Now who can that be at three o'clock in the afternoon? Some errand boy, I suppose, and just when I was about to show you . . .' He got up crossly and pottered towards the door. I stared out of the window keeping my eyes peeled for ankles, thick or otherwise. My perusal was cut short by a voice from the hall only too gratingly familiar.

'My dear Claude, *so* sorry to descend on you like this but it is a matter of some urgency – essential that I make a telephone call and I can never get the hang of the public boxes. All that pressing of buttons A and B, it drives me mad! Would you oblige, dear fellow . . . awful bore, I know!'

I listened in frozen horror to the tones of my bishop, Horace Clinker.

What the hell was he doing, bursting in like this just when I was about to execute my sleight of hand with the idols! Anyway, why wasn't he at home in the diocese doing episcopal things in the Palace? What brought him up here, for God's sake?

I heard Claude's thin tones directing him to the study where presumably the telephone was. A door shut and then my host re-entered the room. He looked peeved.

'Clinker,' he announced. 'I suppose he'll want to use the lavatory next! Anyone would think I was some sort of club or public facility. Haven't seen the fellow for five years and now he suddenly takes it into his head to use my telephone. Typical of Horace – always did take liberties! . . . Did *you* know he was up in London?' (Said in slightly accusing tones.)

I cleared my throat nervously. 'Absolutely not,' I replied. 'Rather a coincidence!'

'Oh well,' he observed scathingly 'we shall just have to put a brave face on things.'

'Ah, that's lucky!' the bishop's voice boomed from the doorway. 'Actually managed to get through. Thanks, Claude, saved my bacon! I –' He suddenly saw me, broke off and recoiled. 'Good God, Oughterard, what are you doing here!'

I was about to mumble something about just passing, when Claude said pointedly, 'Francis and I have had a most *restful* luncheon and I was about to show him my rampant pig.'

'Show him your *what*?'

'My Poona pig.'

Clinker looked startled and said cautiously, 'A pig, eh? Where do you keep it?'

'Well, it's rather precious, so I prefer to house it in the study – too public in here.'

'I see,' said Clinker slowly. 'I, er, don't think I saw it . . .'

'Probably not,' replied Claude carelessly, 'after all, it's not everyone who would recognize the Beano Pig, and of course it's quite small so –'

'Oh,' cried Clinker, relief and recognition dawning, 'you mean you got it out of the *Beano*! I remember. Wonderful little creatures! Mind you, it was three weeks' pocket money plus four tokens, but well worth it. So you've still got yours, have you? Lost mine years ago. Well, I never!' And he laughed loud and long. Claude did not.

'I have no idea what you are talking about, Horace,' he replied stiffly. 'Suffice it to say, I did not get this remarkable objet d'art out of some comic! Fortunately Francis is a connoisseur in these matters. You evidently are not.'

To give Clinker his due he was quite unfazed. 'Sorry, old chap. Put my *trotter* in it there, didn't I!' And he let out another bellow of mirth.

Claude Blenkinsop raised his eyes to the ceiling, sighed heavily, and between what I took to be gritted teeth said, 'Well, Horace, since you are here and are obviously in need of some enlightenment perhaps you would like to see the item in question.' And so saying, he herded the two of us out of the drawing room and into the study.

Unlike the tiny dining room this was surprisingly spacious. It had the same elegance as the rest of the flat, but apart from a large roll-top desk and a couple of bookcases, was largely taken up with display cabinets and a vitrine table. Gesturing towards the latter, he turned to me and said, 'At least *you*, Francis, will recognize my treasure!'

I did indeed, and was rapidly working out how on earth I should manage to make the switch. It hadn't occurred to me that the thing might be kept under glass – a detail that Nicholas had helpfully omitted to mention. Clinker's presence was also a dratted encumbrance. However, I made all the right noises and peered closely at the glass top, trying as it were to get a closer look.

'Just a moment,' murmured the proud owner, 'I'll take it out.' And touching a knob at the side he slid back the glass panel, took out the little pig and placed it on a side table.

'I like the green eyes,' observed Clinker appreciatively. 'Do they glow in the dark?'

'Certainly not,' snapped Claude. 'It's not a lighthouse, you know!'

'May I pick it up?' I asked.

'By all means.'

I made a great show of examining the object, and ran my finger down its back and then, unobtrusively, along its underside. It seemed perfectly smooth. I tried again, this time with my nail – and yes, Nicholas was right: the ridge was there! A mere hairline in the bone, but definitely there. It was the real thing all right!

I continued to regard it solemnly, still desperately wondering how I was going to effect the change. Then miraculously Clinker exclaimed, 'I say, Claude, is that a genuine Toledo dagger over there?' And together they moved towards one of the display cabinets. In a trice I plunged my hand into my jacket pocket, fingers poised to grip the replica . . .

But even as I did so I knew the act to be futile, that my hand would grasp nothing but the coat lining: for the Singer's glove box had flashed before my eyes, and I realized with the certainty of doom that I had forgotten to remove the replacement. Such had been my elation in finding a parking spot that all other thoughts had vanished, and I had strolled blithely up to Blenkinsop's flat with the object of my mission still stowed in its place of safe-keeping!

With hand stuffed pointlessly in my pocket, I heard my father's voice intoning, 'Head full of sea air, Francis – nothing but air!' He had been right.

In helpless dismay I gazed down at the idol while Claude instructed Clinker in the intricacies of Toledo dagger patterns. What could I do? Request another visit? But why on earth should that seem necessary? Make some lame excuse and rush downstairs to the car, get the idol and try to re-enact proceedings? Impossible. Return to the flat disguised as a plumber or tax inspector? . . . These and other absurdities raced through my mind as I stood there bleak and wretched, cursing myself and cursing Nicholas. Finally I slumped down on the sofa bored out of my mind and longing to return to Molehill. The other two prosed on in front of the cabinets, and I shut my eyes . . .

Suddenly I heard Clinker saying, 'Oh, I think that's quite all right. No trouble at all, dear fellow. As a matter of fact I was going to ask Oughterard here if he wouldn't mind giving me a lift to Victoria. I have rather important business to attend to there, but there's plenty of time and we could easily drop it off.' And then turning to me, 'That won't take you out of your way, will it, Francis?'

'No, I shouldn't think so,' I replied vaguely. 'Er, sorry, where are we going?'

Clinker sighed. 'To drop off Claude's pig at the jeweller's – it's got an eye loose. Didn't you hear!'

'The right eye, is it?' I asked absently.

'Well, as a matter of fact it is!' exclaimed Blenkinsop. 'How did you know that?'

I had of course remembered Ingaza's tale of Beano's wife hurling it at the fender with the resultant dislodging of one of the emeralds. Reset it may have been, but the damage was done, and a hundred and fifty years later it had presumably worked itself loose again.

'Er, I . . .'

'Sharp eyes, that's what you've got, my dear chap. A fellow enthusiast, I can see that!' And he nodded appreciatively.

I smiled modestly and gave thanks for major mercies. To think that, after everything, the pig was going to drop into my lap just like that!

But not quite – for my offer to carry the package had been pre-empted by Clinker who seemed intent on taking the box himself, assuring Claude of his utmost care in the matter. Thus somehow, between our departure from the flat and arrival at the jeweller's, it would have to be detached from the bishop's grasp.

We said our goodbyes to Claude, and with Clinker carrying the package and me pondering logistics, made our way downstairs and out into the street. As we went I noticed that in addition to the pig in its box, Clinker was carrying a dark mackintosh. I recalled Mrs Carruthers' reference to his incognito garb, and wondered if the 'important business' near Victoria involved a few rounds of surreptitious tiddlywinks.

However, such speculation was cut short for I had something else to think about: the weather. It had started to rain. Clinker gave a tut of exasperation, stopped in his tracks and began struggling to put on his raincoat. With the box grasped in one hand, he was having difficulties. The rain was suddenly pounding the pavement and I leaped to assist.

'Here, give me the box, sir . . . and I tell you what, if you stand under this portico I'll run on and get the car. Shan't be a second!' And not waiting for a reply I rushed round the corner clutching the precious package.

I scrambled into the Singer, wrenched open the glove box, and with frantic fumbling switched the two objects. I had just done this when a thought struck me – 'God almighty! I've forgotten the damned eye!' The original pig's emerald orb had worked loose, hence our visit to the restorer. Its fake counterpart, to be eventually returned to Claude, would have to show similar damage! I looked around wildly for some gouging instrument. None came to sight or mind. Rain poured, sweat oozed. And then suddenly I remembered – under the dashboard, Pa's Swiss army knife! He had foisted it upon me just before the final hospital sojourn, and cluttered with other problems and impedimenta, I had left it there long since forgotten . . . I took the pig, seized the knife, and attacked the eye. Then executing a sprawling three-point turn, swung the car round and headed back to the sheltering Clinker.

'Most thoughtful, Oughterard. Thank you,' he exclaimed, stuffing himself into the passenger seat. 'Can't stand this erratic weather, you never know what to expect.'

I grunted sympathetically and passed him the bogus pig. 'You'd better hang on to this, sir. Claude Blenkinsop would take a dim view if anything happened to it!' And I laughed wryly.

'Hmm,' he replied, 'Claude Blenkinsop is an old woman – always has been. And why he has to live in an apartment without a lift I cannot imagine. As to this pig, can't see what all the fuss is about. I've seen more riveting things in Woolworths!'

We drove briskly until my passenger pointed out that we were fast approaching Paddington Station. 'Rather disorientated, aren't we, Oughterard?' he observed. 'I think you will find Victoria approximately a mile *south* from here.'

In the face of interesting gestures from cab drivers, I managed to turn the car and join the cortège moving in the opposite direction. It was the rush hour, and reaching Victoria a frustrating business; but we eventually got there, and to my surprise had little difficulty in finding the jeweller's, which was tucked away in a corner behind Westminster Cathedral.

Making a rather laboured joke about entering upon popish precincts, Clinker levered himself out of the car, and clutching the pig box disappeared into the shop. It would, I suppose, have been courteous to offer to go in myself; but my companion had seemed perfectly happy to complete the mission. And in any case, I reflected, the less I was seen to have anything to do with things the better!

Five minutes later the bishop returned to the car and in imperious tones directed me to the Vauxhall Bridge Road. About halfway down he suddenly said, 'All right, you can stop here now, Oughterard. I'll walk the rest of the way. The – ah – office is only just round the corner.' And barely waiting for me to draw up, he was out on the pavement muttering thanks and buttoning his mackintosh; and then with a vague wave in my direction started to walk purposefully towards one of the side streets. As he went he turned up his coat-collar and pulled from his pocket a sort of crumpled black fedora. He crammed it on, and looking like a squat Mafioso, quickened his stride and disappeared out of sight.

I was about to start the engine when, glancing in the mirror, I saw a car draw up a few yards behind me. The passenger door was flung open: and swathed in furs and furbelows, out stepped Mrs Carruthers. I had been right after all!

The noise started immediately she put foot to pavement, as with whoops and cackles she struggled to prise from the back seat a female companion, who eventually emerged into the air as might a grey porpoise. The driver also emerged – one my father would doubtless have described as 'rather a common little man', sporting a small moustache and a very loud check jacket. He was carrying a wicker hamper. The porpoise lady was also carrying something: a large shiny wooden box with brass corners. Mrs Carruthers carried nothing except a tightly furled pink umbrella with an enormous spike. Chatting and clattering, the three of them tottered towards the corner around which Clinker had disappeared.

I looked at the hamper, the wooden box, and my watch. Nearly six o'clock – *l'heure bleue*: the cocktail hour. Obviously time for tiddlywinks and tequilas!

Thus with my mind filled with visions of genteel riot and roguery, I left the Vauxhall Bridge Road and braced myself for the Brighton run.

9

The Cat's Memoir

As I had predicted, the vicar started making preparations to go up to London. Clearly the Brighton type had tightened the screws and our addled master was now once more in the role of reluctant lackey. I cannot say that his discomfort would have bothered me unduly – the risible blunders of humans deserving of some small penance. However, in this particular case the penance would not be confined to F.O. If his project aborted *we* should be involved, and that was not something that I found amusing. Life was precarious enough as it was without the vicar's antics fouling things further.

As I pondered the matter I felt a sulk hovering and began to make my way to the holly bush where I settle at such times. However, my path was blocked by Bouncer. Last seen he had been skulking around the tool shed, but he had evidently observed me emerging from the rhododendrons and was now standing barring my way and panting loudly.

'I say, Maurice,' he gasped, 'you'll never guess – he's cleared away my bones and blanket. It's not right!'

I observed that there were very few things of F.O.'s doing which were right, and would he kindly mind removing himself from my path. He said that he did mind actually, as he had some urgent things to communicate and would appreciate my advice. I am of course renowned for giving good advice and can rarely resist an appeal to my helpful sagacity. Thus I agreed to listen to the dog's complaints. These were not easy to follow but seemed to involve the church, the vestry, the Briggs woman, and some unpleasant-sounding ham bones.

'. . . so I had gone to all the trouble of making this cosy kennel,' he gabbled, 'and put all my stuff there, even the blanket, and it was a really good little den. I'd been going there for weeks, and then F.O. messed it all up and locked the door. It's not fair!'

'Nothing is. Besides, you never told *me* about it!' I replied irritably.

'Thought you would probably cut up rough,' he explained.

'Nonsense,' I said. 'I am not in the habit of "cutting up rough", though doubtless I would have questioned the wisdom of the venture.'

'That's what I said – cut up rough.'

I let that pass, and instead asked how on earth he had managed to transport the blanket unobserved. 'Must have been quite cumbersome. Did you do it at night?'

'Didn't do it at all. It was O'Shaughnessy. He's got a bigger mouth than me. Besides, it was his idea in the first place. Said I would be as snug as a bug next to the hot pipes and only an eejit would think of looking there. A "darlin' little hidey hole" he called it.' I might have known. Trust the setter to be at the bottom of things!

'Well, nice while it lasted, I daresay,' I observed. 'But you'll have to find another place now – though why you can't just stick to the crypt I do not know!'

'Ah, but you see, Maurice,' he replied solemnly, 'in life it's always good to ring the changes.'

And having cast that philosophical pearl, he went sniffing off among the bushes.

Abandoning my sulk, I promptly called him back. 'Your bones matter little in the general scheme of things,' I observed sternly. 'They are merely ciphers which –'

'What scheme?' he asked.

58

'The Brighton type's scheme to manipulate the vicar and destroy our chances of an easy life – not to mention the police putting their hulking hoofs in everything! It is all going to be exceedingly tiresome.' And I emitted one of my more ear-freezing miaows. The dog winced, but before he could bound off again, I remarked casually, 'Anyway, he's definitely going up to London and thence down to Brighton – and this time has no plans to take *you* on the outing.' (I couldn't resist mentioning that, as the dog gets cocky when given preferential treatment.)

'What!' he yelped. 'What about my grub?'

'There won't be any,' I said. And waited.

As anticipated, the reaction was violent and theatrical. Indeed, such was the volume that even the phlegmatic sparrows took flight, and I could hear the baby next door wailing in protest.

I suffered the drama for a while, and then raising my voice above the din let it be known that it was just one of my playful jests, and that of course F.O. would never go off without making the necessary arrangements, and that all was in hand for the dog's culinary needs.

'Yes, yes, but will I get my GRUB?' he bellowed.

'Yes, Bouncer, you will be fed, i.e. f-e-d, FED!'

'Well, that's all right then,' he said. And promptly lay down and went fast asleep.

10

The Dog's Diary

I had a jolly good day yesterday, JOLLY GOOD! In fact it was so good that it made up for me losing my new cubbyhole in the church vestry which O'Shaughnessy had kindly helped me with. When I told him what had happened, about the vicar putting the kybosh on things, he said that in his experience that is what owners generally did, and the name of the game was not to be downhearted but to rise to the challenge and find something else to fox them with. He said that was one of the things that made it fun being a dog: always something to keep you on your toes and your snout in good order! I think O'Shaughnessy talks a lot of sense, though the cat can be a bit sniffy about him – but then Maurice is sniffy about almost everything. He enjoys it. I suppose that's his bit of fun. Mine is racing about or eating – and I did a *lot* of both yesterday!

You see, F.O. had gone swanning off to London, and then down to Brighton, where the Type comes from, so we were without him for almost twenty-four hours (didn't get back till nearly two in the morning – at least that's what Maurice says; I'm not too good on clocks myself). So that meant I could do pretty well just what I liked! Mind you, when Maurice first told me of F.O.'s plans and that he had no intention of taking ME with him, I was pretty miffed. After all, what about my mealtimes? The cat made one of his *un*funny jokes, saying there wouldn't be any grub! Well, you can bet that upset me. I mean to say, no self-respecting dog is going to go all day without his Bonios and Muncho. So I made a bit of a scene. Scared the daylights out of Maurice, who then had the brass neck to say he had been pulling my leg. SOME STUPID JOKE!

Anyway all was well, because the vicar had organized the woman from over the road to come in and give me the necessary. I made a great fuss of her – grinning all over my face, wagging my tail nineteen to the dozen, staring fondly into her eyes, and even sitting up and begging. (I didn't use to be able to do that, but think I've got the knack now, and it's JOLLY handy!) She was so impressed that she gave me extra dollops all round, plus masses of chocolate cake – which F. O. never allows me. She said I was the sweetest little fellow she had ever seen! Maurice said it all made him feel rather sick.

In between the noshes I went and played with O'Shaughnessy in the graveyard and beat him *twice* in our race round the tombstones! Maurice said that the setter was just holding back to let me win, but *I* know different. Bouncer knows a thing or two when it comes to crafty obstacle races! After that we paid a visit to the organist's aunt – the one whose Yorkie was murdered by the bulldog belonging to the vicar's friend, Mrs Tubbly Pole. I told O'Shaughnessy that if we were to get into the garden without the old girl seeing us he would have to be very quiet and tread carefully. He said he would be as quiet as a Celtic fairy. Like hell he was! Great paws crashing everywhere, and all the time laughing his head off fit to bust! Don't know how Tapsell's aunt didn't hear us – deaf, I suppose. Anyway, we had a good time doing her dustbins over, and then had a bit of digging practice outside the drawing-room window. The earth is quite soft there and we were able to make some really big holes. There were lots of those bulb things all strewn about and O'Shaughnessy tried to eat some, but he made awful faces and spat them out, and then rolled about waving his legs in the air making gagging noises and pretending to have tummy-ache. It was good fun – but it was even more fun when the aunt's cat appeared. That really stretched our legs and lungs! We were just on our second lap round the garden when I saw the owner at the window, purple in the face and shaking her fist. Suppose she thought her pet was about to go the same way as the Yorkshire! Anyway, we ditched the cat and got out smartish.

On the way back I asked O'Shaughnessy if he would like to come home for tea and have some chocolate cake (assuming Maurice hadn't hidden it in his litter); but he said that he thought it was nearly time for his mistress to come back from the hairdresser's all permed up, and that he must go to his usual post at the front gate and put on a forlorn face ready for her return. I asked why the face. He said this always makes her feel guilty for leaving him so long, and he would be much petted and given titbits for the rest of the evening. I thought of trying that with the vicar, but knowing him he would probably walk straight past me and never notice a thing!

Still, it was just as well that O'Shaughnessy didn't come back, because as I began trotting up the front path who do you think was coming *down* it? The rozzers: the fat one and the weedy one!

'That's his dog,' said the fat one – March, I think his name is. 'Hello, Bouncer old boy! Where's your master then?' (Damn fool question. Did he really think I was going to say anything?) 'Gone off and left you, has he? Eh?' He patted my head and I gave him one of my soppy looks.

'Nice little chap, this one,' he said, turning to his mate.

'No he's not!' the weedy one snapped. 'Don't you remember when we were here interviewing Oughterard last year? Him and that cat, like fiends from hell they were! Nasty beggars, the pair of them.' And he glared. I was going to glare back but then thought it better if I stayed looking soppy.

'Come off it, Sidney,' said the fat one laughing, 'they were only having a game.'

'Having a game? That's not what you said at the time, sir. What you said was –'

'Yes, yes, all right, Sidney, no need to be so literal ... besides, we're not here to discuss his domestic pets. What we want to know is when's he coming back so as we can have another go at him. That's what we've got to consider.'

'Well, you won't get it from the dog, that's for certain!' And he gave me another sour look.

They went babbling on, but I was feeling sleepy after playing with O'Shaughnessy and it was quite a strain keeping my ears cocked, so I didn't catch much else. (You have to listen really hard when humans talk to each other – and most of it's gobbledygook anyway.) Then after the fat one had written something in his notebook and told me to 'be a good dog then', they went on down the path to the gate. I was glad to see them go as they were standing in the way of me getting at that cake – which I did NOT have to share with O'Shaughnessy!

11

The Vicar's Version

It took ages getting out of London, not helped by the fact that I discovered the petrol gauge was teetering on empty and filling-stations perversely self-effacing. However, I found one at last, and feeling a trifle more relaxed could concentrate on negotiating my way to the Brighton road.

This eventually achieved, I started to think about Nicholas and presenting him with the pig from Poona – or the Beano Bone Idol as it was officially known. I had to admit to being rather pleased by my 'coup' and trusted that he would be duly grateful. After all, he could hardly accuse me of making a cock-up this time, and might even offer to stand me supper or certainly a couple of drinks at the Old Schooner where we had arranged to meet. After the dramas of the day I suddenly felt rather in need of strong libations and glad we were meeting in the warmth of the hotel and not in the dubious domesticity of his home (wherever that might be, for I still didn't know). I wondered if he would bring the so far faceless Eric, but hoped not. For a reason I could not quite define, I was reluctant to confront either his pad or his pal. Perhaps anonymity on both counts helped to preserve the sense of unreality and keep the nightmare in check . . . the more I could keep aloof from the grasp of their raffish world the better!

I pushed on through the gathering dusk, and once

beyond Hickstead began looking for a telephone box from which to announce my arrival. Naturally no such thing materialized until the precise moment when I had a large saloon with blazing headlamps right on my tail. But I was loath to miss the opportunity and, quickly signalling, swerved a trifle abruptly into the kerb and came to a skidding halt. With screaming klaxon and flashing lights the saloon roared past, and despite the gloom I had a brief glimpse of an irate driver and fulminating passenger. For a tense moment I thought they might stop and come back and remonstrate – or worse! But fortunately it sped on, still hooting, into the night.

Muttering oaths I scrambled out on to the grass, and was halfway towards the kiosk when I remembered the pig in the glove box. I suppose I was becoming paranoid, but after the earlier fiasco I was nervous of letting the thing out of my sight until 'safe' in Ingaza's avid grasp. I returned to fetch it, found the requisite coins, and after some fumbling was able to get through almost immediately.

'Wotcha, Francis,' bellowed Eric's voice, 'so you're on yer way all right! Got the goods, 'ave yer?'

I assured him that I had the goods.

'Righto. I'll tell His Nibs to look smartish. In the bath he is – always likes a good sluice before doing business, especially with an old mate! Anyway, I expect he'll be there before you. Can't hang about, old son, big darts bash at the Anchor. I'm their only 'ope!' And with a thundering guffaw he rang off.

I was relieved about the darts match, annoyed at being cast as 'old mate'; but didn't know whether to be flattered by Ingaza's careful ablutions, or piqued that unlike me – harried by the drive and the day's events – he had the leisure for such matters. I could have done with a relaxing bath myself – but even more so with a relaxing drink! And spurred by that prospect I returned to the car and pressed on to the south coast.

* * *

65

Eighteen months previously the Old Schooner had played a brief but major part in my muddled life. It was there that I had fled after my terrible event in Foxford Wood; and it was there that I had encountered Nicholas – last seen a decade earlier making a handcuffed exit from the portals of St Bede's – following *his* event in the Turkish bath.

I pushed open the revolving doors and, caught in a swirl of strange and painful memory, wandered into the bar. This time, instead of the early evening sun flooding the room, the curtains were closely drawn, the lamps lit and the corners dim. But the pianist was there just the same, tinkling away in an alcove – and, as predicted by Eric, so was Nicholas: draped on a bar stool, thin fingers caressing a cocktail, and exuding his customary air of raddled elegance. I had been cursing him all day – while soft-soaping Claude, kowtowing to Clinker, negotiating the mayhem of Croydon's rush hour, and nearly getting myself blitzed by some hurtling limo. But suddenly seeing him there, sveltely poised in the mellow warmth of the Old Schooner, I experienced a pang of almost pleasurable familiarity. I say 'almost', because Nicholas, however occasionally engaging, is invariably dangerous. But it had been a hard day and my defences were down. So I responded to his languid wave with a broad grin, triumphant that my mission was accomplished, and moved quickly to greet him.

I was thus slightly put out by his opening words: 'Christ, Francis, you're not wearing that, are you!'

'Wearing what?' I exclaimed.

'The dog collar of course. Not exactly the sort of thing to help you melt into the crowd, dear boy! I should think they've mapped your progress all the way from Wigmore Street to the Royal Pavilion. Cover it up, for God's sake!'

I had a scarf in my raincoat pocket and obediently wound it round my neck.

'Got it, have you?' he asked briskly.

'Yes, yes,' I replied, 'but what about a drink first? I've had a hell of a time!'

'Let's see the pig first,' he said evenly. 'And then, old cock, you can have anything you want . . .' He smiled slyly.

'A Scotch will do,' I said quickly . . . and then groaned, remembering that yet again I had left the thing in the car. So much for careful resolutions! He raised a caustic eyebrow, and, feeling a prize idiot, I gabbled an apology and hurried back out to the sea front.

When I returned with the precious box Nicholas had moved from the bar to a nearby table. There was a drink lined up for me – not the requested whisky, but a cocktail glass containing what looked to be the same concoction as his own.

'What's this?' I asked suspiciously.

'Between The Sheets.'

'Between *what*!' I exclaimed.

'Sheets. They've only just caught up with it down here, and it's become all the rage. Try it and see.' He raised his own glass encouragingly.

I took a tentative sip . . . and then another. And then, just to be sure, a third. He was right: it was very, *very* good. And accepting the proffered Sobranie, I settled back in the chair savouring the taste, and feeling all the pressures of the day slip from my shoulders . . .

'Well, I'm going to have a quiet shufti at this thing – got to make sure you've brought the right one!' Nicholas announced.

'Of course I have . . .' I started to protest; but with box in hand he had already got up and was making his way to the cloakrooms.

I stared after him indignantly. However, my attention was diverted by the arrival of three men at the next table. Loud-suited and loud-voiced, they carried beers and whisky chasers, and were smoking cigars of impressive proportion. I took them to be local bookies on the razzle. However, judging from their conversation, which was not difficult to overhear, it transpired that two of them had recently come down from London and, having joined the third, were en route to catch the Newhaven night ferry, stopping off at the hotel for a bracer before embarkation. I hoped that this would not be a protracted affair as I had been enjoying the soothing drink and found their noisy laughter grating.

The most florid of the three, who seemed to be in the chair, asked if the others had had a good journey: 'Cut it a bit fine, didn't you? Thought I'd have to catch the boat on my tod.'

'Lights at the level-crossing stuck as usual. Besides, bit of luck we're here at all after that blithering idiot braked when he did, stupid sod!' exclaimed the one sitting nearest to me.

'Looked like some priest,' the other added, 'got one of those collars on.'

His companion grunted and flicked the ash from his cigar. 'Might have guessed. Heads in the clouds . . . lethal they are! If we hadn't been in such a hurry I'd have stopped the car and rammed the collar down his bleeding throat. That would have got him to Kingdom Come all right!' He gave a coarse laugh and the others joined in.

I could feel myself going scarlet, and nervously wound the scarf more closely around my neck. I resented his use of the word 'lethal', feeling that, all things considered, the Church and its ministers probably did slightly more good than harm. I was about to ponder this further, when it struck me that as applied to myself – and from Elizabeth Fotherington's point of view – the term was unnervingly apt. I contemplated my drink soberly, took two more large sips, and then began to feel rather less sober . . .

Nicholas returned from the Gents, took one look at my muffled neck and said scathingly: 'Well, you don't need to overdo it. You look like some invalid in the last throes of laryngitis!'

I grimaced, and muttered out of the corner of my mouth, 'If you don't mind I think we should move elsewhere – not too keen on the present company.'

'Look, old boy, it's not that I'm deaf or anything, but if

you must mumble into your scarf like that you can't expect me to understand a word you're saying!'

'I am going to the *bar*,' I announced – rather more loudly than intended – and got up sharply, promptly knocking his drink over.

'Good thing too, old sport, you can buy me another while you're there!' He followed me over, instructed the barman to mix two more doubles at my expense and resumed his position on one of the stools. From the distance I heard one of the voyagers observe, 'What's wrong with him, then? Must be your voice, Cyril. Enough to scare the pants off anyone!' There was a volley of laughter and another swirl of cigar smoke.

Settling myself on the stool next to Nicholas, I tentatively loosened the scarf a couple of folds, and with back firmly turned to the group at the table, reapplied myself to the cocktail. It really was rather good!

I sensed Nicholas watching me, and in the mirror caught sight of his sardonic grin.

'Thought that might slip down well,' he observed. 'You can always trust Old Nick in these matters!'

'About the only ones,' I said drily.

'Now, now, don't sulk, Francis. You've actually done well this time – the pig's the right one all right: and it's going to make me a moderate mint. Congratulations, dear boy, Bishop Clinker would be proud of you.'

'Clinker?' I exclaimed. 'What on earth has he got to do with it?'

'Don't you remember at St Bede's how he was always saying that he didn't mind his clergy being simple-minded as long as they were *efficient*? Well, at long last it seems you're beginning to show the missing ingredient. My compliments.'

I scowled and was about to retaliate, but somehow both the drink and his accompanying laughter were infectious, and instead I started to giggle. 'At least the Spire Fund can get its rake-off – you did mention a cut, I recall!'

'A modest one, yes. Enough anyway to keep that inebriate female of yours tanked up on brandy for a while . . . God, that was awful!' He closed his eyes, looking suddenly haggard.

Clearly the memory of Mavis Briggs simperingly and insatiably consuming his finest cognac had entered deep into Ingaza's psyche. It was not the first time he had mentioned it.

'That was nothing,' I said, taking another sip, 'you want to be there when she's spouting her verses, nothing beats that . . . Anyway, she is not *my* female, simply a prep-posterous parishioner!' I had a little difficulty with that last phrase and wondered vaguely if Between The Sheets was taking its toll. I can't say the matter bothered me unduly . . . but his next words certainly did.

'Ah, but not as preposterous as the other one,' he murmured silkily, 'Elizabeth Fotherington.'

This time it was I who closed my eyes. 'No,' I said shortly, 'not as bad as her.' There was a pause. And then I expostulated, 'Do you really have to bring that up now, Nicholas? I am only just beginning to thaw out – it's been a very taxing day!' And to underline the point I threw down some more of The Sheets.

'Sorry, old man – a bit like a twingeing dental cavity, I suppose.'

I stared at him open-mouthed. 'A twingeing frigging cavity? Are you out of your mind? Have you *any* idea!'

He raised an enquiring eyebrow, offered me another Sobranie, lit one for himself and said smoothly, 'Just testing, that's all . . . intriguing really. You know: the psychology of it all.'

'Oh yes,' I retorted acidly, 'like some curious specimen. Doubtless I provide you and Eric – whom I presume you've told – with endless speculative material! As it happens, there's nothing remotely intriguing about it – she just got on my fins, that's all, and I did it. Took me by surprise.

In fact, if you want to know, I've been feeling bloody surprised ever since!' I pushed my drink aside and started to get off the stool to go to the Gents.

He caught my arm, and in a low but firm voice said, 'Listen, Francis, I'm not too keen on spreading dynamite around, one tends to get blown up oneself. I have told no one, so get that out of your addled head! Now, go and pee and then we'll have supper.' And so saying, he reached for the menu and started to scan its limited fare.

I left the bar feeling partly reassured and yet in a way even more unsettled. Naturally it was a relief to learn of his discretion (if that was really the case), yet his use of the term 'dynamite' was a painful reminder of my looming peril. Not that I needed reminding, but having it defined by someone else was a confirmation I could do without.

I peed dispiritedly, and with waning appetite returned to the bar. Nicholas, however, was clearly bent on having a full supper and was already moving to the dining room. I followed him in and we sat at a corner table. The cocktails had begun to cloy and I was glad that he had ordered a bottle of house claret.

'Cuts the sweetness. You look as though you could do with something a little more astringent.' And he poured me a large glass. 'So who shall we drink to this time?' he enquired genially.

'Can't think of anyone.'

He shrugged. 'Oh well, it will just have to be My Lord Bishop again.' And we solemnly raised our glasses to Clinker. Reference to Clinker made me think of Claude and the wretched Bone Idol. Theft seemed a bagatelle in comparison to murder.

'Better toast the pig,' I said. He agreed and placed the box between us. We duly drank its health, while I fervently hoped that this marked the end of my 'assignments'.

He pushed the menu in my direction murmuring, 'I don't advise the macaroni, dear boy, it has the texture of a dead Durex.' I blushed and hastily chose the beef.

71

In fact the food was better than expected. What with that and the absurd toasts, my mood and appetite were restored; and feeling more relaxed again, I began to embark on a richly coloured version of the day's events. Indeed I think I must have grown quite expansive, for when I announced airily that I might start my journey home by way of the South Downs, Nicholas hastily urged that I stick to the conventional route.

'No bloody fear, Francis, not at this time of night! In your state you'll only end up at Beachy Head or drive into a chalk pit or something, and then there'll be headlines in the *Argus* – "Vicar found drunk and disorderly in dew-pond: claims he was delivering a pig to distinguished Brighton art dealer."'

I was about to retort that, drunk though I might be, the term 'distinguished' was the last I would be likely to use. However, the riposte was never uttered, for suddenly I had the shock of my life . . .

There *she* was – sitting at a table at the far end of the room, lumpish and unmistakable: Elizabeth Fotherington's dreadful daughter, Violet Pond!

12

The Vicar's Version

'Whatever's wrong?' he asked. 'You look as if you're having a seizure!'

'I am about to,' I gasped. 'It's her, the Pond woman – Elizabeth's daughter, the one who kept plaguing me about the will . . . I told you . . . seemed to think I'd rigged the whole thing and duped her mother into adding the codicil in my favour. Relentless, she is!'

'Put your head down, she may not see you.'

'Too late,' I groaned, 'she already has. Oh Lord, that's all I need!'

'Me too,' agreed Nicholas. 'I'm fed up with your marauding females. Time I was off!' Grabbing the pig, and hastily throwing down a small share of the bill, he melted towards the door leaving me to the larger part and the tender charms of the Violent Pond.

She was halfway across the room, bearing down with purposeful stride. I affected not to see, grabbed a passing waiter, thrust far too much money at him, and with equally dedicated stride headed for the foyer. With luck I could reach the sanctuary of the Gents before she caught up . . . Useless. My path was blocked by a couple of dithering guests, and before I had time to change course and achieve the exit she had tapped me smartly on the shoulder.

'If I am not very much mistaken, it must be the worthy Vicar of St Botolph's, Francis Oughterard!' This was said in a tone of accusing acidity.

'Canon, actually,' I corrected mildly (might as well make use of the few straws I had).

'Well, whatever it is – canon or vicar – I see that you are enjoying the fruits of my mother's money – and the wines too, I shouldn't wonder.' She glanced at the claret-stained napkin still trailing from my waistcoat buttonhole.

I removed it hastily and said in as dignified a voice as I could muster, 'Mrs Pond, it is always a pleasure to meet you, but as I invariably have to point out, I had absolutely nothing to do with your mother's will, and –'

'Except receive what was rightfully Violet's,' a voice said quietly in my ear.

I spun round, and was confronted by a plump moon-faced man standing uncomfortably close to my shoulder.

I was about to ask who on earth he thought he was, when Violet Pond said preeningly, 'This is Victor, my new and delightful husband. He is *such* a support! We're on our honeymoon.' And she gave me a look of simpering smugness.

New he may have been, but he looked far from delightful to me – squat and shifty and, from my possibly biased viewpoint, wearing a look bordering on imbecility.

'How do you do,' I said stiffly. 'I fear you are rather misinformed about the will – but trust that you and Mrs . . . er, will be very happy.'

I was about to turn on my heel and walk away, when Pond cut in: 'Crumpelmeyer, that's my name now, and we've just bought a large house near Godalming – although of course it could have been even *larger* had my poor late mother's wishes been properly regarded.'

'They were,' I said shortly. 'Now, if you would excuse me, I really must be getting back to Molehill. Busy day tomorrow, five funerals.'

My departure was not quite as smooth as intended, for I became entangled in the unusually brisk movement of the revolving door, and rather embarrassingly found myself circulating twice prior to reaching the pavement. However, once there I raced hell-for-leather towards the Singer, couldn't find the key, and slumped panting and distinctly woozy upon the bonnet. I expected to hear pounding footsteps behind me, but mercifully there was nothing, and for a few moments I remained thus: staring out at the darkened sea, listening to the gentle slap of surf on shingle and the moan of distant foghorns.

After a few moments of such repose, I located the car keys in an inside pocket and climbed thankfully into the driving seat. Heeding Ingaza's injunction not to take the Downs route, I drove at stately pace through the centre of Brighton and on to the homeward road.

There was something unreal about that journey which haunts my mind even now. It had been a long eventful day, and latterly bibulous. The sky was black and the roads deserted; and as I drove through the enclosing night in a haze of claret and muddled memory I felt detached both from my surroundings (too dark to define anyway) and even from the pressures of my situation. I thrust forward in a vacuum of unclear purpose and curious calm. Certainly Ingaza was a pain, the Pond woman impossible, my prospects dire – yet somehow, on that solitary midnight road, such things melted and nothing really seemed to matter . . . until, of course, I took a wrong turn and crashed the car.

Actually it wasn't a real crash, rather an ungainly shunting into a ditch as I overcorrected the steering wheel having missed my way at a roundabout. Fortunately there was little damage, and after some revving and sliding I was safely en route again. But it was enough to sober me up and focus the mind on achieving Molehill and bed.

This I eventually did at about half-past one, and stumbled into the kitchen glad – and slightly surprised – to be home. I was also slightly surprised to see that

Bouncer was not in his basket by the boiler, but assumed it must have been one of his nights for the crypt . . . And then I heard the faint sound of canine snores issuing from my bedroom. Maurice, however, was there – awake and unusually chummy, greeting me with a couple of thin miaows and sharp head butts to the ankles. I wondered if he had been at the haddock again, but was too tired to check; and giving his tail a friendly tweak retired thankfully upstairs where I collapsed beneath the blankets and the dog.

13

The Vicar's Version

The next day, despite my reference to the five funerals, there were in fact only two – one at the crematorium and one in the graveyard. I prefer the burials. I suppose it is that raw proximity to the earth that chastens and induces feelings of awe and – oddly enough – comfort. Our roots are with the primitive, and it is that tacit recognition, felt in the touch of mist, rain, snow and sod, which anchors the mind and soothes the spirit.

Maurice enjoys burials too, and it is rare for such a service to occur without some glimpse of the cat's inquisitive presence. Mostly he watches from afar, crouched on his favourite tombstone from where he keeps gimlet sentinel; but sometimes he moves in close and you catch brief sight of twitching ear or darting tail. Only once has he intruded, and that was in connection with Mavis Briggs. Some months previously a local dignitary was being interred and thus Mavis was inevitably at the forefront of things – or had contrived to be so – insinuating herself among the family mourners until she was virtually on the rim of the grave. I had noticed the cat lurking quietly in the shadows, when suddenly, with lightning flurry, he was at Mavis's ankles tweaking her shoelaces with rabid playfulness. The result was mild mayhem – shrieks from Mavis as she teetered on the brink, titters from the mourners, and an oath from one of the pall bearers. It was an unseemly interruption and I was none too pleased. However, it had had the happy effect of keeping Mavis well away from funerals for some considerable time. Even she, it seems, is capable of embarrassment.

Anyway, the current afternoon's obsequies over, I returned to the vicarage to catch up on paperwork interrupted by the previous day's exploits. I was still tired from the driving – not to mention my encounter with Violet Pond – and had hoped to pursue the pen-pushing undisturbed.

It was not to be. A telephone call from the police station enquiring if I was at home announced the imminent arrival of March and Samson. I groaned and grimly braced myself for what, in view of the Whippet's earlier appearance, had been only a matter of time.

They turned up at four o'clock, and if Samson had been expecting more chocolate cake he didn't get any. I had not seen March for a few months and in the interim the portly figure seemed to have gathered additional girth, the fawn raincoat looking more strained than ever, although its wearer's genial phlegmatism appeared unchanged. The Whippet was as always: thin and morose.

His superior coughed, fumbled for his notebook, perused it slowly, and then in a tone of apology said, 'Bothersome business, sir, isn't it . . . but you see, our Mr Slowcome has just arrived down here from the Met and he's a great stickler for procedure . . . a great stickler. And he's got this bee in his bonnet that the case involving your friend Mrs Elizabeth Fotherington was not conducted entirely to his exacting standards and that there are still a few trailing ends. Well, of course it's not for me to say – but you know these London officers, they have a different way of looking at things from us so-called "country bumpkins". Always going on courses and then coming back with ideas which don't seem to connect with anything much!' He cast a glance at Samson. 'Isn't that so, Sidney?' The latter said nothing.

I didn't much like the allusion to my 'friend' and was about to explain that she wasn't so much friend as parishioner, but he continued to rumble on: 'So you see, we've got to run over a number of statements again, and in your case there are just a couple of things that need straightening out.'

'Such as?' I asked casually.

'For example, this legacy she left you – the money you say you gave away. It was quite a tidy little sum, wasn't it, sir?'

I conceded it was indeed quite a tidy little sum, and naturally I had given it away – as he might well recall. And in any case, it could surely be verified by checking with the recipients.

'Oh yes, sir, we've done that already, discreetly of course; but you see, what needs to be established is how *much* of the funds was thus allocated. After all, it's only human nature, isn't it, sir, to keep a little back . . . I mean, just for a rainy day, as one might say.'

I regarded him coldly. 'It may generally be human nature, but in this particular case it was not *my* nature. I can assure you, Inspector, I gave away every root and branch of that legacy.'

'Jot and tittle too, I daresay,' intervened Samson snidely.

'As it happens, yes. And if you have any doubts on the subject I suggest you peruse my bank statements.'

'I was coming to that, sir,' said March. 'You see, our Mr Slowcome is very particular about that sort of thing – fancies himself as an auditing wizard, and whenever there's any doubt in the matter what he always says is, "Check their accounts, March, check their accounts!"'

I looked at him steadily. 'I am sorry if I appear a trifle dense, Inspector, but who exactly are you and Mr Slowcome referring to when you say "their"?'

March blinked and looked vague, opened his mouth and was about to say something when he was pre-empted by Samson.

'What they are referring to,' barked the Whippet, 'are the *suspects*.'

There was a brief silence while I glanced out of the window at the sparse lawn and lacklustre privet, and then at Maurice who returned a glassy stare.

'I see,' I said slowly, turning to March. 'So you think I murdered Mrs Fotherington?'

'Well, not as such, sir . . . that is, not entirely.'

'Not entirely! You mean I only half did it, and someone else came along and finished her off? What are you talking about, March!'

He cleared his throat. 'No, sir, you misconstrue my meaning. What I am saying is that all those interviewed previously are being asked to furnish further details. What you might call filling in the gaps, so to speak. All part of the general routine. As I said, it's Mr Slowcome, he –'

'So I am *not* a suspect?' I snapped.

'Ah well, sir, that was Samson's word. Very keen, is Sidney – makes him use rather colourful language sometimes. Leastways, that's what I would call it.' And turning to his companion he smiled indulgently. Samson scowled.

'Well,' I replied stiffly, 'using monochrome language, perhaps you or the detective sergeant would be good enough to explain what "gaps" you are seeking to fill.'

'It's principally this legacy aspect, sir. A formality really – but you'll understand that what with it being so large a sum and the codicil appended only a few days prior to her death, it is something that has to be given precise scrutiny, especially with you being the chief beneficiary – contrary to all the daughter's expectations. It's what we call a bit of an anomaly, really. So you see, it just needs that extra bit of checking . . . sort of belt and braces, if you get my meaning!'

'I would hardly call it an anomaly, merely a common or garden coincidence. As I explained at the time, my appearing in that codicil came as a bolt out of the blue, and it is clearly my ill luck that she should have met her unfortunate end so soon afterwards!'

'And hers too, I suppose,' muttered Samson.

I affected not to hear and continued to address March. 'And why she should suddenly have favoured me over her daughter, I have absolutely no idea; but it is my experience – and doubtless yours, Inspector – that people are full of whims and fancies for which there is no accounting. It is just one of those things!'

He smiled patiently. 'I expect you're right, sir, but we'll have to check those bank statements all the same. Mr Slowcome is most particular in these things. Likes it all tied up neat, he does.'

'Well, the last thing I want is to obstruct the punctilious Mr Slowcome – nor indeed you, Inspector, so you are perfectly welcome to scrutinize my accounts to your heart's content. I can assure you that every bit of that legacy was deposited with the said charities and that not a single penny was retained for my personal use.' I spoke in a tone of careless confidence – a state genuinely felt, for I knew that as far as the legacy was concerned I was absolutely in the clear. If that was all they were bothered about I was as safe as houses!

March nodded, apparently satisfied, and closed his notebook. 'Thank you, sir.'

'But there is something else,' added the Whippet flatly. (Something else? What more, for God's sake!)

'Oh yes,' I said smoothly, 'and what might that be?'

'The time that you say you left the house to go on your jaunt to Brighton. Now that *is* an anomaly. You see, in your original statement you said that you left at dawn – it being such a nice day and all that. But we have a witness that says you left at lunchtime.'

I felt sick, but also perplexed. What witness? Surely there hadn't been a soul about. I had used the short cut on to the A281 and I could swear blind there had been no sign of vehicle or pedestrian. Admittedly, at the time I was in a rather dazed condition and hadn't taken any particular precautions of concealment. Nevertheless, I was pretty sure the roads had been totally empty. Indeed it was precisely this recollection which, on my return from Brighton and in a panic of self-preservation, had prompted me to give my departure as being earlier rather than later. The forensics had established Elizabeth's death to have occurred between 8.30 and 9.30 a.m. Thus at the time the lie had seemed a sensible precaution. Now, of course, I saw it for what it was – foolishly crude and highly dangerous.

Naturally Samson wasn't going to hand it to me on a plate, i.e. naming the witness and thus giving me a chance to formulate my response. Instead he paused, gazing out into the garden, leaving me to flounder in limbo unsure whether to stick to my story or adjust it as best I could.

It was March who spoilt his tactic. And even now I can remember Samson's look of fury as his superior pronounced the name of the local errand boy, and thus unwittingly gave me the merest chance to collect my wits.

'Young Charlie Fenton. Says you came out of your gate at a right old lick at about midday and nearly knocked him off his bike. Says he wobbled so much that two loaves fell out of his basket!'

I didn't recall the bread part, but March's words suddenly jogged my memory into seeing the look of startled indignation on the boy's face as I swung the Singer into the lane, wrenching the wheel to avoid the dawdling bicycle. I remembered too the heat of the noonday sun, the smell of the car's warm upholstery, and the revving of the engine as I took off from the vicarage in a vortex of fear and numb denial.

I forced a laugh. 'Oh yes, Charlie – I'd quite forgotten. Nearly sent him flying, I'm ashamed to say! Mind you, he's pretty lethal on that bike of his – should think he's been knocked off many a time!' And I laughed again, desperately wondering what I could dredge up next.

'You are probably right, sir,' replied March ponderously, 'but you see, what we are wondering about is the *time* – it being lunchtime and not dawn, as you first said.'

'Exactly,' interposed Samson sharply, 'it's the time factor. You will observe the discrepancy between the two recollections. Quite a difference, I should have thought, between dawn and midday. They don't tally – do they, sir?' And he cast one of his blank yet penetrating looks.

'No,' I answered, sounding rueful, 'they don't tally, and I'll tell you exactly why. Sounds ridiculous, I know . . . but I set off from Molehill first thing, dawdling here and there to enjoy the scenery and sunshine; and then when I had done about three-quarters of my journey I suddenly realized that I had left its whole purpose on the kitchen table!'

They looked uncomprehending, as well they might, and I continued blithely: 'Yes, the essential point was that it was to have been a reading holiday – so much to catch up on, you know! And I had left all my books and papers in my briefcase right in the middle of the kitchen table. Would you believe it!' (Not anyone in their right mind, I hear you say.) 'It was useless continuing to Brighton without them – waste of time really. So after a comfort stop and some coffee from the thermos, there was nothing for it but to turn round and drive all the way back. I got home at about eleven thirty, picked up the books, read the post, and then set off again in a mad hurry. Which was when I bumped into young Charlie!'

There was a silence, and then March cleared his throat. 'I see. And it escaped your mind to mention this to us when the matter was first discussed?'

'Well,' I replied blandly, 'I am not sure I would say it was *discussed*, Inspector. I mean, I seem to remember that you asked me what time I started off for Brighton, and I told you – before breakfast, which was indeed the case. I don't recall subsequent details being requested, and we got on to other things, I think . . .' I trailed off, beaming ingenuously.

There was an impatient grunt from the Whippet and the bullet was fired: 'These books that you *say* were left on your table . . . What were they?' Sharp. But for once I was ahead of him (must have been the adrenalin flowing!).

'*Tractatus Bensonii*,' I replied without hesitation, 'King James's *Basilikon Doran*, and a volume of Herbert's early devotional verse. One or two others, I think, but I really can't quite remember now . . . Oh yes, Newman – such a stimulus!'

He looked sour and was about to say something but was cut short by March. 'Doesn't sound like your kind of reading, does it, Sidney? Not yours at all!' And turning to me he added, 'Hank Jansen, that's his favourite . . . though personally I always say you can't beat a good Edgar Wallace. At least he's British!' I nodded in sympathy. 'Anyway, Canon, thank you for your time. We'll be off now – but yes, as I said, we'll still have to check those accounts at the bank, if you don't mind. Mr Slowcome, he –'

'Of course, of course . . .' I replied benignly, stooping to tickle the cat's ears. And then burbling something about the inclement weather, I opened the front door and watched them proceed down the path. They seemed to be talking intently – or at least the Whippet was – and I wondered if they were discussing their literary tastes.

14

The Cat's Memoir

'First of all he spins an absurd tale to that fat policeman and looks at me as if expecting confirmation, and then, if you please, starts yanking my ears about!' I exclaimed to Bouncer.

'It's a hard life, Maurice,' observed the dog. 'But did he get away with it?'

'Well, if he tries it another time he won't,' I replied with some asperity. 'I mean to say, I had only just completed some rather delicate grooming. Had to start all over again!'

'Bugger your grooming! Did he pull the fur over the flat-foot's eyes?'

I flicked my tail impatiently. 'Just because you give no thought to the finer points of personal toilette – or indeed even to the grosser – there is no call to be dismissive of those who do! Admittedly fastidiousness is not within your –'

'MAURICE!' he roared.

I sighed. 'If you mean did F.O. succeed in convincing the police officer of his innocence, I rather doubt it. However, he would appear to have averted immediate disaster – for which naturally we must be thankful.'

'Hmm,' the dog growled sombrely, 'it's a bit hairy, isn't it?'

'Yes,' I conceded, 'it is somewhat hairy.'

There was a brief silence as we reflected upon the hairiness of things . . .

'There's something else,' he said.

'What?'

'Well, I was talking to the poodle, Pierre the Ponce, this morning, and he says – '

'Always a mistake,' I admonished.

'Oh, come on, Maurice, he's not as bad as all that. I mean, I know he's a soppy French dog and walks in a funny way but he's quite nice really and is full of ideas, and –'

'Exactly! And some very peculiar ideas too!'

'Ah, but this time he might just have something.'

I raised a quizzical whisker. 'Go on.'

'He has seen the old girl's daughter!'

'Which old girl? There are a number.'

'The one that F.O. did in – your mistress, Fotherington of course!'

'But the daughter went off ages ago!' I exclaimed sceptically. 'Got fed up trying to contest the will. Probably in Timbuktu by now.'

'No,' he replied, 'in Godalming.'

I did not like Violet Pond, considering her offensive and uncouth. For a brief period after my mistress's death she had moved into Marchbanks House, encroached on my domain and conducted herself in an even more tiresome way than her mother. Indeed, at one point she had actually had the gall to refer to me as 'that poisonous cat'! Only ill comes from types like that, and I was annoyed to hear that she had returned to the neighbourhood.

'So what is she doing there – apart from taking up unnecessary space?'

Bouncer grinned. 'According to Pierre she's got a chap in tow – a new husband called Crumplehorn or some such.'

'Oh well,' I observed indifferently, 'she'll be far too preoccupied with him to bother us – or F.O.'

'Ah,' replied Bouncer, 'but *you* haven't seen him. The

poodle has. And *he* says he wouldn't like to meet him on a dark night!'

'Pierre the Ponce is notoriously highly strung and absurdly imaginative. You would be wise to treat his words with a crumb of biscuit.'

'My bones tell me different,' the dog said darkly. '*I* think there could be trouble.' And picking up his rubber ring he ambled off to the kitchen making grunting noises.

I sat and considered. What trouble? It was enough having the police hanging around again just when we thought all was well. Surely Pond and this Crumplehorn person couldn't present any threat, could they? Obviously Bouncer was in one of his histrionic moods – too many hours in the crypt. Such excess always makes him go a little peculiar. Nevertheless, I was disquieted – too disquieted in fact to develop a proper sulk. One needs concentration for that, and for the moment I felt quite distracted. Instead I embarked upon the sparrows. They had become more than usually complacent of late and it was time they were unsettled.

15

The Dog's Diary

I've been doing a lot more thinking lately – mainly down in the crypt where it's nice and quiet. Not as comfy as my basket in the kitchen, of course. But sometimes it gets a bit loud in there what with the kettle whistling, Maurice hissing through the window-panes at the birds, and F.O. effing and blinding over his sermons. A dog just can't get his thoughts together. Still, I'm a bit tired now because all this thinking is quite difficult! Makes me hungry too – but I like that because I can sort of store it all up and then have an extra old guzzle in the evening. Maurice says I'm greedy – but then cats don't think as deeply as us dogs so they don't need the grub as much. Mind you, *he* wouldn't agree with that – doesn't agree with anything really – and keeps calling himself an *inter* something or other. Well, I tell him I am inter lots of things so what's new? But he just smiles that slippery smile of his and slinks off into the potting shed.

Anyway, the point is I've worked out one or two ideas down in the crypt, and I DON'T LIKE THE LOOK OF THINGS. Not one bit! You see, I bumped into that poodle the other day, Pierre the Ponce, whose owner's brother lives in Godalming, so he's always being taken over there on visits. Tells me it's 'tray snob' and full of 'lay bo john' – or some such French lingo. Don't understand what he's talking about half the time (I don't with Maurice either!), but what I *did* understand is that that Violet Pond has got herself a fancy man called Crumplehorn. According to Pierre he's a nasty piece of work and would put the frighteners on you at the drop of a Bonio. (Matter of fact, the cat's right there – Pierre *is* a bit of a ninny and it doesn't take much to set him off, but he's not a total fool, not like that idiot bulldog we met last year.) Of course, Pierre doesn't know what F.O. did in Foxford Wood – naturally I haven't told him. I mean, it's not right for a dog to let on about *all* his master's funny habits. But he warned me that he was pretty sure that Pond and thingammy were up to no good where the vicar was concerned, and that they had it in for him and were PLOTTING!

What do you think of that! Well, that's exactly what I asked Maurice. Needless to say he didn't think much at all; but he will. These cats, they have to . . . uhm, what's the word? . . . Oh yes, *re-flect*, that's what he's always saying. You'll see – when he's done a bit of that *re-flecting* he'll start showing an interest and begin bossing me around and telling me what's what. But I shan't mind that because, unlike with bones, two heads are better than one, and we've got to stick together if we are to keep the vicar safe and DEFEAT THE ENEMY!

16

The Vicar's Version

'Parried that one!' I muttered to Bouncer after they had gone, and collapsed gratefully on the sofa immersing myself in wreaths of smoke. The dog stared gormlessly and then applied himself to his bone. The steady gnawing had a curiously soothing effect, and stubbing out my cigarette I closed my eyes and drifted into sleep.

When I awoke it was nearly time for supper, and I was just about to forage in the kitchen when I remembered to my horror that I shouldn't be at home at all, but in the car en route to Archdeacon Foggarty's inaugural drinks party. Now safely spared the appalling prospect of Rummage's elevation, I felt moderately disposed to Foggarty and was perfectly ready to raise a thankful glass to his future ministry. After all, he could only be better than Rummage, and being relatively young surely less stuffy than Blenkinsop. The evening might even prove mildly congenial – unless by the time I got there half the guests had left, food scoffed, and the drink desolate! Thus I scooted upstairs, scattering Maurice on the landing, and in barely ten minutes had managed to clean my teeth, shave, and struggle into a fairly uncreased suit. Fortunately the Singer had petrol, and without more ado I took off speedily in the direction of Guildford.

My destination was St Elspeth's Church House, a Victorian Gothic building used principally by the authorities for their frequent and interminable meetings, but very occasionally, as on that particular evening, for some brief jollification. The former events were invariably sombre, the latter largely sober. Still, a spot of recreational sobriety was surely preferable to sitting at home cursing the police and fretting over the newly designated Violet Crumpelmeyer!

Despite the crush of cars, I managed to park fairly close to the building and made my way quickly towards its heavy doors. I was in the middle of hanging up my raincoat in the vestibule when a voice in my ear said acidly, 'Ah, Canon, I was just saying to my husband that you were bound to have forgotten all about it. Still, better late than never, or so they tell me . . .' And waiting for neither excuse nor greeting, Gladys Clinker pounded on her hefty way towards the door marked *Ladies*. I glared after her and hoped the cistern fell on her head.

I walked down the draughty corridor and entered the dining hall. It was very full and – unusual for such gatherings – the mood appeared to be almost teetering on the brink of gaiety. There was a convivial buzz of conversation and even an occasional gust of muted laughter; and much to my relief I noted that there still seemed to be plenty of food around, and in addition to the inevitable fruit squash, a fair supply of alcohol. No gin of course, but one couldn't be too picky; and studiously avoiding something calling itself Spanish Sauternes, I opted for a large glass of tolerable sherry. With this secured, and balancing a plastic plate of tinned crab and Coronation Chicken, I found a seat in a sheltered corner and embarked on supper.

It is my experience of such occasions that it is well to attend to these matters on immediate arrival, failure to do so invariably leading to short commons as one is collared by some earnest lay-reader, or worse still, the bishop. In fact I noted that Clinker was safely rooted at the other end of the room and heavily occupied with Gladys, who, despite my hopes, had evidently returned from the Ladies unscathed. But I kept my head down just the same, for fear of lurking lay-readers.

91

Supper demolished without hindrance, I felt more relaxed; and emerging from the shadows went to replenish my glass and begin to circulate. Out of the corner of my eye I saw Mavis Briggs sporting a vapid smile and puffed sleeves. Next to her stood Edith Hopgarden wearing neither smile nor sleeves but fearsome in acid yellow. I kept my distance from both and turned in the opposite direction.

I had not gone far when I was caught by young Rothermere from Alfold. I say 'caught', but as a matter of fact despite his overly boisterous manner he is quite an engaging fellow, and during the Rummage rumpus had been a compliant ally.

We chatted briefly and then he said slyly, 'That was a near miss, wasn't it? Just think, we could have had someone else in our midst tonight instead of old Carrot Top!'

'Old *who*?' I enquired, perplexed.

'He of the red hair – old Foggarty.'

'The new archdeacon,' I reproved, 'is neither old nor red-headed, he is merely –'

'Looks pretty ginger to me! And he's not exactly young, is he?'

I replied that the colour of Foggarty's hair was immaterial to his pastoral duties, and that in terms of age he was a mere two years older than myself; an observation which brought the cheery response: 'Sorry, Francis! Forgot you were a canon now – and shall I get you another drink?'

'Yes, Rothermere, you may get the canon another drink,' I replied, 'and be jolly quick about it!' I turned and was confronted by Blenkinsop.

'Ah,' he exclaimed lugubriously, 'thought I might see you here. I've got a message from Claude, something about a bone idol.'

I mentally groaned. The last thing I wanted was a message from Claude. The shenanigans with the pig still haunted me; but the less I heard of it, or its owner, the more I could persuade myself that the whole thing had never happened.

'Oh,' I said bleakly, 'really?'

'Yes, wants you to talk about it.'

'What does he mean, "talk" about it?'

'Don't know exactly. He twitters on – I never listen much. Something to do with a conference on ancient Indian curios – wants you there as the honoured guest speaker. Says he's been mentioning you to a number of his cronies and they are fascinated to hear about your researches ... I must say, Oughterard, can't think where you find the time for all that sort of thing. Should have thought that your obligations to the diocese were more than sufficient to keep you occupied, especially considering your recent advancement – in which,' and he coughed delicately, 'I played some modest part.'

Insufferable Blenkinsops! Why couldn't they both just go *away*!

'Absolutely!' I agreed. 'First things first. Much too involved with matters here for jaunts up to London jawing about some minor personal indulgence. As you say, considerably weightier things in the diocese to attend to.'

'My views exactly,' he replied. 'But of course, Claude has always been frivolous. Still, I suppose you had better contact him, otherwise he'll keep nagging at *me*, and I'm far too busy for that. After all, I've got enough on my plate steering Foggarty in his new ministry. Nothing like sound advice from an old hand!' He nodded sagely, agreeing with his own comment, while I felt sympathy for Carrot Top.

I had even more sympathy for myself. The prospect of being further embroiled with Claude Blenkinsop and the pig business was too awful to contemplate. Surely he wasn't going around telling people I was some sort of expert on Beano or Indian folk art, or both. The embarrassment would be dreadful, shaming! Supposing he had already set up this conference and indicated that 'The Revd Canon Francis Oughterard, noted authority on bone effigies and eighteenth-century British explorers' was likely to attend and answer questions on his current researches and 'work in progress' ... Nightmare!

I steadied myself. No, the thought was absurd. My imagination was clearly overwrought. Pa had always complained of it – 'To quote the great Bard, my boy, "That way madness lies!"' And thus to allay the madness I procured myself another helping of Coronation Chicken and cursed Ingaza. It was all his fault!

I was brooding on Nicholas and his machinations but enjoying the chicken, when somebody sat down next to me. It was Wattle, Rector of St Elspeth's and, despite Clinker presiding, technically our host.

'Good evening, Canon,' he began breezily, 'glad to see you here. Don't think we've met for quite an age. Up in London, wasn't it? One of the Brompton things. But there's always such a multitude one never really gets a chance to have a sensible word with anyone! How are things going at Molehill? Such a peaceful place, I always think.'

It would be, I thought bitterly, given half a chance! . . . Besides, what did he mean by 'peaceful'? A veiled hint about my having a soft ride? I looked at his smiling face and ingenuous eyes, and immediately felt ashamed of such cynicism. Getting paranoid, that's what! I returned the smile and congratulated him on the success of the party.

'Yes,' he agreed, 'people do seem to be enjoying themselves, and it's a nice way for the new archdeacon to be launched.' He paused, and then added in an undertone, 'I suppose Foggarty is what one might call a merciful release – given the other possibility!' And he chuckled benignly.

We talked briefly and lightly of Rummage and the vicissitudes of church politics, and I was enjoying his company until he suddenly said, 'I tell you what I've been meaning to ask you, in fact nearly rang you up about it. You remember that unfortunate parishioner of yours who was murdered in a local wood?'

I nodded guardedly.

'Well, you'll probably also recall the fracas over the burial. The daughter was hell-bent on having her mother interred here at St Elspeth's instead of at your place. She made quite a thing of it, and it was a bit tricky as at the time we were short of space and I didn't particularly relish people from other parishes muscling in and pinching all the best places.' He laughed. 'Still, as you know, we managed to accommodate her in the end, and all was well.' (I certainly did know. The news that my victim would be buried in the neighbouring parish and that I should be spared the necessity of conducting her funeral had been the one bright spot in the whole frightful affair.) 'However,' he continued, 'it's been rather odd recently.'

'Odd? What do you mean, odd?' I enquired nervously.

'Well, despite all the kerfuffle about the funeral arrangements, ever since the service itself neither the daughter nor any family member has appeared again. I mean there's been no sign of anyone coming back to tend the grave or anything, and yet –'

'But that's hardly unknown,' I broke in. 'In fact I should think far more graves are left fallow and abandoned than are properly cared for. There's an initial flood of mourning or dutiful observance, and then what with one thing and another, it all rather peters out. Something to do with attention span.'

'That's true,' he acknowledged, 'but you see, in this particular case there's been a rather startling *upsurge* of attention, quite perturbing really!'

I was beginning to feel perturbed myself. Elizabeth Fotherington's grave was not a subject I cared to dwell upon, let alone discuss. What you might call too close to the bone ... Shifting uncomfortably, I lit a cigarette and asked him casually what was the problem.

'Well,' he began, 'it's a bit delicate really ... you see, they want to exhume the body.'

'Exhume the body!' I gasped. 'What ever do you mean?'

'Exactly what I say. The daughter – I think her name was Pond, though it's different now, Crumpel something ... Anyway, she and the new husband are demanding that her mother be resurrected as there is an object they need to get their hands on.'

'Get their hands on what?!' I cried, dropping ash and singeing my trousers.

'A diamond bracelet apparently.'

'A *bracelet*? I should have thought it was a bit late now,' I expostulated. 'Besides, what is she doing wearing diamonds in the grave!' (Typical of Elizabeth, always excessive!)

'You may well ask,' he replied drily.

'That's just what I am doing. Come on!' I exclaimed impatiently.

He was about to tell me, when we were interrupted by the arrival of Bishop Clinker who, looking a trifle worse for wear (an overdose of the Spanish Sauternes – or Gladys possibly?), drew up a chair and sat down between us mopping his brow.

'All very splendid, these things, but they take their toll, don't they? I wouldn't mind being at home now in my study with the phone off the hook, cat on my lap, and door safely locked!'

We nodded in dutiful sympathy. And then Wattle said, 'As a matter of fact, my lord, I was just telling Francis about the Fotherington affair – you know, the exhumation question . . .'

'Oh Lor', not that again!' groaned the bishop. 'Thought you had sorted that out by now. The whole thing's ridiculous, all that bracelet nonsense . . . I mean, who does she think she is, Queen Nefertiti?'

Wattle cleared his throat and said gently, 'Well, sir, I don't suppose she thinks anything at all – er, at least, not *now* exactly.'

Clinker glared. '*She* may not think anything but the daughter clearly does! What are you going to do about it, Wattle?' The latter said nothing but regarded the remains of my Coronation Chicken as if seeking inspiration.

Despite reluctance to become involved, curiosity got the better of me, and I said, 'I don't understand. Surely all jewellery would have been removed prior to the interment.'

'Normally yes,' replied Wattle, 'but in this case Mrs Pond – as I think she then was – particularly requested that it be buried with the deceased. Said it was a worthless paste job but much beloved of her mother, and since she herself had no use for it thought it a nice idea if it went into the grave with the wearer.'

'So what's changed her mind?' asked Clinker brusquely.

'That's just it, I don't know really. Couldn't quite make it out. A confusion apparently – but they seemed to think that Francis had got something to do with it . . .'

'Me!' I yelped. 'Why me? I wasn't even there!'

'No,' said Clinker, 'gadding in Brighton if I remember correctly.'

There was a pause, and then I said meekly, 'It was my official term of leave, not exactly gadding, sir. I was visiting my sister – a few days' respite, that's all.'

'Well, whatever it was, you weren't there, and now we've got all this palaver,' retorted Clinker grumpily. 'In any case,' he added, turning to Wattle, 'it's your grave and Oughterard's parishioner. You'll have to sort it out between yourselves. I've got better things to do than deal with families who cannot decide whether to leave their relations' belongings *sub* or *supra terram*!' With that he got up, and jangling his car keys removed himself to the far end and rounded up Gladys.

There was silence. And then clearing his throat, Wattle observed, 'Well, no guidance from that direction . . . I had expected more.'

'Not where Violet Pond is concerned,' I said. 'He had a dust-up with her some months ago, and he's not getting caught again.' (I refrained from explaining that the dust-up had been in connection with Mrs Pond's complaint over me featuring so prominently in her mother's will. Like the deceased, some things are best left undisturbed.)

'I've not actually been involved in an exhumation before,' he continued. 'Don't know the protocol – perhaps the new archdeacon can shed some light.'

'Oh yes,' I said grimly, 'that'll test his pastoral initiative all right!' And then added, 'Probably the best thing is to do nothing, perhaps they'll get bored with the whole idea and go away.' But I spoke with little conviction. Knowing Violet, and having encountered Crumpelmeyer, I had small hope that they would just disappear – a doubt that Wattle confirmed.

'They don't seem bored at the moment!' he exclaimed. 'According to Hawkins, my sexton, the two of them have been prowling around her grave for the last three evenings: not engaged in anything like bringing flowers or doing a spot of tidying, just wandering about talking and staring. In fact Hawkins said it was as if they were eying it up, sort of taking its measure ... but then one doesn't want to believe everything Hawkins says, he's got rather a lurid imagination. It's the work, I suppose.'

'I should think he has,' I cried. 'He'll be telling you next that they've been seen with picks and shovels!'

'No,' he replied, 'but we may see them appear with a magistrate and a permit to disinter.'

I closed my eyes and shuddered. This really was the last straw! And then I shuddered again: what on earth had the Crumpelmeyers meant by saying it was something to do with *me*! What dread horrors now lay jostling in my path?

Gripped by that question, I bade goodnight to Wattle, said a few encouraging words to Carrot Top, and then made my way to the car and home. It had been a dreadful evening.

17

The Cat's Memoir

'Bugger me!' exploded the dog. 'If that doesn't take the cat's litter!'

I stared angrily. 'Is something troubling you?' I enquired.

'I should say so,' he growled. 'Look what he's gone and done – put his great hoof in my grub-bowl and mangled all the best bits. It's too bad!'

I regarded the bowl. Its contents looked worse than usual. 'Ah,' I said, 'that must have happened last night when he returned from Guildford. I thought he was in a bit of a state – blundering about everywhere and muttering his head off. Something about graves and bastards . . . the usual sort of thing.'

I resumed my grooming and hoped the dog would be quiet. He wasn't. Instead he embarked on a long saga involving O'Shaughnessy and his latest escapade, which seemed to feature the milkman and two dozen broken eggs. Whatever it was, Bouncer clearly found it highly risible, and at least it diverted him from F.O.'s gaffe with his feeding bowl.

I let the tale sweep over me as I brooded on our master and his current preoccupation with matters subterranean. What *was* it he had been muttering? I raked my memory, and then it suddenly came back to me – yes, something to the effect of '. . . dig up the damn grave and shove Pond in too!' I winced. Surely he was not planning *another* assault!

The upheaval would be dreadful and I should have to rethink my entire routine . . .

Such bleak thoughts were suddenly interrupted by the dog bawling, '. . . and then, Maurice, what do you think O'Shaughnessy did? Lapped up all the milk AS WELL!'

I closed my eyes but nodded appreciatively. 'Remarkable!'

'Thought you'd like it,' he replied cheerfully. 'And what's more –'

'Bouncer,' I said hastily, 'there is something rather serious we have to consider.'

'Well, if you mean my grub-bowl, I think he's even chipped a bit off!'

'No,' I said quietly, 'it is not your bowl, but our prospects. I think he may be gearing himself up for another disposal.'

There was silence for a few moments while he appeared to cogitate. And then he said, 'So who's for the high jump this time?'

I told him I thought it was the Crumple woman. He didn't answer but lay down and chewed his paw.

This went on for some time and I began to get impatient; but eventually he said, 'Oh no, Maurice, I don't think so; you've got it wrong.'

'I beg your pardon?'

'Yes, you're miaowing up the wrong tree there.'

'How do you know?' I exclaimed.

'Well, I don't *know* exactly, just sort of feel . . . in my bones, you might say.'

'No, I wouldn't actually. It is not an expression I care to use. Presumably you will be saying it is your sixth sense next!' (A claim he invariably imagines to be his trump card.)

'Something like that,' he agreed. 'But things are going to be a bit dicey all the same, mark my words.' And with that oracular observation, he rolled over and went snoring off to sleep.

I stared at him irritably. Dicey? Things had always been 'dicey' living with the vicar, there was nothing new in that . . . But what in particular was looming to make F.O. quite so agitated? He hadn't been in such a state since the incident with the cigarette lighter.* I sighed, and carefully circumventing the dog's tail, I too lay down and took my ease.

* See *A Load of Old Bones*

18

The Vicar's Version

The morning after Foggarty's party I woke early with a headache and a distinct sense of foreboding. The few hours that I had managed to sleep had been battered with dreams of earth mounds and shovels and the constant drone of Inspector March's voice repeating incessantly, 'It's like I said – he should never of gone and done it!' A view with which in my waking state I thoroughly concurred.

Downstairs in the kitchen I made strong coffee, lit a cigarette, and ruminated. Technically, of course, the question of Elizabeth's exhumation did not concern me: she was in Wattle's domain, not mine. And despite Clinker's reference to her having been my parishioner, the actual burial location surely carried more weight in such matters than the customary place of worship. Yes, in that respect the whole matter was undoubtedly Wattle's pigeon. Nevertheless, the possibility of her resurrection was something which I found far from congenial . . . indeed, not to put too fine a point on it, grotesque! And the less I knew about it the better. But in this rather closeted part of Surrey grapevines flourish, and – assuming it was ever sanctioned – I doubted whether I could escape hearing of the gruesome event.

Besides, what was immediately worrying was Wattle's comment that the Crumpelmeyers thought that I had something to do with the buried bracelet. What on earth had they meant? Perhaps the rector had got the wrong end of the stick or misheard them. But then again, perhaps he had heard only too well. My encounters with Violet Pond had suggested a woman of wild and improbable imaginings; and emboldened with a new husband what fresh vagaries might she not indulge! It was all very dispiriting.

To assuage anxiety I toasted two thick slices of bread and smothered them in peanut butter and marmalade. Watched intently by Bouncer, I was about to embark on the first piece when the telephone rang. Irritably I put down the toast and went into the hall to answer it: some officious member of the congregation requesting alteration to the time of the Sunday services. Did I not think it would be better to hold the eleven o'clock sung Communion at ten o'clock, thus releasing worshippers to attend to their leisure pursuits sooner rather than later? I replied that, no, I did not think so; that eleven o'clock was the traditional hour, and that in any case, the scheduling of church services could hardly depend on the recreational plans of random members of the laity. I hung up briskly and returned to the kitchen. It was amazing what people occupied themselves with at that hour of the morning!

Settled once more, I reapplied my mind to the exhumation and my toast. A slice was missing and Bouncer nowhere to be seen. I cursed. Wretched dog! Presumably I should be grateful for his courtesy in leaving me the one remnant.

Thus the day started in tiresome mode and continued so until lunchtime and an encounter with Mavis Briggs and Edith Hopgarden, when it took a further lurch downwards.

They were in the High Street together, with Edith marching and Mavis trailing. As they approached (Edith in her clattering heels and Mavis in the flat wide-strapped sandals so despised by Claude) I wondered vaguely what had occasioned such sorority. They were not noted for their

103

mutual admiration. I paused and stared fixedly into a draper's window hoping they would miss me. Quite the reverse.

'I cannot imagine what the canon finds so riveting about ladies' corsets,' announced Edith's penetrating voice. 'Dog collars more his line, I should have thought!'

I swung round, flushing and flustered. She was quite right, there were indeed two peach and bursting under-garments thrust close to the window-pane, which in my haste to remain unnoticed I had somehow failed to register.

Mavis tittered, while I laughed weakly, explaining that I had been looking for vests.

'In that case,' said Edith, again loudly and pointedly, 'you had better try the *other* window, they've got plenty there, nobody could miss them!' I did not like her tone, but then I rarely do.

Mavis started up. 'Oh Canon,' she bleated, 'you remem-ber those gurgling noises in the vestry pipes I told you about?' I nodded. 'Do you know, they've completely dis-appeared. It's such a relief, I was getting really worried! It was almost ... almost *uncanny*. You could hear them every Friday morning – most strange. You must obvi-ously have done something very clever!' She simpered up at me.

'Yes,' I replied, 'I took a hammer.'

Back in the safety of the vicarage, I imbibed a liquid lunch and made a vigorous assault upon the keys: the old favourites, 'Honeysuckle Rose', 'Stardust' à la Errol Garner, lush and plangent, a jaunty little rendering of 'After You've Gone', and then some rather clumsily executed snatches of Schubert. After that I felt considerably better; indeed suffi-ciently inspired to start hunting for receipts with which to mollify the church auditors. This was a long but neverthe-less moderately productive chore, and the afternoon closed on a note of relief.

However, it was a relief somewhat dissipated by my sister Primrose. She telephoned on the dot of six to announce she would require a bed for the night on her way north to visit friends. I was still a trifle frayed by our last encounter and asked diffidently if she intended bringing the chinchillas again, Boris and Karloff.

'Certainly not!' she exclaimed. 'They have barely recovered from their dreadful ordeal last summer!' That made three of us.

I brightened. 'Well, I am sure that should be no difficulty. When do you want to come?'

After some negotiating in which Primrose was the chief protagonist, we settled on four days hence. I wondered whether she might appreciate a little company at supper, and considered inviting the Savages or even the church-warden Colonel Dawlish. But I swiftly banished the idea. My sister's abrasiveness would be too much for the gentle Savages, and too similar to Colonel Dawlish's to make for an easy evening. No, Primrose alone was the best bet – and in any case it was a prospect not totally uncongenial. Although sharing a degree of mutual exasperation, on the whole we relate moderately well – provided distance is kept and meetings are few – and despite her bossiness and what she clearly regards as my muddle, enjoy a wary friendship (albeit recently severely tested by the chinchilla débâcle).

The following day was Sunday. Many can stay abed; vicars cannot. Thus I roused myself early and prepared for the three morning services, two quick and one long. The latter is by far the best, for apart from a short Evensong it marks the end of the day's commitments, and carries the prospect of lunch and an idle afternoon with newspapers and the Third Programme. So the Sunday ritual took its customary course: two short Communions, and finally the Sung Eucharist at eleven o'clock.

It had been a rather agreeable service – good attendance, doughty hymn-singing (so different from the previous week's dirge-like quaverings), a resolute reading from Colonel Dawlish, plenty in the collection plate, and above all a gratifying attention to my sermon. Just occasionally I can pull the rabbit out of the hat and make them sit up and take notice, and that day's particular theme – The Fruits of Merriment – seemed to have caught their fancy and kept them moderately awake. Certainly there was a show of beaming bonhomie in the porch afterwards, and once the usual nods and pleasantries were over I was able to return to the vestry feeling almost buoyed up.

Occasionally on Sundays I am invited to lunch by one of the congregation, but sometimes I prefer the solitude of the vicarage and the prospect of a large gin and a long snooze. That day it was going to be the latter, and I walked down the path and out through the lychgate looking forward to both and wondering vaguely what I should organize for supper when Primrose arrived.

Thus occupied I did not see them at first. But as I stopped to unwrap a peppermint I noticed a couple coming towards me: she square and heavy, he shorter with plump and pallid face. The Crumpelmeyers advanced remorselessly up the lane.

I cast around wildly for an escape hatch. There was none, not even a lurking chorister whom I could button-hole and engage in protective chatter. They approached frozen-faced, while I composed my own features into a smile of ingratiating benevolence. I would take the bulls by the horns.

'Good morning!' I greeted them, 'How's the new house at Godalming? Settling in all right, are you?'

'In the circumstances, yes,' replied Violet distantly. I raised an enquiring eyebrow.

'What my wife means,' murmured Crumpelmeyer, 'is that we would be settled considerably better had you not chosen to interfere with the late Mrs Fotherington's selection of jewellery.'

I stared at him literally open-mouthed. 'Interfered with her jewellery! Whatever do you mean?'

'Exactly what I say. You gave her gratuitous and officious advice which she was fool enough to take, and from which we are now all suffering.' He sniffed assertively and adjusted his tie with podgy hand.

What on earth was the man babbling about? I certainly did not recall offering any advice to Elizabeth – being generally far too preoccupied in trying to extricate myself from her crushing overtures! Besides, how could my advice have possibly affected the Crumpelmeyers? I was to learn.

'If you had exerted less influence over my poor mother,' broke in Violet, 'that diamond bracelet kept in her bank strong-box would have had some useful value. As it is, it has proved worthless! Not content with inveigling yourself into her will and denying me much of my rightful patrimony, you had the gall to tell her to switch the paste bracelet for the genuine article! The stupid old – the poor dear lady went about wearing the *real* diamonds while all the time the paste ones were safely and pointlessly tucked up in the bank vault. We took them to be valued a few weeks ago and were horrified to hear they were utterly bogus – paste through and through. And it's all *your* fault!'

Shocked by the speed and volume of the onslaught and still trying to recollect my part in the matter, I said thoughtlessly, 'So where are the real ones?'

'In the grave of course,' snarled Crumpelmeyer, 'in the rotten grave!'

Ah yes, the grave. But I was still utterly perplexed about my part in the business. And then as I gazed at the lowering faces in front of me, I suddenly remembered.

It had been a Sunday, and for once Elizabeth had succeeded in persuading me to return to Marchbanks House for some sherry after the service. We had talked of this and that and nothing in particular. I had dutifully admired her flowers, her etchings, the budgerigar, the querulously staring cat (Maurice). But just as I was about to take my leave, the bracelet she always wore slipped from her wrist. I picked it up, and, as with the other items, paid the appropriate compliments. She explained rather ruefully that it was merely a copy, the original being deposited with the bank at the insistence of her daughter. I had said something to the effect that it seemed such a shame for lovely things to be locked away – surely they were made to be displayed and enjoyed; and I remembered making the vulgar quip, 'If you've got it, flaunt it!' She had gone into peals of tinkling laughter and said perhaps she might just do that. . .

'When I asked the bank to explain itself,' continued Violet, 'the head clerk airily announced that my mother had exchanged the bracelets about six months prior to her death, saying that the vicar had advised her to do so. Is there no end to your intrusions, Mr Oughterard?' (Or my penance? I wondered.) 'So when I requested the bracelet be buried with my mother I had no idea that it was the original. Worth several thousands! Naturally, had I realized, I should never have –'

'It's not that we are mercenary,' Victor Crumpelmeyer interjected quickly, 'it is simply a matter of principle and justice.'

I nodded. 'Ah yes, of course, principle and justice . . .'

'Yes, and we're going to get it!' cried Violet. 'Just because you've robbed a poor weak woman of her full inheritance don't imagine you can deny her the family jewels as well . . . Mother is going to be dug up!'

I cleared my throat and said quietly that the last thing I wanted was to deny her access to the family jewels, but wasn't an exhumation going perhaps a trifle far? And did she, in any case, think her mother would have approved the project? To which she replied that it had nothing whatever to do with her mother and all to do with rights.

I did not dispute the point but murmured that I rather doubted whether they would obtain the necessary permission as the authorities were rather tight on that sort of thing.

'Ah, but you see it's simply a matter of knowing who to approach and how,' said her husband confidently. 'I am rather a dab hand in such matters – fouling the system, tweaking this and that. I generally get my way in the end.' He stared at me blankly and then gave a slow fat smile. And exchanging smug glances they sauntered off. The Fruits of Merriment were turning distinctly sour.

19

The Cat's Memoir

'Cor!' exclaimed Bouncer. 'Something's got at him all right, shaking like a leaf and silent as the grave! Usually when he's having a bad time all hell's let loose. But not now – frozen into his armchair he was. In fact I thought we'd got a corpse on our paws!' He emitted a throaty chuckle.

'It is no laughing matter,' I reproved. 'I happen to know what it's about.'

'Well?'

'Well what?'

'What it's all about, *Maurice*!'

I took a few more leisurely laps of my milk and sleeked my whiskers. They really are rather fine – but clearly the dog did not think so.

'Leave your whiskers and spill the beans!' he roared, thrusting his hairy snout under my nose.

I backed away. 'The Crumplehorns ... they have put – as you would doubtless say – the frighteners upon him.'

'How do you know?'

'I was there,' I replied casually, 'taking a little Sunday constitutional, and I happened to witness the whole encounter. Intriguing in its way: further evidence, if such be needed, of the absurdity of the human species.' I turned my attention to my tail which Bouncer promptly grabbed and pulled.

'All right, all right,' I protested, 'I'll tell you . . .'

After I had finished there was a long silence. And then he said solemnly: 'Oh lar-lar.'

'What's that supposed to mean?'

'It's what that poodle, Pierre, is always saying.'

I waved my tail. 'Pierre the Ponce has a bizarre and Gallic vocabulary not suited to normal communication.'

'You mean he uses funny words?'

'Precisely.'

I heard him muttering something to the effect that Pierre was not the only one, but it was not clear to whom he was alluding.

'So what's he going to do?' he went on.

I shrugged. 'The usual presumably, panic.'

'Oh yes, that'll get us everywhere,' the dog snorted, and with more mutterings sloped off to the kitchen.

I remained, staring at the sparrows and wondering how they could be so stupid, and brooding uneasily upon F.O.'s similar affliction.

The affliction became only too apparent later that evening when I heard him spluttering down the telephone to his sister: 'It's all very well your saying that,' he chuntered, 'but I'm the one who has to cope with it!'

There was a silence as Primrose presumably gave tongue to her views. Obviously I could not hear these but they provoked further gnashing of teeth.

'Of course,' he snapped sarcastically, 'that's bound to do the trick – make them as meek as the lambs in your paintings, I don't doubt!'

What the reply was I could not gather, but it went on for some time and seemed to have a stabilizing/chastening effect. The conversation concluded with him saying: 'All right then, see you Thursday. I look forward to it.' Judging from his face after he had replaced the receiver, I rather doubted that last claim.

Thursday arrived, and in preparation for the sister's arrival the house had been tidied from head to toe: things shoved higgledy-piggledy into cupboards, the kitchen table raked of its usual debris, ash swept under the carpet, newspapers moved from one pile to another, Bouncer's unsavoury basket thrust out of sight (one mercy at least) and, in a rush of energy, my woollen mouse placed tantalizingly on a top shelf. I considered having a sulk about that but in his current state it would probably have been wasted. Something was fortunate at any rate: this time she would not be accompanied by those ridiculous chinchillas and one would thus be spared the dog's frenzy!

I have observed that quite often the sister's presence has a subversive effect on F.O.'s psyche, and in view of his recent contretemps with Pond and Crumplehorn I envisaged an evening fraught with tension. Thus to prepare myself for this I decided to take an afternoon nap on my favourite tombstone. When I told Bouncer of my plans for the little siesta he said he hadn't realized they held little ones, and that personally he always found fireworks a bit frightening, and rather me than him. I ask you!

20

The Vicar's Version

The days preceding my sister's visit were a period of great disquiet. Ambushed by the Crumpelmeyers, plagued by thoughts of Claude Blenkinsop and his wretched lecture, telephoned by the verger re matters of little worth but great tedium, and generally put upon by the Vestry committee and its doleful complaints, I felt ill prepared to face the advent of Primrose.

This time, however, minus the giant chinchillas her arrival caused none of the commotion of the earlier occasion. She appeared punctually with minimum of fuss or luggage, spoke kindly to Bouncer, admired the kitchen's polished tidiness, and even presented me with a bottle of (somewhat acrid) sherry. And although one never quite knows how things will proceed with Primrose, I was beginning to feel a moderate pleasure at the prospect of a 'family' evening.

Hat removed and nose powdered, she returned to the sitting room grinning broadly. 'I made a nice little packet on the sheep yesterday,' she announced. 'Sold four to some visiting Americans who seemed to think that English lambs looked so much "cuter" than the home-grown variety and ordered another two to be shipped at the end of the month. *Very* lucrative, Francis!'

I observed that since she invariably painted her subjects grazing and gambolling in the shadow of some picturesque downland church, possibly their faces reflected the piety of their context. She thought about that for a moment, and then replied that as long they brought in the spondulicks she didn't care what their faces reflected, and in any case she had not noticed the proximity of St Botolph's illuminating my own features.

I laughed, and asked how the plans for her latest exhibition were coming along.

'Pretty well actually. Managed to bag a private room in the Brighton Pavilion, and a couple of big gallery scouts are likely to be there from London. Should be quite a good show. You can come if you like – though you'll have to buy your own ticket, naturally.'

Naturally. Primrose rarely misses a financial trick.

I explained that, much as I would like to, I was currently under rather a lot of pressure from parish matters, not to mention having to cope with the threatening Crumpelmeyers and the exhumation business.

'Yes, that does sound grim,' she replied. 'You were in a dreadful state on the telephone, but as I said at the time, I think you are exaggerating. I doubt whether anything will come of it. Crossing too many bridges – always did, even as a boy.' She gave a superior smile.

'Huh,' I said morosely, 'it's rather worse than you think.'

'Oh well, we can talk about that at supper ... Now I'd like some more sherry, please, and then I want to go outside and find that awful cat of yours. I'm determined to make it like me!'

Fortunately Primrose's intended overtures to Maurice were thwarted for he was nowhere to be seen (presumably skulked off to the graveyard). This was a blessing really, as given their shared stubbornness the encounter might have proved embarrassing.

I rootled in the kitchen while she started to lay the table, grumbling from time to time about the tarnished state of the cutlery but occasionally exclaiming with pleasure when

114

she discovered some relic from our childhood home. ('So that's where that pepper pot went to, I often wondered. Pa was so ham-fisted with it!' and 'Fancy you keeping those table mats – Mother's pride and joy, though pretty grisly, I always thought.')

Eventually I got the supper on the table, and while it was pleasant enough, things were somewhat clouded by further talk of the Crumpelmeyers and their determination to blame me and get at the bracelet.

Primrose was stout in my defence, asserting the pair were as mad as hatters and – despite her own mercenary leanings – indignant at their ruthless pursuit of Elizabeth's diamonds.

'You must stand your ground, Francis!' she declared. 'On no account should you let them get their snouts in the trough, or for that matter in the grave!' She paused, and then added, 'Anyway, as I said, I'm convinced they will never get away with it, the regulations are far too strict.'

'But I told you – the husband seemed convinced he could beat the system; obviously he's an old hand at confounding the authorities and has probably got some sort of trump card up his sleeve.'

'Poppycock. Delusions of cleverness ... Anyway, Francis, just suppose he *did* succeed, would it really affect you that much? After all, it wouldn't be happening in St Botolph's graveyard, would it? I mean, I realize it's a bit murky to think of a corpse being dug up, especially of someone you had actually known, but when all's said and done, it's in the other parish – *you* aren't the one that buried her.'

'In a manner of speaking, I suppose I am.'

Perhaps it was the wine or the comforting warmth of the kitchen, or the fact that it was one of those rare occasions when the two of us were together in a sort of collusive intimacy reminiscent of our youth – but the years seemed to melt away and we were back at home again, wrangling, bantering ... confiding. Thus when she asked what on earth I meant by that remark, I heard myself saying as if from a distance, 'Well, if you do away with somebody I suppose it could be said that you *had* put them in the grave – wherever its site happens to be.'

There was a silence, and then, 'I don't know *what* you are talking about. I suppose you'll be saying next that you were the one that murdered the old trout!'

'Yes,' I said meekly. 'I was.'

'Francis, how *could* you!' Primrose exploded. 'Are you mad? What on earth would Mother say!' She had gone quite pink in the face.

'Fortunately Mother is no longer with us so we shall be spared those particular dramas. And as to my being mad – well, yes, I probably am, but it's too late now to do anything about it. I've rather burnt my boats, I –'

'Blow your boats! What about my reputation? Nobody will buy my Sussex sheep scenes if it gets out they've been painted by someone with a murderer for a brother. How can you be so appalling!'

'As a matter of fact,' I said, 'that might increase their value, people like that sort of thing, I gather.'

'Don't bet on it!' she snapped.

I tried to mollify her with the offer of a cigarette. It was waved aside.

'Can't you see I haven't finished my parsnips yet? And kindly pass me some more.' She heaped up her plate and launched upon them with avid intensity.

After a while she put down her knife and fork, and grabbing the bottle and refilling her glass said, 'So whatever made you do it? Hardly a crime of passion, I imagine!'

'Well, no . . . I mean to say, it was a mistake really – all happened rather quickly.'

'Mistake, my arse. Monumental disaster! Really, what I have to put up with!'

I said nothing and gazed down at my napkin and then at Bouncer who wagged his tail cheerfully.

'I'll have that cigarette now.' She took it from me, pushed her chair back and strode to the window where she stared out at the garden, drumming her scarlet nails on the sill.

'This must never get out,' she declared. 'It must be suppressed at all costs! Do you hear me, Francis?'

'Of course I hear you! What do you think I've been doing for the last eighteen months – wandering about with a sandwich board advertising it to all and sundry in Oxford Street?'

'No need for sarcasm,' she replied icily, 'I was merely offering you some sisterly advice.'

I studied a perambulating spider on the ceiling and looked at Bouncer again, envying the dog its uncomplicated life. And then, clearing my throat, I asked diffidently if she would like some coffee.

'Yes, but only if it's the proper thing, not any of that ersatz stuff you usually have. And then I want a clear blow by blow account.' She paused, and suddenly gave a thin giggle. 'Well, not a blow by blow *exactly*, if you see what I mean.'

I smiled wanly and asked if she wanted black or white.

'And so you see it's all been rather difficult,' I concluded.

'Yes,' she said, 'but it makes a jolly good story, doesn't it?'

'Only if you are not the perpetrator,' I replied grimly.

'*Or* related to him!' And she started to frown again.

I sighed. 'Well, so far so good, I suppose . . . I mean, as long as I can go on keeping it quiet you should be all right.'

'But *can* you keep it quiet? I do take it you haven't told anyone else,' she added sharply.

In for a penny, in for a pound. 'Er, as a matter of fact,' I said quietly, 'there is somebody else in the know. But,' I lied, 'I don't think that should be a problem.'

'I might have guessed,' she exclaimed. 'You are hopeless, Francis! Who, for God's sake?'

I told her and as feared she hit the roof.

'Not that dreadful specimen you knew at St Bede's – not the one found in flagrante in the Turkish bath!'

'Well, yes, I suppose so –'

'You suppose so! With a name like that of course it is him – *Nickerless* In Gaza. I remember the whole case, it was disgraceful. Trust him to be at the bottom of it all!'

'But he isn't,' I protested, 'I merely informed him after the event. It was difficult not to. You see, he provided a sort of alibi – been quite useful in his way.'

'Huh! That's as may be, but you know Ma and Pa always warned us not to consort with types like that. Pa would have called him a blackguard – in fact I think he did from what I remember.'

'Probably,' I agreed drily. 'It's what he called most people.'

'Anyway,' she went on, 'this Nicholas person, he could be dangerous.' (Didn't I know it!) 'But on the other hand, he is obviously what I believe they call an "accessory after the fact" so he had better watch out!' And she blew a righteous smoke-ring.

'Actually, Primrose,' I reminded her gently, 'so are you.'

'Christ!'

21

The Vicar's Version

I was relieved that I had told Primrose. Ingaza's knowing was less of a relief – more of a penitential uncertainty. But despite the fumings and drama which had inevitably ensued, having Primrose as confidante gave me an odd comfort. Something primitive, I suppose, to do with bonds and consanguinity. Whatever the reason, I felt strangely unburdened, and after she had departed took time off to go into Guildford and sample the new cream cakes at the Angel.

I was just easing myself into one of its deep leather club chairs and reflecting upon patisserie pleasures, when a voice from the adjacent sofa said, 'Ah, so this is where you come to prepare your sermons, is it? A sort of canon's bolt hole!' Colonel Dawlish emitted a shout of laughter and a billow of pipe smoke.

I don't dislike Dawlish, and as a churchwarden he is exemplary; but I was annoyed nevertheless to be interrupted in my solitary hedonism. However, I smiled genially and said something to the effect that I had happened to be passing and thought I would just look in to see how their new extension was coming along. For some reason I was reluctant to admit the hotel was a regular refuge and that his term 'bolt hole' was pretty apt.

'I come here once a month,' he volunteered, 'always the first Monday' (I made a mental note to avoid) 'while I'm waiting for Tojo to have his regular spit and polish. Rather an absurd name really, The Pets' Beauty Parlour, but they clean him up a treat. Little blighter doesn't know himself when he gets out. Worth the money and the wait . . . you ought to take your hound there. On second thoughts, beyond redemption, I shouldn't wonder!' There was another gun-crack laugh.

I was trying to think of a suitable riposte, when leaning forward he said, 'Extraordinary, you know, them opening the Fotherington case again. Apparently not the flasher after all, poor bugger – some other crank, I suppose. Still, bound to be well away by now, unless of course he's the type that lurks around. Some of them do, I gather. They get a sort of perverted excitement in remaining in the crime area, watching the police watching for them. Funny really, the criminal mentality . . . What do you think, Canon?'

I thought he was barking but refrained from saying so. 'Perverted excitement' my foot! What about the sleepless nights and abject terror?

'Yes, it's puzzling,' I replied vaguely. 'Rather beyond me, I'm afraid – not terribly good on that psychology stuff, a bit over my head!' And I gave a weak laugh.

'Oh, I don't know,' he said grinning slyly, 'I think less goes over that head than sometimes appears.'

I was not quite sure how to take that (and am still not), but beginning to feel uncomfortable stood up, saying something about going to look for the waitress. Dawlish also got up, and collecting his *Times* and trilby said it was time to fetch Tojo from the beauty parlour. I had a vision of the West Highland bounding from the doorway sparkling and irascible, and felt rather glad that my own charge was the tousled, matey and unredemptive Bouncer.

In fact I did not seek the waitress. My companion's reflections on the Fotherington case and the workings of the criminal mind had somehow soured the prospect of cake, and leaving the hotel I returned home in sober mood.

* * *

Sobriety gave way to twitching angst when, two hours later and as I was in the middle of grappling with the Sunday school rota, the telephone rang. Mavis Briggs had been threatening to contact me about the sequel to her nauseous *Little Gems*, and I picked up the receiver with failing spirit.

'Hello, old cock!' breezed the voice. 'How's tricks?' Evidently not Mavis.

'Ah . . . hello, Nicholas,' I replied guardedly. 'What can I do for you?'

'Well actually, dear boy, it's not so much what you can do for me but rather what yours truly might do for *you* – or at least for your talented sister.'

'Primrose?' I exclaimed. 'But you don't know her.'

'Not as yet, no – but it might be *arranged*.'

'Who by? What for?'

He cleared his throat, and said severely, 'If you mean, Francis, by whom and for what purpose, the answer is by you and for the purpose of helping your sister.'

'Primrose doesn't need helping, she never does.'

'All artists are interested in financial patronage, and I don't imagine your sister is any different from the rest.'

Too right she wasn't – but what on earth was he getting at? I was to learn.

'You see,' he went on, 'my Cranleigh chum has a rather useful Canadian contact who just happened to mention that for some bizarre reason the art denizens of Ontario have recently conceived a passion for paintings of sheep and churches, and there is an enormous demand for them out there. Don't ask me why, a more boring subject I cannot imagine! Still, that's the Canadians for you . . . Anyway, they are paying high prices for consignments from all over Europe: Switzerland, Holland, Italy etc. So my Cranleigh pal told *his* chum that he thought he might just be able to lay hands on a likely source of supply, and none of this bland Continental stuff they're being palmed off with, but really good *British* sheep and decent native churches . . .'

'Oh yes?' I said bleakly.

'Yes – you see my drift, don't you, dear chap?'

I said nothing but nodded dismally down the telephone.

'I mean to say, if your sister could keep up a steady trickle – preferably stream – of said paintings, I would ensure that she was richly rewarded ... after the usual deductions, of course.'

'Of course,' I murmured.

'What do you think?'

'We-ll,' I said slowly, 'she might be interested, I suppose, but I don't know that –'

'There's only one *slight* snag, and that is that what they really like is original eighteenth-century stuff: you know the sort of thing, rural idylls with pious peasants loitering by crumbling chapels tending their sheep, and painted by obscure pastoral artists of whom nobody has ever heard. I can tell you, dear boy, a *mint* is being made over there!'

'Oh well,' I said greatly relieved, 'that lets Primrose out then, doesn't it!'

There was a pause. And then he said quietly, 'Well, not necessarily ...'

Ingaza's proposal that my sister should supply the Ontario art market with fake eighteenth-century pictures was both risible and outlandish, and I told him so in no uncertain terms.

He seemed unruffled by my outburst and said it was merely a suggestion and that doubtless some accommodation might be reached. I told him that I was not too keen on his 'accommodations' and knew for a fact that Primrose would not be in the least receptive.

'If you say so, Francis old boy, if you say so. Just a thought.'

The subject was dropped and we moved to safer matters: specifically Eric's recent triumphs in the Brighton darts championships.

* * *

The rest of the week was taken up with the usual parish duties, although evading Mavis Briggs had been one of the principal preoccupations. Such evasions are normal but this month I had particular reason for keeping a wide berth. The second volume of her *Little Gems of Uplift* had been unwisely published a couple of weeks previously, and I knew that this would eventually involve an evening of lugubrious recitations in the church hall. I suspected that her immediate mission was to commandeer me, fix a definite date and ensure that I gave the event my endorsing patronage. Naturally I did all I could to postpone the inevitable, but she caught me in the end: outside the sweetshop where I go periodically to buy packets of slab toffee.

I had just slipped a large and particularly jagged piece into my mouth, when I heard Mavis's winsome tones: 'Oh, Canon, at last I have found you! Might you possibly spare a minute?'

Jaws firmly clamped by the toffee, I nodded silently. She beamed and launched into a breathless résumé of her literary endeavours and of what she evidently imagined to be the finer points of some of the poems.

'And so, Canon, when I talk about hearts being "sprinkled with lissom sprites and fanned with lace-wrought doilies" and "the south wind bloweth all wet and weeping" the audience will immediately grasp the underlying *significance*, don't you think?'

I shifted a piece of toffee from one side of my mouth to the other, got it stuck on a molar and nodded again.

'And then you see, the simile "like phalanxes of plangent cows moaning in the plaintive morn" is bound to strike a chord in the souls of the more . . .'

She broke off and looked at me quizzically. 'Oh dear, I didn't realize. Have you just been to the dentist? You must be in great pain – your cheek is all swollen!'

I swallowed unsuccessfully, tried to speak and resorted to spluttering into my handkerchief. Inadvertently this had the desired effect, for Mavis, full of solicitations and squeaking about rest and oil of cloves, took herself off, saying she would catch me at a more propitious time. A brief reprieve, and I scuttled home gratefully.

The telephone rang. It was Wattle.

'I've got the exhumation sewn up,' he announced.

'Ah.'

'Yes, it's off – absolutely. The municipal authorities won't stand for it. Thought you'd like to know ... Mind you, there's been a hell of a rumpus, but the Crumpelmeyers had to climb down in the end.' He paused and then chuckled. 'Better watch your back, Francis – they're gunning for you!'

'Oh yes?' I said wearily.

'Yes. They are convinced you've hatched some dire plot to deprive them of the wife's inheritance. Apparently being balked of the bracelet was the last straw. Crumpelmeyer used some pretty choice language in the matter. Speaking personally I'd put in for a sabbatical!' He chuckled again.

'Very droll,' I muttered.

Something to be thankful for at least. The possibility of Elizabeth being disinterred had been weighing on me heavily and it was certainly a relief to hear of the project's veto. For once the executive had proved its worth. However, the ire of the Crumpelmeyers was still in prospect ... Clearly a time for some rousing Brahms. And, lighting a cigarette, I made for the genial haven of the piano.

22

The Dog's Diary

That Primrose was here the other day; stayed the night again and made a lot of noise. I quite like her really, and she often feeds me titbits when F.O. isn't looking. But I've noticed that whenever she comes, or we go there, the vicar goes pale round the gills and gets sort of ratty – like I do when I've lost a bone. Mind you, sometimes they are on jolly good form with lots of laughing and alcohol swilling about, but generally one of them seems to say something that sets the other off and then there is a contrytomp. (That's Pierre the Poodle's word for a buggers' shindig.) Well, they had one of those the night she was here, and a right little up and downer it was too! Maurice was in the graveyard and missed it all and is spitting mad that I only tell him about it in bits – one haddock-head at a time, as you might say. Really gets him going!

Anyway, from what I could make out, F.O. told the Prim that he was the one who had bumped off old Fotherington. And oh my backside, didn't the balloon go up! She didn't half give him an earful: said he was stupid and that it was going to jep – something or other, her artist's reputation. I think she meant she would lose some lolly if people got to hear about it. So she went ranting on and then demanded details. But when he had finished the story she started to giggle. The master didn't think much of that and said it was all right for *her*! They went wrangling on for another hour and then stomped up to bed. The next morning things had calmed down a bit, and she went away and he took himself off to Guildford. I know where he went – to stuff his face with cream buns at the Angel. It's where he usually goes when he's on form – or off. Off generally.

Since then he's been up and down like a cat's tail. I think the Brighton type telephoned, and that seemed to put him in another spin, though I couldn't quite make out why. And then there was somebody called What-Ho, and that was GOOD news because the vicar went to the piano and started pounding the keys like crazy. I liked that and tried to join in – but he didn't seem terribly keen.

While all this has been going on I've made a new friend – newer even than O'Shaughnessy. This one is huge, much bigger than the setter, though she comes from the same country as him – that place over the western seas where they all gabble their heads off. But she's much easier to understand than O'Shaughnessy, and in any case doesn't speak as *much*. She is grey all over, with a shaggy coat and a big head, and I think she is VERY NICE. I shall talk to Maurice about her, but knowing him he'll probably be snooty and not want to know. But I can tell you, if she puts a paw on him he'll know all right, so he had better watch out!

23

The Cat's Memoir

I had passed a very agreeable afternoon basking on my favourite tomb in the graveyard. It really is a remarkably comfortable place of rest, better even than the large gatepost gracing the drive of my late mistress's abode. That was highly convenient as it afforded such a broad view of The Avenue and thus kept me well apprised of Molehill's business. It had been, you might say, my civic watch tower.

However, perched on a knoll overhanging the vicarage lane, the tomb too has sentinel properties. And it is from here, well camouflaged by the mounds of ivy, that when in curious vein I can glean all manner of useful information. I know for example that the organist Tapsell is not the only romantic interest in Edith Hopgarden's life: she now has her eye on the verger! I don't think F.O. is aware of that, but on at least two occasions I have observed them sidling past, gazing at each other with expressions not usual to those discussing the exigencies of church maintenance. Nor has it escaped my notice that sundry members of the preparatory school choir regularly congregate under the sycamore tree to smoke and play gin rummy when fleeing the summons of their music mistress. The lane is also favoured by Mavis Briggs to practise those verses so abhorred by the vicar. He has a point. Never in my nine lives have I witnessed such ludicrous sounds and gestures! Then there are the antics of the animal species: the cavortings of fellow felines, the absurdities of dogs, the stupid posturings of pigeons . . . Yes, a veritable charivari passes my basking-place and I do not regret the transfer from gatepost to tomb-top.

However, there was one thing I did regret. Being thus engaged, i.e. watching the pavement cabaret, I was not at home on the night that the vicar's sister came to stay and when her addled brother confessed his role in the Fotherington assassination.

Bouncer was insufferable in providing only a partial account, a garbled version proceeding in fits and starts and stopping at the most crucial moments. It was tantalizing, and, I suspect, deliberate. However, being sharp-witted and accustomed to the dog's ramblings, I quickly grasped the import of his words and made the appropriate comment – an observation to the effect that our master was showing even greater signs of derangement than usual. The dog replied that he wasn't sure about that and perhaps the vicar had felt the need of an ally. Allies are all very well, I replied, but it rather depended who they were. Some allies – Irish setters for example – could be a distinct liability; whereas others, such as cats with fertile minds, could be of singular asset.

He stared blankly and said that, since the vicar's sister was neither a setter nor a cat, he didn't know what I was talking about.

Some time later the dog returned from wherever he had gone and seemed to be in an excitable state.

'I've just been talking to our new neighbour,' he announced, 'the one that's moved in with the people opposite the vet's. I met her a couple of days ago but she was on the lead so I didn't get a chance to say much. But just now she was wandering around on her own and we got on jolly well.'

'You mean the Irish wolfhound?'

'Yes, she's *huge* but very pretty, with a nice kind face.'

128

'Well, evidently an improvement on that foxy little Pomeranian, Flirty-Gerty, you were always pursuing! Nevertheless, Bouncer,' I admonished, 'she's clearly out of your league. Too tall and too educated. Do not get ideas above your station – it will only end in distemper.'

'Oh, I don't know,' he replied airily, 'I think she rather fancies me.' And he gave a cocky flick of his back leg.

I sighed. 'So what is her name?'

'Florence.'

'Florence? Florence! That's no name for a dog.'

'Oh, yes it is,' he growled. 'And it's a jolly good name – but then cats wouldn't know about such things . . .'

I mewed irritably and stalked off to the potting shed.

I had not been there long when I heard the door creaking open, and turning round was startled to see a very large and very grey head poised upon the threshold. I stared in some perplexity, and the head moved slowly in my direction followed by an immense, angular and shaggy body and long sweeping tail. I retreated a few steps, nervously weighing up the apparition.

It sat down splaying and then crossing its forelegs and fixed me with a mellow gaze.

There was a momentary silence, and then it said, 'Good afternoon. I am Bouncer's new acquaintance and I believe I have the pleasure of speaking to his good companion Maurice. My name is –'

'Florence,' I said.

She beamed and slowly moved her tail in a sort of stately wag. 'How clever of you to remember . . . I mean, I know you are a very *busy* cat and it cannot be easy recalling everything Bouncer tells you.'

'Oh,' I purred modestly, 'it's just a knack, you know . . .'

'Ah, but it is not a knack everyone can cultivate, only those with *very* sharp minds.'

I smiled self-deprecatingly. For a dog, she struck me as being remarkably well informed and I was disposed to speak with her further. Thus wafting a paw, I said that I gathered she was one of our Hibernian cousins and had she met Bouncer's other friend, O'Shaughnessy? She explained that she was *Anglo*-Irish but so loved the setter's Cork accent and didn't I think he was no end of a sport!

I wasn't quite sure how to answer that, O'Shaughnessy's sporting activities being largely confined to putting his gallumphing feet into his garrulous mouth and goading Bouncer to ever-increasing heights of ludicrous horseplay. As to his accent, one was hard pressed to understand any third word he uttered! However, I mewed graciously and said I trusted she would settle down well in the neighbourhood. She thanked me gravely, unfolded her paws, and rising to her full height (which was very full indeed) said what a pleasure it was to have met so civilized a cat and how fortunate Bouncer was to have such a friend. And thus saying, she turned around and glided off into the dusk.

It is rare to meet dogs of such breeding and intelligence. I remained for some time in the potting shed, lingering rather longer than usual over the evening ritual of washing my face and sleeking my ears.

When I returned to the kitchen Bouncer was already gobbling his Muncho, and I informed him that I too had just had a very agreeable encounter with the wolfhound.

'Hmm,' he said between mouthfuls, 'she's the goods, isn't she?'

'If you mean that the lady possesses fine manners, style and good sense, then I agree. But I fear they are qualities entirely unsuited to your proclivities.'

'We'll see about that,' he growled, and resumed his chomping.

24

The Vicar's Version

Sunday morning again. There had been a good attendance and some lusty hymn singing, and thus I mounted the pulpit steps confident that my sermon – rigorously cut to the bone – would meet with their approval. The opening paragraph was quite dramatic in flavour, and noting the stir of interest, I continued with a degree of pleasure . . . until my glance fell on an alien face: Victor Crumpelmeyer's.

He sat fatly in a central pew, his pallid skin and hair contrasting starkly with the tightly buttoned black raincoat. His eyes were fixed unswervingly on the pulpit – or to be more exact, on me. Wretched man, why wasn't he at home in Godalming with the newly acquired Violet? Surely he had better things to do on a Sunday than come traipsing over to Molehill to listen to my words of wavering wisdom! I started to glare; and then remembering he was not the only member of the congregation, hastily adjusted my features to a more amiable cast.

Things continued to progress well enough, but Crumpelmeyer's presence had unsettled me and I concluded both sermon and service in a mood of disquiet. What the hell was he doing there!

Fortunately he was not among the loiterers in the porch afterwards, nor was there sight of him elsewhere – for which I was certainly thankful. On the other hand, if he had not come to harass me further about the bracelet, what on earth was his purpose? Devotion to Sunday worship seemed unlikely, but in any case if he wanted to do that sort of thing there was a perfectly good church in Godalming. It was peculiar, and I did not like it at all.

I walked home disconsolately with Wattle's warning – 'they're gunning for you' – echoing in my mind, fed the dog his Bonio and embarked on a long snooze.

This was pleasant except for the latter part, which was punctuated by dreams of Ingaza, Primrose, and a miscellany of her po-faced sheep sporting diamond bracelets and wandering around the plains of Ontario bleating hymns of ovine joy . . .

I awoke stiff from the sofa's confinements and was just about to turn on the six o'clock news when there was a loud knocking at the window. The whey face of the telegraph boy peered in. My heart sank. There was only one person I knew who still used that particular service – Primrose; and on such occasions the content invariably spelt trouble.

I put off opening it for as long as I could – long enough at any rate to pour a whisky and hunt for my cigarettes. And then, having no further reason to delay, I slit open the small yellow envelope. My surmise was correct.

ARE YOU TRYING TO BLIGHT MY ARTISTIC CAREER QUESTION MARK KINDLY DO NOT MEDDLE IN YOUR SISTER'S AFFAIRS STOP TELEPHONING STOP PRIMROSE

I took the receiver off the hook and ruminated. Evidently Nicholas had already got at her, put his proposal and indicated that I had been sceptical of her interest. Foolishly I had overlooked the fact that where there was a conflict between Primrose's high-minded pride and her interest in money, the latter would invariably triumph. Wearily I replaced the receiver and waited. It did not take long.

'You get a stipend for life,' she stormed, 'little to do, *and* a free parsonage. While your poor sister has to earn her crusts by the sweat of her brow and her talent. I consider your words to that Ingaza person officious in the extreme. It is entirely *my* affair what commissions I choose to take!'

'Well, yes,' I rejoined, 'but in this case the plan is a bit dodgy, isn't it? You know – painting fakes for gullible Canadians –'

'Not half as dodgy as something else I could mention,' came the swift reply.

I considered that well below the belt but said nothing; instead, remarked mildly that I thought she had always held an aversion to Nicholas.

'Most certainly I do – a distinctly unsavoury type. But this is *business*, Francis, something I couldn't possibly expect you to understand!'

'So what are you going to do?' I asked. 'Flog the frauds and let your agent take his cut? He sets a high price, I can tell you!'

There was a pause, and then in icy tones she said, 'Well, I gather you know all about that. And in any case, they will not be frauds – as you so delicately put it – but items of singular taste and artistic skill which any discerning buyer would be grateful to hang on their walls. In the world of culture, Francis, there is always space for imaginative, creative licence. Kindly remember that!'

'Yes, Primrose.' And then I took a gamble: 'Tell me, how are the chinchillas? Eating well, are they?'

It did the trick, and we spent an amiable ten minutes engrossed in the exploits of Boris and Karloff and execrating the inanity of show judges who failed to appreciate their remarkable distinction.

Gardening is not my forte, and other than responding to the occasional summons from Primrose, I avoid it whenever possible. But that Monday morning with the sun shining, and suddenly struck by the rabble of weeds romping over the sun dial, I had felt that a little clearance was in order. I was also prompted by Edith Hopgarden's scathing remark two days previously, that the vicarage lawn was fast resembling the back end of the Garden of Eden – wholly wild and uncultivated. She had been with Mavis Briggs at the time and thus the jibe had lost its edge by the pun having to be laboriously explained. However, the memory still rankled and I attacked the weeds with irritable energy.

Heavily absorbed in this, I did not at first register their presence; but I suddenly realized that I was not alone. People were standing behind me – specifically March and Samson.

I started to rise from my crouching position while March made some jocular crack about the Reverend spending so much time on his knees. I smiled falsely and asked what I could do for them. March seemed in no hurry to enlighten me, and instead embarked on an involved disquisition concerning the relative merits of two popular brands of weed-killer. Having dispensed this information, he turned his thoughts to the quality of my trowel, the recalcitrance of slugs and the best kind of ground cover for north-facing corners. I listened with polite interest while the Whippet scanned the distance with sullen eye.

Eventually the horticultural treatise changed tack. 'Ever been to France, sir?' March asked suddenly.

I was startled, my mind occupied by visions of slugs and paraquat. ' Er . . . no. Well, not recently at any rate. We had a family holiday in Brittany once when I was a boy . . . but why do you ask?' (Surely they weren't going to resurrect the art theft business all over again! Or was he about to suggest the efficacy of garlic as a weed suppressant?)

'So you are not familiar with the Auvergne?' cut in Samson curtly.

My knowledge of France and its geography is limited, and so it was with genuine puzzlement that I told him that I hadn't a clue what he was talking about.

'You see, sir,' continued March, delving into his briefcase, 'we've got Mrs Fotherington's diary here, and –'

'Yes, yes,' I replied impatiently, 'you've shown me that before.'

'Ah, but *this* isn't the same one. It's an earlier one, written quite a few years previously.' He spoke with patient satisfaction. 'And if you wouldn't mind, sir, I'd just like you to cast your eye over this here passage.' He thrust the notebook at me, and I took it, thinking him mad. How could a diary dated well before my arrival in Molehill have any conceivable relevance either to me or to their investigations! Dutifully, however, I 'cast my eye' over the entry. It read as follows:

So tiresome – Ernest is eager to go to the Auvergne again to see that crumbling monstrosity built by his father – 'La Folie de Fotherington' as the locals insist on calling it. Having been dragged there once I certainly don't propose repeating the visit – a most dark and sinister place; and as for that tale about buried Nazi gold, I've never heard such nonsense!'

I looked at him blankly. 'What on earth's all that about?'

'So it doesn't ring any bells, then?' barked Samson aggressively.

I turned to look at him, replying coldly, 'No, Sergeant, it does not ring any bells. And I cannot imagine why you should think it might!'

He was about to answer but March got there first, and in conciliatory tone said, 'You're right. By itself it doesn't amount to much, but when set alongside the letter, things tend to cohere ... as our Mr Slowcome would say.' He beamed. I did not. Was I participating in some ghastly Kafka novel? What 'things' and what letter, for crying out loud!

'Show him the document, Sidney,' directed March. The Whippet put his hand in his raincoat pocket and pulled out a crumpled page which he passed to me in sour silence.

I looked enquiringly at March. 'It's the start of a letter apparently addressed to someone called Mildred,' he explained. 'You'll note that it's dated a couple of weeks prior to the lady's unfortunate end. Looks as if she put it aside meaning to continue later. But as things turned out, she was . . . er, overtaken by events.' He coughed discreetly. 'Anyway, have a read of it if you wouldn't mind, sir, and I think you'll find the matter becomes clearer.' It did. Clear and disturbing.

My dear Mildred,

Such an exhausting day! Spent the whole morning in Guildford shopping for knitting wool and bird seed for Freddie, and then in the afternoon rearranging my will. Can't find the deeds to that awful ruin of Ernest's that I was telling you about. Not that it matters really . . . had once intended to give them to the dear Revd Purvis (*such* a Francophile!) but alas, he passed over before I was able to. Perhaps Francis would be interested should they emerge, a nice little present for him. Apparently people are developing a taste for that kind of archi-tecture – becoming quite fashionable they tell me. Can't think why! But in any case, the land itself might have some value – several acres, you know, or *hectares* as they say over there! Violet, of course, can't abide the French and wouldn't be remotely interested – and, besides, she'll have quite enough as it is. Yes, I shall definitely offer them to Francis and really must renew my searches! I don't think Freddie likes the new bird seed. He was a very naughty boy this evening, had a tantrum and bit my finger. It's quite sore!

Friday
Would you believe it, Mildred, dear. Having scoured the house from top to bottom, I've found those deeds! Stuck in a pocket of one of Ernest's old suitcases. Can't think how they got there. Anyway, the moment I see Francis I shall present them to him! I'm sure the dear man will be delighted for I doubt if he has many surprises in his life. It will be a lovely moment for him. Oh, drat! Have just

seen the butcher boy wheeling his bicycle straight across the asparagus bed. If I don't catch him now he'll only

Presumably at this point, and in a flurry of indignation, Elizabeth had downed pen and rushed out to remonstrate with the asparagus despoiler.

I continued to stare at the words on the page, certain of one thing: whatever her intentions, she had omitted to present me with any such 'surprising' deeds (as if I didn't have enough shocks to contend with!) or even mention the existence of that inelegant though possibly valuable ruin. *I* knew that, but how to convince others? At the time of my 'event' I had spent much energy in devising means of ridding myself of the embarrassment of her legacy, and had finally rested secure in the knowledge that in no way could financial gain possibly link me with her death. But then I had not reckoned on the chance of even later posthumous gifts!

I stared at March in bewilderment. 'I know nothing about it,' I said blankly.

'So at no point,' he said slowly, 'did the deceased hand over these deeds to you?'

'No, never!' I exclaimed.

'And we take it that there was no mention of the documents or her intention?' Samson interposed.

I was about to assure him of that, when he continued quickly, 'You see, sir, we wouldn't want any misunderstanding like last time, would we?'

'What do you mean "like last time"?'

'That little mix-up over your times of departure to Sussex on the day of the murder. You forgot to mention to us that you had started out twice, i.e. returned once and set out again.'

'No, Sergeant. As I explained to you, I did not forget – *you* omitted to ask and then proceeded to another line of enquiry. I think we need to be clear about that.' I fixed him with the sort of look that would just occasionally quell Edith Hopgarden. No such luck with the Whippet of course.

137

He was about to respond, when March cut in hastily: 'You're right, sir, clarity is of the essence, and that's why it's imperative that nothing can be misconstrued about these deeds . . . You are absolutely certain that they were never in your possession and you knew nothing of them?'

'Absolutely certain, Inspector.'

He nodded to Samson and pocketed his notebook. 'Ah well, that's it then, Sidney, isn't it? That's another item we can cross off Mr Slowcome's list.' He turned towards the path, cast a critical eye over the rose bed, and added thoughtfully, 'Take my advice, sir, they're too old. Root 'em out and put in begonias instead – nice splash of colour in the summer . . .' He seemed to ruminate for a moment, and then said briskly, 'Anyway, Reverend, won't keep you any longer, that's all we need.' And so saying, he began to lumber towards the gate.

'For the time being,' murmured Samson.

Bastard.

After they had gone I sat down on the rusting lawn roller and pondered. It was a mercy at least that Elizabeth had never foisted those wretched things upon me. And I wondered idly what had delayed her and where they were in any case. Still, a lucky escape all right! But it was maddening that the matter should have come to light at all, and my name be linked with hers yet again. To have this added to the bracelet business was the last thing I needed. I wondered gloomily whether the Crumpelmeyers knew about this latest development . . . Bound to. Doubtless March would have informed them. Or more likely it was they who had found the letter and diary in the first place and, incensed and triumphant, presented them to the police. I groaned. It was true – not one jot of peace for the wicked! There was only one thing to do: bash up Beethoven. And crunching a peppermint, I threw the trowel aside and marched indoors to the piano.

25

The Vicar's Version

Later that week I had a luncheon appointment: one of the bishop's 'intimate' At Homes given periodically when Gladys has a social rush of blood to the head. In fact, they are generally far from intimate – chilly, cumbersome affairs from which few depart unscathed. However, having missed the last one, and in view of my new canonical status, I thought it politic to attend.

Besides, hope springs eternal, and after the abrasions of Primrose and the Crumpelmeyers, the prospect of taking lunch in civilized surroundings – even among the Clinkers – was not without appeal. There would be a reasonable dose of wines and liqueurs, and even the possibility of congenial conversation with the other guests. The real snag was Gladys, but to mollify her I had armed myself with a large box of very expensive Charbonnel et Walker chocolates, hoping they might help parry the brickbats. Thus, dressed even more soberly than usual and bearing my gift well to the fore, I presented myself at the episcopal portals exactly five minutes after the prescribed time, and rang the bell.

Surprisingly, it was Clinker himself who opened the door and beckoned me in with what I can only describe as a furtive finger. This he put to his lips and said in a low tone, 'Glad you could get here, Oughterard. I might warn you that Myrtle is with us and the lamb is burnt.'

I was nonplussed by this information but produced a sympathetic smile and a muttered 'Ah yes.' Who Myrtle was I had no idea. Was she perhaps the new cook tested and found wanting by the main course . . .?

'Yes,' he went on, still *sotto voce*, 'she flew in yesterday from Brussels, since when life here has been purgatory!'

Comprehension dawned. It was the dreaded sister-in-law from Belgium. This was grim news indeed. The prospect of Gladys reinforced by the fabled sister was unnerving to say the least. However, I put on a brave face and followed my host into the drawing room.

A number of people were already assembled, house guests presumably or near neighbours, but over by the window I espied Archdeacon Foggarty conversing with a woman of mammoth proportion. Caught in the sunlight, his hair seemed more virulently ginger than usual, but his face was white and uncharacteristically strained. Was the combination of office and his predecessor's attentive 'guidance' already taking its toll? Quite possibly. However, there was little time to ponder Foggarty's health, for I was swiftly buttonholed by Gladys and subjected to the usual barrage of patronizing questions. I thrust the chocolates at her, a gesture which momentarily stopped the flow and allowed me to slip sideways to a hovering maid with a tray of martinis. Thus armed, and with vacuous smile, I generously forfeited my place to another victim.

Various people I recognized, and a few whom it was agreeable to talk to. Another martini was offered, and I was just beginning to feel a degree of burgeoning warmth when Foggarty sidled up and tapped me on the elbow. He looked even more harassed than when I had first seen him.

'Good to see you, Francis,' he murmured quietly. And nodding in the direction of my drink asked, 'Are there any more of those around?'

Looking at his strained features it struck me that I was talking to a man in need, and in a moment of aberrant altruism I passed him mine.

He grasped it gratefully and rather to my surprise polished it off in a trice.

'That's better!' he muttered, and then seeing my look of enquiry, smiled sheepishly. 'Rather a tough time, I fear!'

I was about to ask what he meant, when he added with a broad grin, 'But your turn next, I fancy.'

'Sorry – I'm not quite clear . . .' I began.

'You will be,' he replied cryptically, and still grinning sloped off to the far end of the room.

What on earth could he mean? What did Carrot Top know that I didn't? I stood perplexed and then heard Gladys's booming voice chivvying the ladies to lead the way into the dining room. As the rest of us dutifully followed, Clinker caught up with me and, waving a piece of paper under my nose, announced, 'I see you've got Myrtle!'

'Er . . .?'

'You're on her left. It's down here in black and white.' And stabbing a sadistic finger, he pointed to the table plan in his hand. I said nothing, circled the table, found my place card . . . and glanced to my right. She was there, Foggarty's erstwhile companion – vast, billowing and, it would seem, furious.

As I pulled out her chair she glared and said in a loud stage whisper, 'Typical of Gladys, she knew very well I wished to be seated next to Sir Gerald, there is *so* much I need to speak to him about. They are coming to Brussels in September, you know, to the embassy, and there are all manner of things I could have advised him upon.' I glanced down the table at the diminutive Sir Gerald who looked remarkably unperturbed by his loss; indeed, was getting exceedingly chummy with Clinker's niece, a pretty, busty girl clearly commanding all his attention.

Myrtle scowled in her direction and then at me. 'And you are . . .?' she queried irritably.

I gave my name, adding as a vague afterthought, 'Er, Canon actually . . . from Molehill, rather a small place, you probably won't have heard . . .'

'Well, Canon Molehill,' she observed, 'all I can say is I hope you don't have a fondness for meat – my dear sister has wrecked the lamb again. She does it time after time. I gave her an excellent Belgian recipe only last Easter, but will she follow it? Not one jot. Stubborn as a mule – hence my sitting here and not next to Sir Gerald! Oh well, one will have to make do, I suppose.' And so saying, she turned abruptly to the man on her right. Her bulk obscured his identity but I was grateful to him nonetheless.

My other neighbour being also engaged, I busied myself with the soup: Mock Turtle – very mock – and I contemplated with gloom the impending lamb. In fact, as lamb goes and despite the dire warnings, this proved rather good; and fortified by two tolerable glasses of claret I started to experience moderate enjoyment.

However, this was swiftly curtailed by Myrtle suddenly turning back to me and saying, 'I gathered from the archdeacon that yours is the parish where that dastardly crime was committed. My brother-in-law mumbled something about it, but of course I never listen to *him*, and Gladys is rarely to be relied upon. Still, I've managed to glean a few details from the Venerable Foggarty – not that he was particularly forthcoming, spent all the time coughing and clearing his throat. Typical of the clergy, they can never say yea or nay to anything! Now, Canon, what I want to know . . .' She broke off. '*What* did you say your name was?'

'Oughterard,' I answered bleakly.

'How peculiar . . . Anyway, what I want to know is, *who* did it?'

Like Foggarty I also cleared my throat. 'Uhm . . . it's not known really, bit of a mystery, I suppose . . .'.

'Well, it has no business being a mystery! I don't know what the police are doing these days. They're as ineffectual as the Church. All part of this namby-pamby liberalism! Personally I'd have them all castrated.'

'The police?' I exclaimed.

'Not the police, the criminals of course. Murderers, like the one near your vicarage. That would teach him!'

I gasped. 'Isn't that a bit excessive? I mean, what good would it do?'

'Stop them breeding,' she said darkly, 'that's what!'

'Yes, I imagine it would,' I replied, folding my hands nervously in my lap.

Thankfully, at that point the pudding appeared and I hastily began to enthuse about its colour and texture, both of which were dreadful.

With the arrival of the brandy the ladies mercifully withdrew, and for a brief space I was able to relax and listen to the talk around the table. Not that this was exactly scintillating, but after the onslaught from Myrtle and the braying tones of Gladys, conversation of any quality seemed a blessed relief. The departure of the siblings clearly had its effect on Clinker too, for he became genially expansive and started dishing out cigars as if they were liquorice sticks.

I have to admit to not being terribly practised with cigars, finding cigarettes considerably more manageable; however, it would have been churlish to refuse, and after a few false starts trying to light the thing, I began to enjoy the novelty. Thus, wrapped in a pall of fragrant fumes, I took another sip of cognac, settled back in my chair, and prepared to savour the remainder of the interlude.

I was just doing this and trying to keep up with the meanderings of a shaggy dog's tale being told by my neighbour, when I heard the bishop's voice bawling down the table: 'I say, Oughterard, you're supposed to smoke the thing, not chew it! Best Havanas these are, not Wills' piddling Whiffs!' The admonition was accompanied by a snort of mirth signalling general merriment.

My discomfort was partially defused by the reedy voice of Sir Gerald observing that he had once owned a Labrador puppy who liked nothing better than a good dish of buttends for breakfast. This brought further merriment and I was grateful for the diversion, though not entirely pleased to be bracketed with Sir Gerald's puppy-dog.

Despite that hiccup, things proceeded affably enough – until interrupted by a loud hammering on the door and a voice crying, 'Come along now, you've been in there for at least fifty minutes. Kindly come out *at once*, we are waiting!' Gladys.

'Oh well,' said Clinker sighing, 'better go in, I suppose . . .'

Once more in the drawing room, we joined the ladies already engaged on the coffee and liqueurs. I was pleased to note my box of dark chocolates being unwrapped by my hostess, who proceeded to pass them around.

'Personally,' she announced, 'I *much* prefer milk chocolate, plain is so bitter! However,' she continued, casting a wintry smile in my direction, 'we don't look nice gift horses in the mouth, do we?' I returned her smile with one of dazzling sweetness and mentally topped up her glass with cyanide.

On the sofa next to me was a small woman dowdily dressed and amazingly quiet. I took to her like a duck to water. But she blotted her copybook by suddenly saying in an earnest voice: 'I gather you are the great authority on the Bone Idol – you know, the Beano pig. I have always wanted to meet someone who really knows its history!'

I stared transfixed at my coffee cup. And then finding my voice, mumbled something about there being nothing much to know really.

'Oh, you scholars are always so modest!' she exclaimed. 'My friend Claude Blenkinsop says you are a fount of knowledge and a real expert on the subject. Do tell us something about it!'

Bloody Blenkinsop! Bloody Ingaza! Bloody Beano!

All eyes were turned on me. I raked the circle of enquiring faces, desperately trying to recall a few facts from the potted history that Nicholas had forced me to read.

Unwittingly it was Clinker who retrieved the situation. He had obviously overdone the brandy; and flushed of face and glazed of eye, bellowed with laughter and cried: 'Can't think that Francis is a fount of knowledge on anything – except White Ladies perhaps!'

144

'Really? Fancy that! Just shows that canons know a thing or two,' cried Sir Gerald. 'What proportions would you recommend, Oughterard?'

I was able to instruct him with clarity and authority. But even as I spoke, I was pondering the extraordinary fact that Clinker had actually mentioned the name of the cocktails which, eighteen months previously, had rendered him merrily senseless on my sitting-room carpet. It was an incident which ever since had been shrouded in complicit silence – indeed, I had rather assumed it was carefully expunged from his conscious memory. Presumably the brandy (and possibly the trauma of Myrtle) had pulled the bucket from the well. In any event, it was a timely diversion and I was glad.

My sofa companion looked disappointed and seemed poised to pursue the matter further, but by then the party was beginning to break up and I made sure I was among the first to leave.

When I got home, despite feeling a little fragile from the effects of the alcohol and the joint proclamations of Gladys and Myrtle, I managed to put in a couple of hours of much delayed paperwork. And then feeling both tired and virtuous, I gathered the dog and set off for our evening walk.

At first Bouncer was full of beans, straining at the leash, prancing at passers-by and, once let loose, bounding vigorously after ball and sticks. But on the way back as we neared the vicarage, his mood seemed to change. The bounce slackened, his gait slowed and he started to make odd little whining noises. This was strange, for normally on such occasions, once the initial exuberance subsides it is rapidly replaced by a jaunty eagerness as, mission accomplished, we head for home and food. This time, however, he seemed distinctly reluctant, dragging heavily on the lead and with the whines turning into hostile growls. I was perplexed as there seemed no cause for such display, but assumed there must be a fox or alien cat lurking in nearby undergrowth. But then he suddenly stood stock still, back legs stiffened and muzzle projected as if he were some sort of pointer! I had not seen this particular performance before and was intrigued. He continued to emit low growls, and I scanned the bushes trying to discern the object of such charade. There was nothing.

'Oh, do come on, Bouncer!' I protested. 'We'll never get home at this rate.' He looked up briefly, but continued to stand his ground, ears cocked and tail quivering. And then, just for a moment I thought I heard footsteps – which I suppose I must have, for there was the sudden splutter of a car engine revving into life, and an unlit shape loomed slowly around the corner from the vicarage and purred off into the dark.

It seemed to be the dog's cue for action, for instantly the whole street was rent by his frenzied shrieks and barks, and what had been a twitching statue turned into a roaring, dancing dynamo. Deafened and embarrassed, I dragged him the remaining yards and scuttled into the house before attracting the attention of irate neighbours. Just as we gained the sanctuary of the hall, the telephone rang. The dog bounded noisily into the kitchen and I picked up the receiver. It was Clinker.

'Ah, Oughterard,' he said, 'thought I might catch you. That Mrs Pinder who was sitting next to you during coffee – she's very keen for you give a talk to her Ladies' History Guild. Says she wants to hear more about that Bone Idol thing of Claude's, the Beano pig or whatever it's called. Apparently her father was something big in Poona, and so she's especially interested. Gladys seemed convinced you could oblige. Anyway, I've given Mrs P. your number, didn't think you would mind . . . Glad you could get over for luncheon. It all went very well, I feel.' Like hell, I thought.

26

The Cat's Memoir

Another happy sojourn amidst the gravestones! It is gratifying the number of pleasures that can be packed into so short a time: scattering the newly dug soil on the Fanshaw mound, organizing my defences against the intrusion of that foul Siamese, pressurizing the butterflies in the far corner, practising pouncing tactics behind the compost heap, and keeping vigil on my favourite tomb for any irregularities in the lane below. (Regrettably none on this particular occasion, but one always harbours the hope.) Thus I returned to the vicarage well satisfied with my morning's diversions and looking forward to a light lunch.

As I pushed my way through the pet flap, I was met by Bouncer in a state of noisy indignation.

'Some bastard's been here!' he exclaimed.

'Probably the verger. Sometimes he changes his day to Saturday.'

'No, not that bastard, another one. I knew there was something up last night on my walk, but of course you and F. O. wouldn't believe me. There's a very funny smell, very funny indeed!' To demonstrate, he thrust his snout to the floor and rollicked around the kitchen snorting and growling theatrically.

'Calm down, Bouncer!' I admonished. 'You'll wake F.O.' In fact I could already hear stirrings from above, the bed springs creaking and a shoe being dropped or tripped over.

'It's about time he came down,' he muttered. 'I want my grub. Anyway, if he hadn't been snoring his head off this wouldn't have happened!'

'But nothing *has* happened!'

'That's what you think,' he said darkly. 'I know better. I feel it in my bones.'

Just occasionally the dog's bones do seem to exhibit a curious intuition, but it is not something I often acknowledge. Instead I asked him if the smell was confined to the kitchen.

'No,' he replied, 'all over the shop but especially in the study. That's why I know some bastard's been here, and why I've got to go down to the crypt and THINK!'

'What about your grub?'

'After that, of course. You can't think without a bit of nosh in you. I wish he'd *hurry up*!'

'Start baying. That should do the trick.' He took a deep breath and proceeded to let forth. Forfeiting lunch I escaped hastily through the window.

I bided my time lurking in the tool shed for a while, but became unexpectedly embroiled with a colony of mice who had the nerve to assume they could run circles round me. Then having demonstrated otherwise and feeling rather satisfied, I curled up for a brief snooze. In fact when I awoke it was nearly tea-time. By now Bouncer would be well ensconced in the crypt and the vicar busy in church, and thus it might be a good moment to enjoy some belated haddock undisturbed . . .

How easily the best laid plans of mice and cats are foiled! As I glided past the open study door I suddenly noticed an alien shape bending over the desk. Far too squat and fat for F.O., it was clearly a stranger – indeed, an intruder riffling through the vicar's papers! I watched silently, recognizing the portly form of the Crumplehorn, but undecided whether or not to make my presence felt. As I pondered, there was the familiar sound of canine toenails rasping on the linoleum in the hall: the dog evidently returned from his subterranean thoughts. He pottered over to where I was poised by the study door and also stared in. 'Fetch!' I murmured . . .

I must explain that this was a command that Bouncer had last heard when living with his first master, the bank manager Reginald Bowler, who would bawl it out with tedious regularity. I gather that the idea was to train the dog into performing some useful act of retrieval. However, despite Bowler's persistence, the command would remain only partially executed – the dog invariably preferring to concentrate on the preliminaries (involving much sound and fury) rather than the concluding delivery. I once asked him why he never completed the task. 'Boring,' he growled. 'Nothing beats a good bite and a chew – what's the point of handing it over?'

However, the word clearly awoke some Pavlovian instinct, for the dog immediately hurled himself upon the Crumplehorn's bending buttocks, and with whoops of unfettered joy proceeded to devour the ample rump. Loosing a volley of high-pitched oaths, his victim fell to the floor dragging ink and papers with him. Here he writhed, lashing out vainly, while Bouncer, snarling like Ghengis Khan, gave no quarter. I watched with interest; and then deeming that things had gone far enough, called the assailant to heel . . . that is to say, I punctuated proceedings with a falsetto yowl and a claw to the dog's tail. This had the desired effect, and relative calm descended as Bouncer, still looking his bellicose best, stood guard with quivering flanks, and snout within inches of the intruder's ink-drenched face.

I was about to compliment him on his martial zeal, when there was a slight movement from the study door, and turning my head I saw F.O. standing frozen on the threshold mouthing silently and clad (rather remissly, I felt) only in his shirt and sock suspenders. He seemed to be saying, 'God in heaven, what the hell now!' On the other hand it might have been, 'How long, O Lord, how long?'

It was difficult to tell exactly. But what *can* be told is that the Crumplehorn passed out and that Bouncer – evidently overdone by his exertions – trundled on to the hearthrug, curled up, and with a satisfied sigh went fast to sleep. With the two contestants out for the count I was left alone with the vicar whom I fixed with a quizzical stare . . .

He gazed wildly at the comatose Crumplehorn, began to fumble for his cigarettes, shoved one into his mouth the wrong way round, and then cautiously approached the now stirring heap by the desk. He made some initial enquiry which was swiftly followed by an interesting exchange of imprecations, Crumplehorn's being the more explicit but the vicar's the more literate.

I have to admit to being impressed by Bouncer's handiwork: he had routed and cowed his quarry without inflicting anything worse than shallow tooth marks – painful no doubt but far from serious. The victim continued to swear, but gradually levered himself off the floor and then had the nerve to demand that F.O. supply him with brandy! To his credit the vicar denied him the request – though I suspect less on account of principle than because he had demolished the last of the bottle the previous evening. However, he expressed his refusal in a suitably righteous tone and, after further and prolonged altercation, seemed to achieve the verbal advantage. Eventually, sweating and still garrulous, the visitor turned to the french window and withdrew whence he had come.

It had been a perplexing, disturbing little incident and I was not surprised to see F. O. make a stumbling beeline for the toffee tin and thence the telephone . . . Presumably either the Brighton type or the sister was to be the recipient of a spluttered narrative.

27

The Vicar's Version

I had just got home from the church and gone upstairs to change into more comfortable clothes, when the house was suddenly rent by the most appalling noise from below: a bedlam of jungle snarling and human roaring, followed by a stupendous crash. In shirt and socks I tore downstairs to investigate . . . and then gazed transfixed by the spectacle before me, scarcely believing that I was standing in my own study. Was I experiencing some parallel existence – some mode of being hitherto unvisited? Or was it simply the overripe Stilton at lunch that had precipitated such nightmare? Perhaps at any moment I would wake, sweating but sane . . . None of those things. I was only too awake and the study firmly real. And at the foot of my desk, solid, ink-sodden and insensible, lay Victor Crumpelmeyer!

His body was surrounded by a shower of pens and papers and all the accumulated debris which had cascaded from the open lid during what had clearly been the dog's attack. The man's right trouser leg was split from hip to knee. And what had sounded like mayhem as I bounded down the stairs was now replaced by a deadly hush, broken only by the dog's snoring from the hearthrug where he had retreated at my entry. The cat sat grooming himself on the window-seat, pausing now and again to stare at me with a look of accusing curiosity. I stared back helplessly, and then took a few tentative steps towards the figure on the floor.

I cleared my throat. 'I say, Crumpelmeyer, are you all right?' There was silence. And I gazed down at the slumped effigy, wondering what to do next. Police? Ambulance? A cup of tea? Unsure which for the best, I lit a cigarette. Bloody man, what the hell was he doing here – and at my desk too! (It wasn't just its lid that was wide open, I now noted, but also a couple of the drawers.) There was a movement from the hearthrug and Bouncer, evidently rested from the excitement, came padding over to survey his handiwork. I took him by the scruff, but before I had time to get a grip, he had craned forward and started to snuffle and lick his victim's face. That stirred things.

'Get that fucking hound off me!' screeched Crumpelmeyer.

'He is not a fucking hound,' I observed reprovingly. 'He is an extremely efficient guard dog – as I am glad to say you have discovered.'

There followed what might be termed an animated conversation. Until finally, looking murderous and clutching his posterior, Crumpelmeyer girded his loins – or rather hoiked at his trousers – and still ranting, lurched out into the garden. I refrained from following, judging the man to be too incommoded to constitute further threat; but was careful nonetheless to shut and firmly bolt the french windows.

The whole episode had been extremely unsettling, and to soothe my nerves I made a raid on the toffee tin, before sitting down and telephoning my sister to see if she had any thoughts on the matter. A voice of moderate sanity would be welcome.

'It was dreadful!' I expostulated to Primrose. 'He was here, when I came home, locked in battle with Bouncer in the study. The dog had him by the seat of his trousers and there was a fearful noise, and the desk drawers wide open and my papers strewn all over the place. Obviously having a good old rummage, if you please!'

I was about to enlarge on the details of the appalling scene, when she cut me short: 'Francis, are you sure you've got your teeth in?'

'*What?*'

'Your teeth, are they in?'

'What are you talking about?' I replied indignantly. 'I don't have any teeth . . . false ones, I mean!'

'Well, you could have fooled me. There's an awful lot of chomping and gurgling going on, I can barely hear you!'

Swallowing hard, I took a piece of blotting paper from the desk and removed the caramel which had become stuck in a lower cavity, and then resumed my tale.

'Crumpelmeyer – he was here, ransacking my desk! And quite frankly if it hadn't been for Bouncer attacking him I don't know what might have happened. He was in a very nasty mood . . . when he came to, that is. Had the effrontery to accuse me of harbouring the Hound of the Baskervilles and harassing innocent passers-by who had just dropped in for a friendly chat. I tell you, Prim, the man's as mad as a hatter!' Without thinking I broke off another piece of toffee, and was about to thrust it into my mouth when I remembered her previous comment and lit a fresh cigarette instead.

I continued to relate the details of the episode: Crumpelmeyer's absurd and garbled story that he had had a matter of business to discuss with me and, not getting any response at the front door, had come round to the open french windows hoping I might be in the study. Apparently he had just entered and called my name, when the dog suddenly flew in, pinned him to the desk and proceeded to savage his backside. The attack had been so frenzied that in his attempts to remain upright he had clawed at the desk, wrenching at the drawer handles and scattering all the files and papers. 'A likely story!' I fulminated to Primrose. 'He was just snooping, and I can't think why!'

'I can,' she replied coolly.

'Whatever do you mean?' I exclaimed.

'It's obvious: he was after those deeds – you know, the ones for that place in France you were telling me about. Having failed in their bid to dig up the mother's bracelet, he and the Violet woman are now after the deeds – probably think that crumbling pile may be worth quite a penny; sort of compensation for the "lost patrimony" which they're convinced you owe them.' And she gave a dark chuckle.

'But I haven't got the damn deeds,' I moaned. 'Besides, it's not funny, Primrose. Crumpelmeyer is clearly deranged and I am being made the victim of a groundless persecution!'

'We-ll,' she murmured, 'not entirely groundless. After all, you have to admit there's a certain dramatic irony to it all.'

'Look,' I snapped, 'this is not the perishing theatre, it is real life, and I am sick and tired of being pursued by Pond and her fat fancy man or husband, or whatever he is. I just don't know what to do!'

There was a silence, and then she said, 'You could always go to the police, I suppose.'

I sighed in exasperation. 'Given the circumstances, the less I have to do with the police the better. It'll only give them a chance to do more sniffing and questioning about other matters. And in any case, it would simply be my word against Crumpelmeyer's: there's no actual proof to suggest that his cock and bull tale of wanting to drop in for a chat isn't perfectly true. And what's more,' I added, hearing my voice rise an octave, 'I shall probably be accused of keeping a rabid dog in the house . . . and then what!'

'Now look here, Francis,' she said severely, 'being accused of keeping a rabid dog is not as bad as being accused of doing away with Crumpelmeyer's mother-in-law. Do try to keep a sense of proportion and calm down. Sometimes you sound just like Uncle Herbert!' That sobered me. Pa had been difficult enough but his younger brother was impossible, and I did not care for the analogy.

'So what do you suggest?' I asked morosely.

'Well, in the short term I recommend that you go and play on that nice piano of yours. It always does you good and you'll feel much better afterwards.'

She was right. A turn on the piano would doubtless help to soothe the jangled nerves, but it was a temporary palliative and I needed something more far-reaching.

'And what about the long term?'

'That remains to be seen. But meanwhile I think you had better come down here for a couple of days and let the dust settle. The garden needs doing again, and I doubt whether Crumpelmeyer will try another incursion, not now at any rate. From what you've said he's probably just as ruffled as you are and will want to lie low. And as to the pair of them lodging a complaint about Bouncer and it being your word against his, what about his word against *yours*? After all, you're the one who's the vicar – pillar of the community and all that. And by now the police are bound to know all about them having wanted to exhume the grave for her diamonds. That's not criminal intent of course, but it doesn't *look* good . . . No, I should think there is no immediate threat or worry, but it won't hurt you to get away all the same. You sound peaky.'

Peaky! Who wouldn't sound peaky with all I had to put up with? The nightmare event of the woods, March and the officious Samson, Ingaza and the Bone blithering Idol, bloody Claude, the intrusions of Clinker, and now the lunatic Crumpelmeyers: all intent on driving me insane! What else, for God's sake? What else?

'As it happens,' Primrose went on, 'if you were to come down here you could be quite useful – socially, that is.'

'How do you mean?'

'Well, I might be needing a little moral support . . .'

I found that hard to believe, but saying nothing waited for her to explain.

155

'Yes, you see I've got that friend of yours coming over from Brighton – the Ingaza man, to discuss the matter of my paintings going on the Canadian market. You remember my telling you. I must say, he sounds very keen.'

I closed my eyes. When I opened them I heard myself saying wearily, 'You mean the fakes.'

There was a pause, and then in distant tones she replied, 'Francis, I have no intention of explaining to you yet again the difference between crude fakery and artistic adjustment. Clearly these are technicalities far too subtle for your understanding.'

'You bet they are!' I muttered irritably.

Her voice became brisk and managerial. 'Now come along, Francis, stop being such a wet blanket! Your sister needs your brotherly support and you need a rest from those peculiar people. Padlock the house, board the animals, and tell the parish you're going on a course.'

'What course?'

'Christian Ethics, I should think.'

28

The Dog's Diary

He's lucky to have me, you know. Very lucky indeed! I'm what's known as a watch-dog of the first water – as my old master Bowler used to say. (Most of the time he said too much, but now and again he was SPOT ON!) Anyway, I really helped the vicar the other day and even Maurice was impressed. Got that pasty Crump person right down on the floorboards, I did, and gave him what for. Just the job! But *he* didn't like it – not one bite, he didn't!

Mind you, F.O. looked under the weather as well, and started to shake all over just like those posh show dogs at Crufts with their hind legs going like the clappers. Still, he calmed down after a while and went over to the desk and asked Chummy exactly what he thought he was doing. (Silly question really – it was obvious what the basket was up to: CASING THE JOINT! Anyone could see that, but the vicar is a bit slow sometimes. Can't help it, I suppose – humans are made that way.) Anyway, after a right old argy-bargy between the two of them, Fatso gets up and limps out on to the grass, and the vicar bolts the door. Should have done that much earlier, if you ask me, but he never does of course. Far too trusting – or just plain idle.

Of course, I'd known for days that something was going on and that it wasn't the first time that Droopy Chops had been prowling around – he was here a few nights ago when F.O. took me for my bedtime walk. I've got this sixth sense, you see: it's in the bones and you can learn all manner of stuff that way. Maurice says it's rubbish, but then he says that about most things . . . Well, it wasn't rubbish what I did the other evening. It was JOLLY GOOD, and I hope he comes back for another dose. But I don't suppose he will . . . Yes, they're lucky to have me around all right. In fact that's just what I told Maurice – 'Bouncer's the chap!' I said. He didn't answer of course, just flattened his ears and shut his eyes tightly. But I think that secretly he's quite proud of me. After all, it's not every cat that has a top prize-fighter for a companion!

I was telling O'Shaughnessy all about it and it got him really excited, and he said I was no end of a fine fellow and was I after doing anything more like that. I told him not at the moment, but since he'd missed all the fun I would give him one or two demonstrations. That really got him going and he kept chasing his tail and barking, 'Up Dev! Up Dev!' Don't know what he meant by that but he seemed to be enjoying himself so I joined in too, and we raced up and down the road roaring those funny words until a neighbour came out and hurled a bucket of water at us. Missed, of course.

Well, here's a howdy-do! According to Maurice, who was listening to him burbling down the blower, the vicar is going to visit his sister again, and *not* taking us with him. He was talking about boarding us out, if you please! I got a bit shirty when I heard that, but Maurice says it's all right because he has arranged to settle us with those new people down the road who own the wolfhound, Florence of Fermanagh. So maybe things won't be too bad. In fact, come to think of it, they could be a load of all right! That Florence is a very nice lady, and I know she likes me, and even Maurice approves. And what's more, I've heard that her owners are pretty free-handed with the grub. So all in all we might have quite a good few days. I'm just sorry that we shan't be seeing those gormless rabbits again ... but still, you can't have everything. Plenty of nosh and a great friendly wolf should be enough!

29

The Vicar's Version

I brooded on Primrose's suggestion. Visiting my sister was always a trifle fraught, and the prospect of Ingaza's presence of little enticement. On the other hand, my nerves really were shot to pieces by the Crumpelmeyer confrontation, not to mention March and Samson's suspicions about those absurd deeds. And the thought of getting away – if only to dig my sister's garden – was not uncongenial. So when the bishop telephoned to announce that he wished to speak to me on urgent business and would be shortly arriving in the area, what had been merely a mooted idea swiftly turned to firm purpose.

Unfortunately immediate escape was impossible, for in addition to a sudden spate of baptisms and funerals, there loomed the Vergers' Social Evening – a ferocious affair of Colonel Dawlish's devising, invariably conducted with military rigour and sadistic relish. And such were the instigator's powers of persuasion that attendance was by far the simplest course. Thus, willy nilly, Clinker and his vagaries would have to be faced before fleeing Molehill for the sanctuary of Sussex. Still, it was something to look forward to . . .

A few days later my superior arrived, looking decidedly

harassed; so much so that I felt a spark of sympathy. It quickly died.

He cleared his throat, looked shifty, and then said, 'Now look here, Oughterard, uhm . . . it's about Mrs Carruthers and the tiddlywinks.'

Oh Lor', I thought, here we go!

'Yes,' he continued. 'The fact is I have to practise some rather special moves with her. The team is entered in the Neasden Championships, a most prestigious event, and we stand a very good chance of winning. But it's essential to be well prepared – some pretty stiff competition! The trouble is, she's got her nephew staying and he's allergic to tiddlywinks and hates bishops. I wouldn't feel comfortable crawling about on her carpet with him there. But Wednesday evening is the only time I'm free. So I thought your vicarage would be a good substitute for her sitting room. You can easily take yourself off to the cinema . . . They've got *Roman Holiday* showing at the Plaza,' he added encouragingly.

I explained that much as I would like to see *Roman Holiday* and Audrey Hepburn, the vicarage was unfortunately booked that evening for the bell ringers' AGM and they wouldn't be leaving until at least ten o'clock.

'Surely you can shove them somewhere else,' he protested.

'Not really, sir, there's quite a lot of them and the notices have already gone out. Besides, Mavis Briggs is doing the sandwiches and she won't want to –'

'Hell,' he groaned, 'that's torn it! Can't you think of anywhere, Oughterard?'

'Well,' I ventured, 'I suppose there's always your Palace.'

'Don't be facetious,' he snapped. 'You know perfectly well the position with Mrs Clinker!'

I pondered. What on earth would be a suitable venue for the bishop and Annie Carruthers to clamber about on all-fours rattling the dice and flicking bits of plastic at each other? There was a long silence and he drummed his fingers.

'I know!' I said brightly. 'The allotments – there's a vacant shed, third row from the end. A bit cramped, perhaps, but better than nothing!'

'The *allotments*! You mean those big ones by Foxford Wood, the ones behind your graveyard? Are you mad, Oughterard? You can hardly expect me to get down on my hands and knees at dead of night in a potting shed! Most undignified. It's an outlandish suggestion.'

The whole charade struck me as being outlandish, but I refrained from saying so, and instead stood meekly shuffling my papers while he fumed. After a while he calmed down, and enquired the dimensions of the shed and whether it had an even floor.

'I rather think so. It's one of those new pre-fabricated ones, all very neat and shipshape. As a matter of fact it belongs to a friend of mine – our local piano tuner – he lets it out, but at the moment no one's using it.'

'Hmm,' muttered Clinker, 'might do, I suppose . . . well, it'll have to. Got to get something fixed up! But those allotments are huge – you'll have to be there to show me where the thing is exactly. What time are your bell ringers coming?'

I told him eight o'clock.

'Oh, plenty of time then. You can meet me at six, and meanwhile I'll make arrangements with Mrs Carruthers.'

After he had gone I put on my slippers, removed the cat from the armchair, and easing myself into his place closed my eyes. Really, the things one did for one's masters . . .

To my relief Savage was remarkably co-operative about the loan of his property and was only too happy to hand over its key. I had had to explain its purpose of course – the tiddlywinks – but naturally made no mention of Clinker, simply stating that I had a friend whose tastes in recreational pursuits were a trifle juvenile. When I explained that Mrs Carruthers shared those same tastes and would be accompanying him on the shed floor, Savage exclaimed,

'Cor, you don't say!' and started to grin. I was slightly put out by this and felt we might be at cross purposes; but before I could clarify matters Mrs Savage appeared from the kitchen floured and flushed, and insisted I try her latest batch of fairy cakes, and thus the matter was shelved.

Later that day there was a telephone call from Clinker agitating about the forthcoming arrangements. Discretion, he confided, was the name of the game. It would not do for him to be observed accompanying Mrs Carruthers through the portals of the allotments: they would travel separately and he would establish himself in the shed and practise a few special thumb flips while awaiting her arrival.

'But she doesn't know where the shed is,' I objected, 'she'll need guidance.'

'Yes, but not from me, Oughterard. That will be your job. What I want you to do is to take me there first and then go back and meet her at the bus stop in The Avenue. I've told her you'll pick her up.'

'Wouldn't it be simpler if I just met her at the allotment gate?' I asked, inwardly fuming that I was to be involved in these antics at all.

'Not really. You see, she doesn't *know* that we shall be playing in the shed . . . I, uhm, thought it better not to mention it.'

'Why ever not?'

There was a pause, and then he said distantly, 'It is quite evident, Oughterard, that you know very little about the female psyche. Were she to learn that she was expected to crawl about on a hard floor amidst dust and potatoes in an alien potting shed, the ructions would be stupendous and one would doubtless forfeit an invaluable hour of practice. I've set my heart on that Neasden Championship and I don't propose being under-rehearsed because my partner had chickened out on account of her nylons!'

'But she might make an even bigger fuss when she does find out!' I exclaimed.

163

'Perhaps, but it'll be too late by then. Face them with a fait accompli and they generally back down. Having had the benefit of Gladys all these years I know about these things.' There was a grim note in his voice.

I sighed. Yes, I was thankful to be spared that particular benefit. Nevertheless, the prospect of Mrs Carruthers' fury when confronted with the bishop's choice of rendezvous was not a happy one, and I wondered disconsolately if there was any way of getting out of it. There wasn't, of course.

Wednesday evening arrived; and having organized the sitting room in readiness for the bell ringers and added a couple of spare chairs, I reluctantly left the vicarage and made my way to the allotments. Through the gathering dusk I could just discern a dark bulky figure lurking by the main gate: it was clearly the bishop in his incognito garb – black raincoat and face-concealing fedora hat. Fortunately there was no one about for he might just as well have been wearing cope and mitre.

We exchanged a few pleasantries, and in answer to his anxious enquiry I assured him that Mrs Carruthers was all set and I would fetch her as arranged. He was holding a briefcase, presumably containing the tiddlywinks, which he gave me to carry. Then, keeping a nervous eye open for strangers, I led him along the winding cinder paths until we reached the far end and Savage's shed. I took the key from my pocket and went to unlock the door. There was some difficulty as the wretched thing got stuck and wouldn't turn properly. Either it or the lock must have been bent.

'Here, let me try,' said Clinker impatiently. And after some rattling and wrenching it eventually worked, and the door creaked open. He went in and stared into the gloom muttering something about finding a light switch. Then I heard him gasp. 'My God!' he cried, leaping back and crushing my foot. 'What the hell's that!'

164

Standing behind him and in the half-light, I couldn't make out much, and said in some pain, 'It's only the wheelbarrow, it's –'

'Don't be a fool, Oughterard! Can't you see . . . it's a *body*. Look, there are the legs!'

I gazed into the murk. And sure enough, there was indeed a pair of legs – female ones, sticking up in the air propped behind the barrow. As I stared, I could just make out what seemed to be the head and torso sprawled on the floor, the body up-ended in a sort of jack-knife pose. There was a long silence as we peered paralysed; and then I fumbled for the switch.

'Don't!' snapped Clinker. 'Do you want us lit up like Christmas trees? Go and take a look and check if it's really dead.'

I took a few limping steps. Mercifully the face was turned away – but judging from the position of the neck, the rope around it, and the icy stillness of the form, I had no doubt we were in the presence of a corpse. (You may recall it was not the first time I had been in such proximity.)

'Dead,' I whispered, '. . . garrotted.'

'My God!' Clinker gulped. 'I've got to get out of here. This is appalling! Quick, Oughterard, go back to that phone box by the main gates and ring Mrs Carruthers. Fob her off!' And grabbing his briefcase and staying for neither God nor corpse, he pushed past me and floundered down a side path into the dusk and on to the lane. From the other side of the fence I heard the revving of a motor car. And then silence.

Left alone, I stood for some moments in numbed horror, riveted by the legs. Pulling myself together, I stumbled to the exit, tried vainly to lock the shed door, and pocketing the redundant key, started to pick my way back along the cinder tracks. It was nearly dark, but not wishing to risk meeting a loitering plot-holder, I scrambled through a gap

165

in the hedge to the anonymity of the road, and looked for the telephone box.

I spun her a garbled tale of the bishop being overcome by influenza and anchored to the episcopal bed. And then with solicitous squawks ringing in my ears, and still in a state of zombied shock, I began my walk back to the vicarage. I did not get far. Coming up the road was Savage – tapping along briskly and, for once, whistling in a moderately tuneful way. Had I been thinking straight I suppose I might have side-stepped him and he would have continued none the wiser – for the time being at any rate. Time at least for me to collect my wits. But I was not thinking straight, and in any case it seemed only charitable to warn him of what lay ahead.

Thus I coughed discreetly to herald my approach, and as he paused said: 'It's me, the vicar. I say, Savage, I hate to tell you – but there's a dead body in your shed.'

He grinned. 'It's not April Fool's Day, Rev. Pull the other!'

'No, really,' I hissed, 'it's true. Behind the wheelbarrow – dead. Throttled, actually.'

'In my *shed*!' he yelped. 'Have you been on the bottle?'

'Certainly not!' I exclaimed indignantly, and proceeded to give him the few details I knew.

He scratched his head, emitted a low whistle, and muttered, 'A corpse, eh? Well, here's a howdy-do and no mistake. I don't think Mrs S. will like that very much, especially as it's nearly brand new.'

'What is?'

'The shed. We've only had it six months . . . This body, whose is it, anyway?'

'I've no idea,' I replied. 'But it's all rather tricky. You see . . .' And I started to impress upon him how embarrassing it would be if my 'colleague' were to become involved.

'You mean the one that was going to have a dink-donk with the Carruthers woman?'

'Yes – no! Nothing like that! I told you, they were going to practise tiddlywinks.'

166

'I doubt if it was tiddlywinks they were going to practise.' And he gave a sly chuckle.

'Yes they *were*,' I protested.

'If you say so, Rev. Anyway, this friend of yours, he got
more than he bargained for, didn't he! . . . Mind you,' he
added musingly, 'so have I. Better inform the police, I suppose, but I can't do that tonight – not when she's on one of
her baking jags. More than my life's worth! It'll have to
wait till tomorrow. What the eye doesn't see . . .'

I was grateful to Mrs Savage. Her periodic bouts of
manic baking may have been a trial to her husband, but
this particular occasion allowed me time to think: to produce a cogent reason why the Canon of Molehill and his
bishop should be appearing in court as principal witnesses
in the case of what the press would doubtless dub 'THE
ALLOTMENTS SLAUGHTER!' Really, I fumed, as if I
hadn't enough with a murder of my own to cope with,
without having to be dragged into other people's as well.
It was too bad!

I was reflecting upon this irony and wondering just how
I was going to play it, when I heard Savage say, 'What have
you done with the key, then?'

'Oh, it's here,' I said, producing it from my pocket. 'But
it's no use, there's something wrong with the lock or
maybe the key itself, it wouldn't work. Kept jamming.'

'There was nothing wrong before I went off this morning,'
he replied. 'Both were oiled and in good working order.'

'Well, I can tell you, it certainly wasn't working just
now,' I muttered irritably.

There was a pause, and then he said slowly, 'No, and I
can guess why. Whoever did her in had to pick the lock.
How else could they have got access? Either he strangled
her *in situ*, or he brought the body in from somewhere else
. . . Still, that's for the police to decide. In the meantime, if
you've got any sense you'll go back there.'

'But I don't want to go back! Whatever for?'

'That lock you were grappling with will be smothered
in fingerprints – yours and your friend's. Better take a

handkerchief and do a bit of polishing up. Did you touch anything else?'

'No, nothing.'

'Well, that's all right then.' Rather an overstatement, I thought.

'So – what will you do?'

'Oh,' he replied casually, 'I'll go down there first thing tomorrow morning, see what's what and then report it at the police station. I'll say I tripped over it.'

'Suppose they try to pin it on you?'

He smiled. 'No, they won't do that.'

'Unlikely, but you never know. They're so suspicious!' I spoke with feeling.

'Ah, but I've got an alibi. Moorfields.'

'What?'

'The big eye hospital in Middlesex. I go twice a year for a check-up. Spend all day there, hours on end! In fact, I've only just got off the train now . . . And do you know what?'

I said I didn't.

'They think they've seen a bit of daylight. Slight signs of improvement, they say. What you lot would call a miracle, I suppose . . . what I call a bloody piece of luck!'

'Is that why you were whistling in tune?' I asked.

He chuckled. 'Better get on with that polishing, Rev!'

Somehow I managed to weather the invasion of the bell ringers, returning from my polishing in the nick of time to let them in. But I participated little in the AGM proceedings, being too fixated by images of those rearing legs to give much attention to the niceties of chimes and changes, least of all to disputes about the tea-making rota and the venue for their annual supper. My mind was grappling with other urgencies: what to do!

In fact, I concluded, the best thing was to do nothing. Apart from Savage, who had kindly volunteered to tell the police he had tripped over the body, there was no one to know that either I or the bishop had been anywhere near the allotments on that particular evening. The fact that neither of us had anything remotely to do with the affair – innocent bystanders, you might say – was not the point. The last thing I wanted was further parleying with March and Samson, especially on matters cadaverous. All in all, the less said – or asked – the better. And for the next two days I immersed myself in parish duties with a fervour last felt as a callow curate bludgeoned by the forces of 'muscular Christianity'. Indeed, so zealous did I become in pursuit of defaced hymn books and recalcitrant choir boys that Edith Hopgarden was heard to enquire whether I was sickening for something.

Meanwhile not a squeak out of Clinker, and I concluded that he was engaged in comparable activity. The fear of having to account to Gladys for the body in the shed and the tiddlywinks tryst with Mrs Carruthers was enough presumably to keep any bishop silent and busy.

However, in between these bouts of random zeal I did have time to ponder the identity of the lady – and, indeed, who it was that had been so discomfited by her existence as to take the course they had. Apart from the legs, thick and sturdy, I knew nothing about the victim – neither age nor provenance. Undoubtedly it would all come out, but for the time being I was content to bask in discreet ignorance. Not that there was much basking going on, for in addition to parish matters I was much occupied in preparing for my trip down to Primrose: cajoling young Rothermere at Alford to take some services, rescheduling a Vestry meeting, and trying vainly to organize the Boy Scouts to look after Maurice and Bouncer. None was available, all apparently being lured by some jolly camping spree in the purlieus of Surbiton.

Thus I tried the new people with the gigantic wolfhound. For some reason they were very taken with Bouncer, and when I first enquired if they could possibly have the cat and dog as lodgers for a couple of days they had been only too delighted, saying it would be nice for Florrie to have some playmates. Then at the last minute they were called away to attend to some ailing in-law, so there was nothing for it but to take the pair with me again. I just hoped they would be less disruptive than on the previous occasion: enough trouble was likely to be generated by the presence of Nicholas without having to cope with the added burden of Maurice's tantrums!

The next day, luggage and animals carefully stowed, I started for Sussex; but before getting fully under way, I stopped at the florist's to buy flowers for Primrose. If she was still smarting from my 'intrusions' upon her business negotiations with Nicholas they might help soften the blast.

I was just getting back in the car when I was accosted by the breathy tones of Mavis Briggs. 'Oh, Canon,' she gasped, 'isn't it dreadful? Whatever will happen next!'

'Sorry?'

'So terrible – I mean it really stops one sleeping at night!'

'What does?' I murmured irritably, trying to prise Bouncer from the driver's seat.

'But haven't you heard?'

'No.'

'Why, it's all in the papers – another murder, here in Molehill. In a *shed*!'

I gritted my teeth. It had only been a matter of time, but trust Mavis to be in full cry!

'Dear me,' I said, 'that's a bit much. How unfortunate! But if you don't mind, Mavis, I really must be on my way, I've got to –'

'But you don't understand!' she cried. 'It's the daughter!'

'What daughter?'

'It's all happening again,' she wailed. 'Mrs Fotherington's of course!'

Having managed to push Bouncer out of the way I was about to take his place behind the wheel, but stopped in mid-manoeuvre. 'Mrs Fotherington's daughter!' I yelped. 'You mean Violet Pond? Violet Crumpelmeyer as she is – was?'

'*Yes!*' exclaimed Mavis avidly, realizing she had got my attention. 'You see, it's all here in the papers . . .' and she drew a *Telegraph* from her string shopping bag and attempted to thrust it under my nose.

I waved it aside, murmuring, 'Dreadful, dreadful!' And clambering into the seat and engaging the gear, apologized for my haste, and with lurching mind drove off swiftly.

In fact, so ruffled was I by this revelation that I delayed taking the Sussex road, and instead returned to the vicarage where I found some codeine, made coffee and tried to take stock of things. Little came of the stock-taking, and I was just about to leave when the telephone shrilled and I mechanically lifted the receiver. It was Clinker.

'Ah, Francis,' he began (use of my first name invariably precedes a request or a confidence), 'hoped I might find you. I've, er, just been reading *The Times* and there's a small item about Molehill and that, uhm . . . well, about the allotments thing, you know.' His voice trailed off, and I told him that I did know, and that while there might be a small report in *The Times*, I gathered there was a very big one in the *Telegraph*.

'Ye-es,' he said uneasily, 'I thought perhaps there might be.' There was a pause, and then he said in a tone half wheedling and half hectoring, 'Now look here, I think we both realize that this is a matter of some delicacy and I see no reason for the diocese to become involved, no reason at all . . . and therefore –'

'The less said the better,' I completed.

'Exactly! Very shrewd, Francis. Now I take it that your man Savage is discreet . . . I mean to say, I'm sure he wouldn't want any publicity for *you* about – ah – borrowing his shed for example . . .'

'No,' I answered earnestly, 'and neither for its purpose. And fortunately Mrs Carruthers knows nothing and so that shouldn't be a problem.'

There was a brief silence. And then he said rather frostily, 'As it happens, there has already been a problem. Can't think what tale you spun her, Oughterard, but she rang up at nine o'clock this morning enquiring after my health. Said she had heard it rumoured that I had contracted some appalling lung condition and was about to be carted off to the Surrey Hospital for exploratory tests and was unlikely to emerge for at least two weeks. Unfortunately it was Gladys who took the call . . . told Mrs C. that she was insane and that I had never been in ruder health. I must say, Oughterard, the next time you are asked to deliver a tactful message kindly curb your imagination!'

As you may imagine, my journey down to Lewes was not the most placid. The animals were unusually quiet, but my thoughts considerably less so. 'Trust the Fotheringtons to pull a macabre stunt like that!' I blustered. 'First the mother embarrasses me by that wretched codicil, then the daughter gets herself murdered – and by the same method. It's indecent!' It was also very peculiar and I didn't like it one jot.

I reached Primrose in a state of some turbulence, but pulling myself together and having hauled Maurice and Bouncer from the back seat, gave the bell a brisk ring. I had decided to keep quiet about the whole episode. The less my sister – or indeed anyone – knew about my part in the allotment matter, the better: it is amazing how one thing can so rapidly lead to another! In any case, I was still uneasy about having confided to her the details of the original event, and did not want to muddy the waters further by revealing my role – however innocent – in this startling development with Violet. I suppose, too, I still harboured a sort of jaundiced loyalty to Clinker, and felt a sneaking sympathy for anyone faced with an enraged Gladys – not to mention the bemused probings of the Church authorities! With a bit of luck Primrose may have been too busy preparing for Ingaza to have delved into the *Telegraph*'s inside pages, and so be ignorant of the whole affair. Thus I breezed into her drawing room in a state of expansive good cheer, regaled her gaily about the antics of Maurice and Bouncer, asked fondly after the chinchillas and babbled inconsequentially about anything unconnected with Molehill and its murderous associations.

Primrose was mildly welcoming and expatiated at some length about her proposed negotiations with Nicholas. 'Of course, he's a total bounder,' she exclaimed. 'But *art* and fiscal necessity transcend that sort of thing, and one does have to think of the long term.'

I said that perhaps she now understood why I had been forced to get involved with him in the first place.

'Certainly not,' she replied, asserting that there was nothing remotely artistic about me – and that in any case, had I been thinking of the long term I would have moderated my behaviour in Foxford Wood and thus been spared his tiresome attentions. 'Were it not for that absurd blunder with the binoculars he need never have darkened your doorstep!' I was too tired to dispute the matter and asked instead what she was planning to give him for supper.

'Gin, I should think,' was the reply.

After a light lunch we settled down in the sitting room: me struggling with the crossword and Primrose devouring the local *Argus*. I was making little headway with the clues, and was just thinking that I might take a short nap to prepare for the rigours of Nicholas, when Primrose suddenly exclaimed, 'I say, what an *extraordinary* coincidence!'

'What?'

'It's your Molehill again. There's been another murder – the daughter of Elizabeth Fotherington!'

My heart sank. 'Ah, I did hear something about that but –'

'Francis!' Primrose cried. 'You haven't done it again, have you?'

'Certainly not,' I snapped. 'Whatever gives you that idea?'

'Apparently she was strangled with a scarf. Isn't that what happened to her mother?'

'Masses of people are strangled with scarves,' I replied irritably, 'but not all by the same person!' (The usual false reporting: this time rope had been the preferred material, not chiffon, but I could hardly tell Primrose.)

She buried her head in the paper again, and then I heard a gasp. 'Good Lord!' she muttered.

'What?'

'It says here she was found in a shed near Foxford Wood, on the allotments behind your graveyard . . . Are you *sure* you weren't involved?'

'Of course I'm sure! What do you take me for? I haven't got over the first one yet! . . . Besides, I would hardly be stupid enough to use the same area again, would I?'

'Well,' she said doubtfully, 'if you weren't thinking, you might . . . and you must admit, you don't always think!'

'Think?' I cried. 'I do nothing *but* think, and so would you if you were in my shoes! What you are saying is preposterous – I thought you were supposed to be on my side.'

'I am,' she protested. 'It's just that one must make sure one's got the whole picture without any blurring of the edges.'

I groaned. 'No, Primrose, there are no "blurred edges". I have committed only one damn murder and that is my lot – and my doom. And now, if you don't mind, I am going to bed!'

As I mounted the stairs, narrowly missing the basking cat, she called out, 'You'll find some aspirin on the bath-room shelf . . .'

By seven o'clock, washed and shaved and soothed with aspirin, I felt more myself again. Indeed, in a masochistic way I was almost ready to welcome Nicholas when he arrived.

I went down to the sitting room where Primrose had made up a good fire and set out a tray of drinks. I poured a whisky, lit a cigarette and stared at the dog, wondering how on earth the two would get on and what, if anything, could possibly come from their 'business negotiations'. The dog seemed disinclined to shed light on the matter, but I did not have long to wait for there was suddenly an anguished rasping of tyres on gravel, and from the window I saw the familiar and slightly sinister hulk of the black Citroën sprawled in the driveway.

Primrose had obviously heard the din as well, for she came rushing out of the kitchen tearing off a pinafore and crying, 'Oh my God, is he here already!'

My sister is not normally flustered – but then neither is she normally dressed quite so vividly: scarlet sweater dress, scarlet lipstick, high heels with black stocking-seams, and a pair of mother's jet and diamante ear-rings from the twenties. Primrose is tall and the overall effect was distinctly intimidating.

'Do I look all right?' she whispered.

'Er – yes,' I replied, 'very, uhm, *capable*.'

'Capable of cutting a good deal?'

'I should say!'

'That's all right then.' And she clattered off into the hall.

The dog started to growl and I gripped his collar. 'Nothing to worry about, Bouncer,' I lied. 'It's only your nice friend Nicholas. He's come to visit us.' To my surprise, he stopped growling and began to wag his tail. No accounting for tastes, I suppose.

Nicholas appeared in the doorway looking almost distinguished, his frayed elegance only partly dissipated by the brazen tie-pin and over-large silk handkerchief tumbling from his breast pocket. The brilliantined hair was shorter than when I had last seen him, and the sheen on his shoes put my own to shame. He was nursing two enormous bunches of yellow gladioli which he presented to Primrose with a theatrical flourish. He too, it seemed, was intent on cutting a good deal.

'*Enchanté*,' he murmured, flashing her a smile of oiled intimacy. 'I have been *longing* to meet you. Your paintings are a delight, such rare intelligence and . . . but my goodness,' he gasped, 'I've just noticed! Those ear-rings are *exquisite*. Clearly the originals, and they frame your face so beautifully. How clever of you to find them!'

I listened to the patter with cynical amusement. If Ingaza imagined he was going to impress his hostess with that sort of blague he was barking up the wrong tree. My sister was the last person to be so disarmed. And I awaited her reaction with a degree of unease, fearing a tart response. None came. Instead Primrose flushed, cleared her throat, simpered into the gladioli and muttered something to the effect that they were just some old family heirlooms which she happened to have to hand. Then instructing me to offer our visitor a drink, she gathered the flowers and retreated awkwardly into the kitchen mumbling about vases and water.

Left to ourselves I poured him a Scotch which he grabbed with alacrity.

'Christ, what a day, what a journey – all the sods in Sussex on the road!'

'But you've only come from Brighton,' I protested, 'it can't have been that bad.'

'Ah, but I had to go to Eastbourne first to visit Lil. Howling gale! And I tried to get her into the cinema but she wasn't having that – oh no, had to be the perishing bandstand as usual. Freezing cold, no hot-dogs, and now I've got earache.' He took a gulp of the whisky and grimaced. 'Bit heavy-handed with the soda, aren't you, dear boy, or are you on one of your puritan kicks?'

I made good the defect and enquired after the health of his Aunt Lil.

'Never been better,' he replied sourly. 'Playing merry hell with everyone, including yours truly of course. Old baggage still blames me for that disastrous Spendler business. Had the nerve to tell me I was losing my touch and should have stayed in the Church. I ask you!'

I could see the funny side, but to divert him from the tribulations of Aunt Lil said consolingly (albeit a trifle acidly) that doubtless his negotiations with Primrose would compensate.

176

'Ye-es, I think they might. They just might.' He smirked slyly and sleeked his hair. 'Yes, I think your Primrose and I could come to a very useful, not to say lucrative, arrangement. She's a bit sharper than you, Francis, a little more on the commercial ball if you don't mind my saying.'

'Not at all,' I replied drily, 'but kindly count me out, would you? I have no intention of being involved in this dubious transaction.'

'Absolutely, old boy, absolutely! After all, you've got your own little upset to deal with, haven't you? Wouldn't dream of burdening you further.' He beamed ingratiatingly.

I scowled. Like hell he wouldn't dream! Ingaza would dream of anything if it suited him and money was at stake.

At that point Primrose emerged from the kitchen once more her poised self. She poured a dry sherry, accepted one of her guest's Sobranies and embarked on a witty and scathing account of a local art exhibition she had recently attended. Nicholas appeared to hang on her every word, nodding in the pauses and chuckling conspiratorially at the more caustic of her pronouncements. Thus the gallery was played to and duly showed its appreciation. It was a collusive little display in which I formed no part, and instead spent my time brooding on 'La Folie de Fotherington' and Violet Crumpelmeyer's legs in the tool shed.

Supper went remarkably well: Nicholas continuing his role as charming and complimentary guest, and Primrose (presumably buoyed up with the prospects of a lucrative partnership) doing her best – which wasn't at all bad – to sound artistically cosmopolitan and financially practised. My own contribution was descriptions of the grosser gaffes of Mavis Briggs and the romantic shenanigans of Tapsell and Enid Hopgarden. They listened to these with courteous good humour, but it was obvious that each was impatient to get down to business and 'clinch the deal'. Thus, supper over and having done some of the washing up, I made the excuse of walking the dog and left them to it.

It was a pleasant night, soft and starlit; and although Bouncer was clearly intent on visiting the chinchillas, I eventually diverted him out of the garden and into the adjacent fields. Here we wandered about peacefully: me enjoying the silence and the stars, and he in his element sniffing and peeing at every turn. I suppose it was the novelty of the new landscape which produced such sustained activity.

I lit a cigarette and brooded yet again on the extraordinary fate that had overcome Mrs Fotherington's daughter. The coincidence was unnerving to say the least, but it was also intriguing. Who on earth had done it? And indeed, whatever was his or her motive (other than irritation) for taking Violet's life? For a split second I had a pang of sympathy for the newly-weds – the bride's demise so soon after tying the knot being surely singular bad luck! However, such altruism was immediately eclipsed by thoughts of their joint awfulness and the husband's disgraceful behaviour at my desk. I would have pondered the matter further, but by now Bouncer seemed to have exhausted his urinary excitement and was indicating his preference for home comforts.

Thus we made our way back to the house and re-entered by the side door. To get there one had to pass in front of the drawing-room window. The curtains were still open and I had a brief glimpse of Primrose and Nicholas taking their ease in the large fireside armchairs, each nursing a glass of cognac and looking remarkably relaxed. So much so, I noted, that Nicholas actually had Maurice on his lap and was stroking his ears – a situation which normally I would have expected neither to permit! Presumably the Canadian negotiations had gone well.

My surmise was correct. As I entered the room I was greeted with unusual warmth from both parties and invited to share in the brandy.

'You've been ages,' exclaimed my sister. 'Jolly lucky that's there any left!'

'Bung-ho!' said Ingaza vaguely, waving his glass in my direction.

'Bung-ho,' I answered soberly.

There was a pause, and then Primrose said, 'Francis, dear, your friend and I have come to a most amicable arrangement regarding my paintings and I think I can say that we look forward to a most profitable partnership!'

'Oh yes,' giggled her collaborator, 'most profitable – what you might call *artistically* so.' And he downed more brandy.

'Delighted,' I said shortly, taking a small sip.

There was another pause, and then Primrose burst out, 'Oh come along, Francis, don't be so moody. The Canadians are going to love my sheep, and if they are fool enough to think they're from the eighteenth century then that's their lookout. As we say in the art world, *caveat emptor*! I mean to say, when all's said and done, it's the quality that counts, and the quality is very *good*.' She looked at Ingaza for confirmation. 'Isn't that so, Nicholas?'

'Rather!' he replied, taking another gulp. 'Simply superlative!' And turning to me he exclaimed, 'So kind of you to introduce us, dear boy.'

I began to say that I had made no such introductions, but looking at the pair of them triumphant in their mutual resolution, realized I was out-gunned. 'Oh well,' I grunted, 'I suppose it'll be all right – but just keep me out of it, that's all.'

'That's the spirit!' Nicholas cried. 'No worries on that score. As I said before, you're far too heavily engaged in *other* areas to take on artistic matters as well.' And then lowering his left eyelid into a heavy wink, he added, 'Besides, considering the mess you made of things last time, your involvement would be a distinct liability.' This was followed by a hoot of laughter and he offered me a Sobranie. I have a particular liking for Sobranies and also fancied some more brandy; and so despite my misgivings regarding their scheme (let alone the brazen innuendos about my 'other areas'), I accepted his offer and settled back on the sofa resigned to the merriment.

The merriment proceeded for some time; until Primrose suddenly said out of the blue, 'Well now, what about this latest murder, Francis? You can't expect to keep it all to yourself, you know. After all, given the circumstances, you must admit the whole thing's pretty rum!' She looked at me intently and I knew it was something I could no longer side-step.

'Well,' I began uneasily, 'to be frank I don't know much about it, no more than you've already seen in the *Argus* really. I gather that Mr Savage tripped over the body in the morning when he went to prick out some cabbages . . . you know, despite his dodgy eyesight he's awfully deft like that and produces some marvellous –'

'Oh, blow the cabbages,' she exclaimed impatiently, 'what did he do next?'

'Uhm . . . well, I don't think anything very much. He was a bit taken aback, and had to think about it, I suppose.'

'You don't say!' observed Nicholas caustically. 'Sat on a flower pot and cogitated, no doubt!'

'No,' I said firmly. 'Once he had got over the shock he marched straight down to the police station and reported it to the duty officer. And beyond that I simply have no idea. It's all very baffling.' (Which, of course, was entirely true.)

'But you must admit,' said Primrose, 'it does look odd . . . considering your earlier imbroglio with the mother. Are you *sure*, Francis that you didn't –'

'Of course I'm sure!' I expostulated. 'I've already told you, I know nothing about it!'

'But where were you when it occurred?' asked Nicholas softly. 'I mean, can you produce an alibi or anything?'

'I do not need an alibi,' I replied stiffly. 'But if my where-abouts fascinate you so much, as it happens I was out all day; and then in the evening with the bell ringers . . . more or less.'

He grinned, and repeated slowly, 'More or less with the bell ringers. Police will like that all right!'

I glared at him. And then Primrose interjected, 'But Francis, why didn't you tell me about this when you first arrived? After all, Molehill can't have many excitements – I should have thought it would have been at the forefront of your mind.'

'No,' I snapped, 'it was not at the forefront of my mind. I have other things to consider, i.e. that deranged Crumpelmeyer and his dastardly intrusion into my study. God knows what he thought he was doing!'

'We've discussed this on the phone,' she replied. 'He was obviously digging to see if he could find the deeds or any mention of that Fotherington Folly thing which Elizabeth wanted you to have. *Do* you have them?'

'I know nothing about the Fotherington fucking Folly!' I heard myself yelling. There was silence as they looked at me quizzically.

'Steady on, old boy – you're getting over-alliterative,' observed Nicholas.

'And kindly don't shout,' added Primrose.

30

The Vicar's Version

The next morning the guest departed, clearly well satisfied with the way things had gone and urging Primrose to commence her 'creative endeavours' as soon as possible. She needed no encouragement. The combination of outrageous flattery, artistic challenge and the expectation of handsome profit was quite enough to send her scurrying to the studio. Here she closeted herself for most of the day, while I was directed to mow and dig the garden, hack down the convolvulus and build a bonfire. I was also required to feed the chinchillas. Since my previous dealings with those creatures had been mildly catastrophic, I was surprised at this last diktat but assumed that Primrose's zest for the Canadian project had blurred either memory or resentment.

I applied myself to all tasks with uncharacteristic energy. Somehow, grubbing about in the garden, and even engaging with Boris and Karloff, provided a welcome diversion from the strain of recent events; and with Nicholas safely returned to Brighton and the artist absorbed in her spurious pastorals, I spent a few congenial hours communing with nature and the rabbits. I also constructed a very serviceable bonfire.

Eventually, proud of my achievements and the unaccustomed exercise, I returned to the house where, with Primrose still occupied in the studio, I made a cup of tea, pushed Bouncer off the sofa and settled down for a well-earned nap.

I awoke to the striking of the hall clock and the sound of my sister's feet thudding down the stairs. She entered the room in paint-daubed smock, hair dishevelled, and grinning broadly. Her labours too, it seemed, had been productive – though I was still uneasy as to their outcome. But it was fruitless to issue further warning about Ingaza, let alone the thin ice of forgery. Older than me and with a stubborn will of her own, my sister would take scant notice of the moral qualms of her clergyman brother . . . nor presumably of one who had been instrumental in relieving the late Mrs Fotherington of her life.

She was still intrigued about the second murder but mercifully seemed to have got over the idea that I might be in any way responsible. And thus we spent a convivial evening playing gin rummy and inventing an elaborate crime scenario in which Mavis Briggs and the bishop's wife were the chief suspects. Rather to my relief nothing more was said about the Canadian project, but before I left in the morning I dutifully and vaguely wished her good luck with 'things'. She smiled confidently and replied that with her talent and Ingaza's knowledge of the market, 'things' could hardly fail. I was unconvinced of that but refrained from saying so; and gathering cat and dog, and waving a fond farewell, set off for Molehill – and fresh developments.

These were slow at first but once started came thick and fast, and I was hard pressed to keep my head above water – or indeed neck from noose.

The first problem was inevitably the press – the *Molehill Clarion*. This organ of mischief and public righteousness was happily wetting itself in ecstasies of conjecture. 'Obviously,' it assured its readers, there was a clear link between the death of Elizabeth Fotherington and the slaying of her daughter: the coincidence was too great for the crimes not to have been perpetrated by the same hand. A bestial serial killer was on the loose and all doors should be securely bolted at night. Indeed, it counselled, padlocks should be purchased for bicycle sheds and pigeon lofts . . . who knew where the assassin might not lurk!

Originally the press had seized upon poor dead Robert Willy, 'the flasher in the undergrowth', as being Elizabeth's killer; but now with this latest incident his place was supplanted by an unknown (and thus more exciting) predator. Good for the *Clarion* and its readers, less good for the vicar and his peace of mind. With Willy discounted, the way was once more open for all manner of rumour and speculation. This was bad enough in itself, but I also had to contend with the thought that in the fearful event of my being arrested it was highly likely I should be saddled with a *double* murder! I brooded upon the injustice of chance, and then sloped off to practise some scales.

These produced little internal harmony, and quickly tiring of the exercise I decided to take Bouncer for a walk instead. It was not the dog's normal hour, and he clearly resented the interruption to his accustomed routine. And thus we commenced our outing in mutual gloom. Typically the dog swiftly regained his snuffling good cheer. I did not. And thus when I saw Tapsell coming in our direction my spirits sank to further depths.

The organist seemed to share my annoyance and he gave one of his customary glares. I wondered whether in retaliation I should mention Edith Hopgarden. Ever since I had unwittingly surprised them *in medias res*, mention of the one to the other invariably produces red-faced discomfort, a condition which generally works to my advantage.

However, I was in no mood for mischief and prepared to let him pass with a bland smile. I was just composing my features for such when he stopped, and in querulous voice said, 'It's not right, you know – all these murders going on. What are you going to do about it?'

'Do about it?' I said in surprise. 'What do you mean? How can I do anything about it?'

'Well . . . it's your parish, isn't it? You're the vicar – *canon* in fact. I mean, you ought to organize something – vigilantes or a protest group.'

'*Vigilantes?* A protest group?' I exclaimed. 'To whom would one protest, for goodness sake?'

'Huh! The police for a start. In my opinion they've been very slow about the whole thing. Need to smarten themselves up. It shouldn't be allowed – innocent citizens being terrorized in their beds while this vampire's abroad. Not right at all.'

'Vampire? That's a bit colourful, isn't it?'

'Not at all,' he replied indignantly. 'He's done two, hasn't he? There's bound to be a third one, there always is. You mark my words!' He waved a truculent finger. 'Anyway, like I said, it's your parish and you ought to set an example. If it was me I'd take the police by the ears and tell them what's what.'

'I doubt whether that would achieve much,' I observed drily.

He continued to glare, and I was just beginning to wonder whether the time had come to introduce both Edith Hopgarden *and* Mrs Tapsell into the conversation, when he moved closer and in a more conciliatory tone said, '*I* think you ought to hold a rally – or better still, an all-night vigil in the church: prayers, psalms, candles and such – and with me playing the organ. I've got a new composition I want to try out and it would be just the thing for a time like this. Why, we could even get the press to come!'

So that was it, was it? Tapsell angling for limelight and glory in the wake of Violet's demise. Typical! He had never really got over being centre stage at the Elizabeth Fotherington Memorial Ceremony, and now presumably was seeking similar laurels from the daughter's misfortune. Yes, in my next breath I jolly well would mention the wife . . . wife *and* girlfriend! But again I was forestalled.

'In fact come to think of it,' he went on, 'it would probably appeal to the grieving widower – sort of calm him down.'

'What?'

185

'Him – Crumplesheet or whatever his name is; daresay he'd be quite appreciative.' He lowered his voice and added, 'They say he's *stricken* . . . I could have a word with him if you like.'

'No,' I said swiftly. 'That will not be necessary. Mr Crumpelmeyer is not of this parish and I am sure his own vicar and church are perfectly equipped to deal with his grief. We don't want to appear officious, Tapsell, do we!'

'Oh well,' he sniffed, 'if that's your attitude . . . Just trying to be helpful, that's all.' And throwing a look of distaste in Bouncer's direction, he marched off.

Mention of Victor Crumpelmeyer pushed me into further gloom – or rather gloom compounded by agitation. So shocked had I been by the naked fact of Violet's murder, that the victim's spouse had been temporarily erased from my mind. The visit to Lewes and the matter of the Nicholas/Primrose collusion had also had an amnesiac effect. However, Tapsell had jolted disturbing memories and I found myself once more dwelling on the man and his brazen intrusion into my affairs. Had he really been after the deeds to that French property as Primrose was so convinced? And if so, would he launch another 'investigative foray' upon the vicarage? Given the outcome of his previous endeavour it seemed highly unlikely – particularly in view of the current circumstances. With spouse lately strangled, presumably even one as grasping as Crumpelmeyer would be occupied with more pressing concerns.

We had reached the canal bridge and I let Bouncer off the lead to nose about in the bushes while I stared down into the water, brooding. And then I brightened: with Violet gone and the husband 'stricken' perhaps I should be permitted to merge into the background again. I whistled to the dog, who responded with uncharacteristic speed, and we set off briskly back to the vicarage.

The following day I went into the High Street to do some shopping and was promptly accosted by Miss Dalrymple.

'I say,' she began, 'this is a pretty kettle of fish, isn't it, Canon? Two murders, and in the same family!'

'Yes,' I replied vaguely, 'appalling.'

'And of course *he* is frightfully cut up. It's all over the papers,' she added with zest.

'Which papers?'

'Well – the *Clarion* principally.'

'Hmm, the *Clarion* rather enjoys these things. Doesn't do to pay too much attention.'

'Ah, but in this case, Canon, there is considerable truth in it all. There's a full-page spread with photographs and interviews . . . and apparently there's some reporter piecing it all together.'

'What do you mean, piecing it together?' I said sharply.

'Showing the connections between the first murder and the second. After all, mother and daughter – obviously it's by the same hand! But they'll get the savage all right, you mark my words. Oh yes!' And clutching brolly and library books, she strode confidently on her way.

I sloped into the newsagent, bought a copy of the *Molehill Clarion*, and finding an empty table at Miss Muffet's Teashop covertly turned to its centre page. The first thing that loomed up was not one, but three photographs of Crumpelmeyer. (Presumably the editor was short of copy that week.) 'STUNNED WIDOWER GRIEVES', the headline ran. He didn't look at all stunned, merely gormless as usual; but the article underneath milked his bereavement for all it was worth, emphasizing the newness of the marriage and the spirited gaiety of the relationship. The first was a fact, the second an assertion I found hard to credit. In my experience there had been nothing remotely gay about Violet . . . and as for her consort, it would have been difficult to find a more unspeakable pain in the arse. However, she was dead and he evidently bereft. So who was I to raise a sceptical eyebrow? There were more insistent things to ponder: the wretched reporter for example and his zeal for 'piecing things together'. I ordered a cream bun and stared morosely at the porcine features of the grieving widower.

31

The Cat's Memoir

'What's deeds?' Bouncer suddenly asked. I was monitoring the movements of a spider at the time and in no mood to be drawn into the dog's interrogations.

'Another term for actions,' I replied shortly, keeping a lynx eye on my prey.

There was a silence. And then just as I was preparing to pounce, the dog burped loudly and said, 'Oh no, Maurice, I don't think so. More to do with words probably.'

Too late. I missed the crucial moment and the spider scurried off among the lobelias. I glared at Bouncer. 'Thanks to your din that creature has just escaped my paw. Kindly go elsewhere!' He didn't of course, and instead sat down and began to scratch. I scanned the grass clippings for another diversion, and not spying any, asked him what he thought he was talking about.

He stopped scratching, and cocking his ears replied thoughtfully, 'Well, when we were down in Sussex with F.O. staying with that sister and the Brighton type, they all kept using this word "deeds" and talking about them being lost ... You won't remember, Maurice – out for the count on the Brighton type's lap.' (I most certainly was, prostrated by the noise and the people!) 'Anyway, for some reason it seemed to upset the vicar and he got quite shirty. Kept telling them that he hadn't seen them and didn't have them. The Brighton type sounded excited and said that was a pity as these deed things could come in useful and perhaps still might be found ... So you see, Maurice, it can't mean actions. You're wrong there.'

I am not accustomed to being called wrong and was nettled. Nevertheless the dog had a point, so I pondered the matter while trying to look indifferent ... Yes, I recalled, there was another meaning: something told to me in kittenhood by my great-uncle Marmaduke (the gallant hero of the hen-run plunder mentioned in an earlier memoir). I think he had said something to the effect that they were documents showing entitlement to property.

I explained this to Bouncer who nodded eagerly. 'That's more like it,' he said, 'papers with words on, that's it!' He got up, shook himself vigorously and informed me that he was going down to the crypt. It was not his usual hour for visiting and I asked why the hurry.

'Got to think,' he replied mysteriously. And picking up his rubber ring, he dog-trotted off towards the church. I was puzzled, but glad of the peace resumed my surveillance of the lobelias.

An hour later he reappeared. 'I have been THINKING,' he announced.

'Yes, you did mention it,' I murmured.

'These deeds I was telling you about – the sister and the Brighton type seemed to think the old girl was meaning to give them to F.O., but didn't. I think I know where they are.'

'Nonsense,' I laughed indulgently, 'you couldn't possibly know.'

'Yes I do!' he retorted. There was a defiant look in his eye.

'All right then, where?'

'In O'Shaughnessy's kennel.'

'O'Shaughnessy's kennel!' I exclaimed. 'What *are* you talking about? You're imagining things.' And I gave an impatient flick of my tail.

He peered out from the shaggy fringe. 'It's a bit complicated, Maurice. Might take a little time ...'

I sighed. 'Well, if it's going to be one of your interminable sagas we had better discuss the matter over supper. Unless F.O. has been remiss with the shopping there should be pilchards tonight. Perhaps they will aid concentration!'

He grinned. 'Right-ho, Maurice!' And thus later that evening we continued the conversation under the kitchen table.

I was both surprised and irritated to hear what he had to say: surprised because I had had no inkling of the events he described; irritated because yet again the dog had concealed matters of which I should have been informed. It was too bad!

'You remember when I told you about me finding the old trout's corpse in Foxford Wood?' he began.

'How could I forget?' I exclaimed. 'The noise was excruciating. I thought your lungs would explode and my ears be split!'

'No, not then,' he snorted impatiently, 'later, when I got down to the details.'

'About you scoffing the gobstoppers and burying F.O.'s cigarette lighter?'

'That's it. Only there was something else, you see.'

'What else?' I asked indignantly. 'Why didn't you tell me?'

'It didn't seem all that important then. Besides, there was so much to think about I couldn't remember everything . . .' He knit his brows.

'Yes, all right.'

'Well, when she was lying there and I was sort of sniffing around seeing what was what, and after I'd eaten the humbugs, I noticed there was a bulge in the pocket of her dress. And you know, Maurice, it crossed my mind that she might have some biscuits there and –'

'Really, Bouncer! Even in the midst of death you can think of nothing but your stomach!' I closed my eyes in pained displeasure.

190

'That's as may be,' he replied, 'but what I found was pretty interesting. Not then of course, but it is now. You see I reckon what I had found was the DEEDS!' He let out a bellow of triumph causing me to close my eyes again.

When I opened them I asked him to kindly justify his assumption, and he said that what he had dragged out of her pocket had been a wedge of typewritten papers tied up in blue ribbon covered in silver stars. 'Sort of like a present,' he explained.

My quick brain immediately grasped the implications. 'So you think these were the deeds which Primrose thought Mrs F. meant to give him.'

'*Yes!*' shouted Bouncer. 'And she would have if he hadn't done for her first! *That's* why she pursued him into the wood – to hand them over!' He stood panting, gazing at me expectantly.

'Hmm,' I mused, 'you could well be right.' His tail threshed the air. 'But,' I continued sternly, 'having retrieved the packet, what did you do with it?'

'Buried it.'

'Whatever for? After all, unlike the lighter, as far as you knew it was of no significance.'

He explained that he had been in training for a bone-burying contest with some of the neighbourhood dogs – apparently a vital challenge requiring much expertise. And feeling he was a trifle out of practice but determined to win, he had been taking every opportunity to hone his technique by using anything which came to paw. 'Seemed a pity to pass up the chance,' he said.

'Quite,' I agreed drily. 'But tell me, Bouncer, what are the documents now doing in the setter's kennel? Why aren't they still in the ground?'

'Ah,' he said, looking shifty, 'that happened when you got us together to go and dig up the lighter before the sniffer dogs found it. You remember, when –'

'Of course I remember,' I replied impatiently, 'it was that masterly plan of mine to organize the vicar's defences. I accompanied you both to the wood to supervise the

191

excavation, but I certainly do not recall anything about a sheaf of papers being recovered.'

'No,' he answered slowly, 'thought you hadn't noticed.'

'What do you mean? Noticed what?'

He cleared his throat and shifted from paw to paw. 'It was like this: I happened to mention to O'Shaughnessy that I had buried some stuff close to the lighter, and *he* said wouldn't it be a good wheeze if we could dig it up again without you noticing and carry it home along with the lighter. You know, a sort of test of speed and . . . oh, that word you are always using – dexter something or other. Anyway, he bet me it couldn't be done without you seeing. "Betcha!" I said. So when you were busy chasing a pheasant that O'Shaughnessy had put up right across your path, I grubbed up the papers, and he clamped them in his jaws and bounded on ahead – while I trotted along with the lighter just like you told me to. When we got back to the vicarage and met O'Shaughnessy again he had already dashed home and shoved the papers in his kennel . . . Quite a neat little op really.' The dog cleared his throat again and gazed vacantly into the far distance, while I contemplated the monstrous duplicity of the canine race.

As you may imagine, this disgraceful tale put me into a sulk for the entire evening, and it was only by the afternoon of the following day that I could bring myself to even glance in his direction.

32

The Dog's Diary

Maurice is in a right old bate! Hasn't spoken all day and looks at me as if I'm something the cat's brought in. Still, I don't mind really – it's been quite peaceful and given me time to collect my thoughts *and* talk to that nice giant Florence. (She's been most helpful and given me a few ideas to chew over.) Still, he'll come round soon enough because he gets bored if there isn't somebody to trouble or complain about. It's probably to do with that furtive brain that he's always on about – at least I think that's what he calls it – but it could be another word beginning with f. He uses so many I get confused!

So what's bugging him? I'll tell you. It's all the result of our time down in Sussex when he went to sleep on the Brighton type's lap and I stayed awake and listened to them all yapping and burbling. They seemed to be enjoying themselves, or at least the Prim and Gaza persons were, but F.O. looked a bit uneasy. But then he often looks like that – something to do with having done the old girl in, I suppose. He was swigging back the brandy all right and smiling now and again, but I could tell his heart wasn't really in it. Too much on his plate, if you ask me, and not just the Foxford Wood murder either! My special sixth sense (which Clever Claws is always so rude about) tells me that there are some pretty odd things going on – pretty odd. But there you are, if you live with a cat and a vicar what else can you expect!

Anyway, the three of them kept using this word 'deeds' – flying all over the place it was – and the more I listened the more I knew it was VERY IMPORTANT. But the problem was I hadn't a clue what it meant. There are some words you can work out, but this one had me really foxed. So after some hard thinking I gave up and thought about other things: my grub, my new ball, having my toenails cut at the vet's, that nice new patch of smell by the garden gate, the organist's dustbin (you can get some good pickings there all right!), rats and cats – oh and heaps of other stuff! So you see, the deeds thing rather went out of my head, and it was only when we got back home that I began to think about it again. That's when I asked Maurice, and *that's* when he started to get shirty.

He told me that deeds are like the letters humans write: pieces of paper covered in words, except that these tell you that you are the owner of a building or some such – a bit like O'Shaughnessy owning his kennel perhaps. So I went off down to the crypt, thought some more and had a snooze. When I woke up it was nearly ALL CLEAR! These deeds that F.O. has lost, or doesn't have, show that he owns some place which is different from the vicarage. The sister in Sussex kept saying that the old girl, Mrs F., had been going to give them to him, but for some reason never did, and she wondered why. So in the crypt I began to wonder why too. And then, of course, the bone dropped with a great crash: they were probably those papers that *I* had pulled out of the corpse's pocket and then buried! What do you think of that?

So that's what I told Maurice; which in a way was a mistake because then I had to explain how O'Shaughnessy and me had dug the papers up again right under his nose and hid them in the setter's kennel. It had been a joke really, to see if we could get away with it without him noticing. Well, we *did* get away with it, and O' Shaughnessy said it was the best bit of craic he had had for weeks! But of course the cat doesn't see the funny side at all, not at all – which is why he is now crouched under the apple tree looking like the Wrath of God.

Still, as said, he'll soon come round, and in the meantime I'll tell you about Florence of Fermanagh. She's a really nice lady and full of useful advice.

You see, while all this cat-sulking has been going on, I thought I'd just nip out and have a little potter around the block. So I was doing that – sniffing here and there and having a good pee against the verger's gatepost – when I suddenly remembered that I was in the road where Florence lives, and thought I would just trot past her drive and see if by chance she was in the garden . . . And there she was – on her back in the middle of the gravel having a good old roll! (Cor, you've never seen such long legs, stretched up to the sky they did!) So I gave a couple of sharp barks just to draw her attention, and she came lolloping over.

We had a good old gas, and she said she liked living here in Molehill because although there wasn't as much space to bound about in as in that Fermanagh place, she found the neighbourhood dogs really friendly, and the humans not bad either.

'Huh,' I said, 'some are! There are certain types you'd do best to avoid if you can. At least – it's not that they're bad exactly, just mor . . . mor . . . uhm, it's one of Maurice's favourite words. Can't quite remember –'

'Moronic,' she said, wagging her tail.

'That's it,' I barked, 'MOR-ONIC! There's quite a lot of those about, I can tell you!'

She nodded her big head and sat back folding her paws. (Just as I said, those forelegs aren't half long!) 'Yes, I know what you mean, we have a good number of them in Ireland too. Over there things are more spread out so they get sort of lost among the mountains and fields and bogs; but here in Molehill where the population is more concentrated –'

'What?' I said, a bit puzzled.

195

'. . . where there are more people in a smaller space, you tend to notice them more.'

'You can say that again!' I agreed eagerly. 'The place is crawling with them, especially in church on Sunday.' And I told her about how I quite often go with F.O. and sit in the pulpit while he's spouting his sermons, and watch the people below. 'A pretty rum lot, if you ask me!'

She did ask me. 'So who's the rummest?' she said.

I had to think about that because there are so many different sorts of rum. 'Well,' I told her, 'for a start there's that schoolmistress Miss Peachy, the one that keeps white mice in her saddle bag and a bottle of gin in her satchel. I would steer clear of that one if I were you: she doesn't like dogs and has a sort of fit every time you get near. I said hello to her once and there was an awful hullabaloo! And then of course there's the Mayor's nephew – a real nut cutlet and no mistake! And Mavis Briggs who's everywhere and has a weedy voice which she uses a lot, and keeps creeping up on people and reading things to them from a notebook. I've noticed that whenever she appears in the High Street the shoppers start to walk very fast. In fact, one time when I was with F.O. he began to tug so hard on my lead that I nearly choked. And as for –'

'So what about the vicar? Is he rum?'

'Crikey, yes – he's really off his chump! But he's very nice to live with – if you can stand the ups and downs and don't weaken.' She looked puzzled, and I *very* nearly told her all about the Foxford Wood business, but stopped myself just in time. Maurice told me once that I must never, *ever* mention it. Just now and again he's right, I suppose. Anyway, he was very fierce about it, so I try to keep my trap shut. We've got a very cushy number at the vicarage and it would be a pity to spoil it.

Florence unfolded her paws and stood up. And bending her head, she put her nose close to mine and said quietly, 'But there's someone dafter than him, isn't there?'

I was a bit startled by that, and sniffed the gravel while I thought about it.

'Er – I'm not sure . . .' I began.

'It's that fat, white-faced one with the staring eyes,' she explained, 'who lives somewhere else but comes to Mole-hill quite often. My sixth sense tells me he needs watching.'

'Your sixth sense!' I barked excitedly. 'You've got one too?'

'Oh yes,' she said, 'all the best dogs have that.'

That really made my day! In fact I was so pleased that I nearly forgot to tell her about my set-to with Crumplehorn in F.O.'s study – which I then did at some length.

When I had finished I thought she looked a bit sleepy, but I expect she had spent a busy morning: all that rolling around, it can tire a dog out, you know. Anyway, she said I was clearly a very *brave* guard hound and that the vicar was lucky to have me (which I keep telling Maurice, but he just stares blankly). And what's more, she said that if we ever needed any help she would be only too happy to muck in as she knew a trick or two that might come in use-ful. I thought that was jolly sporting!

It was nice talking to her and I am sure the cat will approve, *when* he snaps out of his sulk. I think I'll just go and sniff around and see what's what – it's about time he surfaced.

He did surface and was quite matey, even asked if I had had a pleasant day. I told him it had been jolly good and that I had spent some of it talking to the wolfhound. He said he was delighted to hear that as it could only do me some good. Didn't quite know what he meant by that, but it obviously meant *something* – it always does!

He then said that he had been thinking about those deed things in O'Shaughnessy's kennel, and that on reflection (one of his favourite words) he felt they would be far safer in his custard. (Matter of fact, the cat's not too keen on cus-tard, so why he wanted to put the deeds in it I don't know. Still, Maurice is full of funny ideas and sometimes it's simpler not to ask.)

'Oh yes?' I said.

'Most definitely,' he replied, and the sooner I nipped along and brought them back to him, the better.

I explained it wasn't as easy as that because O'Shaughnessy doesn't like having his toys nicked and was bound to cut up rough. He gave his typical cat smile and said if anyone could do it, I could. Well, of course he was right there. No fleas on Bouncer! Besides, just because he beat me in our last peeing contest O'Shaughnessy has been getting a mite big-headed lately and needs taking down a few pegs. If he's not careful his collar will burst.

So that's what I did – waited till I knew the setter was being exercised in the park, and then sneaked along, dived into his kennel and found the packet stuffed under his bedding at the back, and brought it smartly home to Maurice.

We sat staring at it for a while and the cat seemed very keen to tweak the ribbon with his claws, but I pointed out that the wrapping was already pretty grubby from being carried by O'Shaughnessy and perhaps we had better leave things as they were. For once the cat agreed, and then we took it in turns to carry it back to the house. By that time the package was not just grubby but slobbery too, but with F.O. being out we could dry it by the boiler.

When I asked Maurice if he was going to put it in the custard, he said I must be barking mad, and in any case wouldn't I like to know! Considering it was me who had fetched the stupid thing I thought that was a bit rotten. Still, there are better things to think about than a bunch of soggy papers: bones for instance. I've got a very nice one on the go at the moment, only two days old. But it will be due for burial soon so it's time I started to nose round for just the right spot. In the meantime the cat can go and shove those things exactly where he wants!

33

The Vicar's Version

The next few days passed uneventfully – uneventful that is except for the failure of the church boiler, the verger's unceasing complaints about his lumbago, and Miss Dalrymple bemoaning the fact that there was an even greater presence of chewing gum deposits in the choir stalls than usual. 'It's the American sort,' she grumbled, 'less durable than our own brands and the boys spit it out more often.'

I expressed concern and enquired whether the local sweet shop might be prevailed upon to revert to type. She retorted that it would be far more useful if I could preach a brisk sermon on the perils of self-abuse.

'Self-abuse!' I cried in horror. 'Whatever do you mean, Miss Dalrymple!'

'Well, Canon,' she said, 'as I am sure you very well know, unseemly behaviour often precedes moral turpitude. Can't you deliver a little homily on the use of chewing gum as a prelude to dental decay and sin? *That* would give them pause for thought!'

'Pause for sleep, I should think,' I responded. 'Try bribery, it might be more . . .' Fortunately at that point we were approached by Colonel Dawlish in high dudgeon over some gaffe made by the auditors in the church accounts; and for the next half-hour I was subjected to a heated and technical tirade on the finer details of double entry bookkeeping. Eventually I was able to extricate myself and made my grateful way home relishing the prospect of a good restorative.

As I opened the door I found a cream envelope on the mat. It was sealed but bore no name or address and I assumed it was a circular or some similar trifle. However, before attending to the restorative I slit it open and glanced at the contents. They didn't amount to much. In tiny, black and scrupulous capitals were written the words: 'YOU ARE NEXT.'

I stared down uncomprehendingly. Next? Next what . . .? Puzzled, I turned the sheet over to see if anything was written on the back. There was nothing . . . And then of course the point dawned: a childish prank singling me out as the next victim in 'The Allotment Plot' as one or two of the cruder journals had begun to call it. It was half-term, and presumably the local *jeunesse dorée* had nothing better to do than play silly-beggars with their vicar. I tossed the note into the wastepaper basket and applied myself to gin and perusal of the evening paper.

I hadn't been long at this when Bouncer appeared and started to sniff about the room in a most irritating way. I sighed. 'I suppose you want your supper, do you?' Normally the word 'supper' elicits immediate response, but he seemed not to hear and continued to agitate the air and my nerves. Suddenly with a low growl he made a bee-line for the wastepaper basket, tipped it over with his snout and started to rummage in its contents. 'For good-ness sake,' I expostulated, 'you're not a retriever, you know. Lie down or go out!' He paused, stared at me gorm-lessly, and then thrust his head into the basket again. I had had enough of these antics and, taking the dregs of gin with me, went into the kitchen to do my own foraging.

I awoke later that night with a slight headache and, know-ing better than to lie there vainly hoping it would pass, went downstairs for some tea and aspirin. Both of these I took into the study and was about to sit down when I saw the upturned wastepaper basket lying where Bouncer and I had left it the previous evening. I gathered the strewn papers and began to stuff them back in the basket, when my eye fell on the crumpled anonymous note. Idly I read it again, took the aspirin and settled down with the tea. As I sipped, disquieting images of the rearing legs came into my mind; and although at the moment of discovery there had been too little time and too much panic to examine the rest of the body, now, two weeks after the event, my imagination filled up with lurid details and I was suddenly back in the murk of Savage's fearful shed. What had been intended as a tryst for jolly tiddlywinks had become a place of violent death, and the memory was unsettlingly real.

Abstractedly I swallowed another aspirin and pondered the enigma of why this second dispatch should disturb me – not so much in a *deeper* way than the first, but in a manner more acutely frightening. Presumably, I mused, it had something to do with the fact that in the original incident it had been I who had done the deed, and thus there was neither mystery nor threat. Moral responsibility may weigh one down but it does not induce primitive terror of the unknown. And being perforce in full possession of the facts also reduces the imaginative process. To some degree what we know we can control (however dreadful); but what is outside us – things beyond our ken – can exercise a power of awesome force. In this case what was particularly awesome was the ghastly coincidence of mother and daughter! And surely it *was* a coincidence, wasn't it? Or was there some obscure underlying link which connected me as first assassin with this second, unknown OTHER? Or – horror of horrors – was *I* that Other, and Primrose quite right in her initial suspicions? After all, it was still being mooted that the crime had taken place elsewhere and the body only later imported into the shed. Perhaps at last madness had truly come upon me and I was leading some kind of weird schizoid existence . . .

I glanced once more at the note on my lap, swallowed a third pill, and settling myself in the recess of the chair, drifted into troubled sleep.

I woke early: stiff, chilly and not noticeably rested. But after a hot bath I felt mildly revived, and having engaged in a protracted breakfast was fairly ready to deal with the day's agenda. This as often was a humdrum schedule – although on that day set to culminate in what doubtless would be high drama: taking the dog to the vet to have his toenails cut. Fortunately the appointment was not until four thirty, so in the meantime, soothed by duty and routine, I could prime myself for the impending theatricals.

These when they came were well up to standard, but as usual Robinson handled the subject with phlegmatic good humour. 'Awkward customer, your Bouncer,' he observed. 'Still, nothing compared to the cat – now that one *is* a prima donna! A right old holy terror. Must be the influence of the vicarage.' He laughed good-naturedly. I thanked him for his patience, and clipped and voluble we emerged into the late sunshine.

Our walk home took us via the High Street and we nearly encountered Mavis Briggs traipsing along festooned with dangling shopping bags. I thought at first she hadn't seen me but should have known better, for in the next instant there was the familiar bleat: 'Oh, Canon ...' I affected not to hear, and yanking Bouncer's lead took swift sanctuary in the barber's where I spent an unconscionable time selecting a packet of razor blades. Since it was well after five o'clock and the shop on the point of closing, I think our presence was not entirely welcome. However, there are times when one cannot falter.

The danger over, we went briskly on our way, the dog presumably as keen for his supper as his master. We were just rounding the corner leading to the lane which runs past the vicarage, when a large saloon car glided past, slowed and stopped. As I drew level the rear window was wound down and Clinker's head emerged. The purple waistcoat and chauffeur's presence suggested he was either coming from or going to some formal function. With luck the latter. Hopes were dashed, 'Ah, Oughterard,' he exclaimed, 'just on my way back from Windsor and thought I might catch you at home – but this is as good as anywhere. Now, get in, if you wouldn't mind, there're a number of things I need to discuss.' He opened the Daimler's door and I clambered inside hauling the dog behind. 'I trust that hound hasn't got muddy paws,' he grumbled, 'Barnes has only just vacuumed the upholstery.' I said nothing, thinking that if the bishop chose to go around hijacking people from the kerbstone then he could jolly well put up with muddy paws!

Fortunately the back of the car was spacious and Bouncer, tired from the toenail histrionics, ready to curl up and go to sleep. Clinker leant forward and snapped shut the glass partition, and lowering his voice began. 'Well now, Oughterard, this shed business . . .'

It was really a repeat of the earlier telephone conversation, i.e. urging the necessity for discretion and enjoining me yet again to make absolutely no mention to Mrs Carruthers of what had been the intended venue. He had obviously been brooding on the matter since our last contact and, to quote one of Ingaza's questionable analogies, must have been as fearful as a ferret with its arse shot off. He wanted to know if Savage was 'safe' and whether I knew of any developments in the current police enquiries: 'I mean, for example, Francis, have they found anything in the shed of . . . er, a compromising nature – any trace of there having been *other parties* present?'

I reassured him about Savage, and said that as far as I was aware nothing further had emerged, adding that in any case since we (and specifically he) had spent so little time at the scene it was highly unlikely that there would be any residual traces. 'But there was one thing,' I volunteered, 'which could just make things a trifle sticky . . .'

A flush of colour mottled his cheeks. 'Good Lord, whatever's that, Francis?'

'Well,' I replied slowly and with straight face, 'just by the door I gather they picked up three or four spilled tiddlywinks counters . . . you know, sir, little plastic blue and red ones. They seem to think the assassin may have dropped them . . .'

He stared at me in horror, his mouth opening and shutting like a mesmerized goldfish. And then finding his tongue and his wits, said in icy but slightly shaky tones, 'I take it that is your idea of a joke, Oughterard – you can generally be relied upon to produce some puerile jest at times of serious moment. Gladys was right – why they elected you a canon I cannot imagine!' And so saying he tapped briskly on the glass partition and indicated that the Reverend Oughterard was about to leave and the engine could thus be started.

Bouncer and I climbed out on to the pavement, and raising my hat I bade goodnight to the bishop and watched as the Daimler trundled on its stately way.

'Supper at last!' I said to the dog. 'Come on.'

We entered by the back door, said hello to Maurice and settled to the pleasures of a leisurely meal. It was only much later, having done the washing up and listened to the Light Programme and the absurdities of Ted Ray's *Take It From Here*, that I left the kitchen and crossed the hall to the study . . . On the mat by the front door lay another blank cream envelope.

I stared down despondently, and with a sigh of resignation picked it up and opened the flap. The writing was exactly as before – black ink, obsessively neat capitals. Only the message was different: 'NEMESIS STALKS,' it told me. I recall that my first reaction was one of annoyance. 'Well, it can bloody well go and stalk elsewhere!' I fumed. Nevertheless, despite the melodramatic phrasing, the word 'Nemesis' struck a distinctly uneasy chord, and as I pondered its source and purpose, the more agitated I became.

The first missive could indeed have been the work of some juvenile prankster cashing in on the current excitement. But this second one held a pertinence altogether too close to the bone, and I suddenly found myself shaking uncontrollably. Who could possibly know? *How* did they know? And above all, what were they going to do about it? These were questions that whirled and swirled in my mind making me feel quite faint with anxiety.

As so often in times of stress, the piano beckoned; and I hastily approached the keys trusting they might yield up some fortifying balm. They didn't. My fingers were heavy, my shoulders tense, and even Bouncer seemed less than impressed by the resulting performance. After the fourth wrong note he lost interest and ambled back to the kitchen.

I retired to bed, my imagination engulfed in pictures of the scaffold and Albert Pierrepoint.

34

The Vicar's Version

The public hangman pushed firmly to the back of my mind, I got on with my clerical duties. Sunday passed unremarkably, but Monday brought an avalanche of tedious post: a proliferation of bills, circulars, church notices, approaches from charities, an invitation to attend the annual dinner of the Guildford Temperance Society (no, thank you!), an unwelcome note from Archdeacon Foggarty reminding me that the time for the Canonical Address was nigh and would I please submit my theme as soon as possible (naturally I had none such), and finally a handwritten envelope in crabbed script postmarked central London. Seeing that last one nearly gave me a heart attack as the small handwriting suggested the anonymous letters, and such was my agitation that I was ready to fear the worst.

In fact it was from Claude Blenkinsop asking me to telephone him immediately as he had some intriguing news. I doubted whether there was anything pertaining to Claude that could be remotely intriguing, but nevertheless made a mental note to call him that evening.

The day proceeded busily, and I became immersed in the usual run of meetings, telephone calls, home visits and other sundry commitments of the parish. The early evening brought bell-ringing practice, an event that, despite the strenuous exercise, I find curiously soothing; and I arrived home satisfied with the day and looking forward to my armchair and a nice spot of supper. I was just beginning on the latter when I suddenly remembered Blenkinsop's request to telephone him. I was tempted to put it off until later, but preferring to eat in a mood of ease decided to get it over with. So after returning the pie to a low oven and putting a lid on the mash, I went into the hall and dialled his number.

'Ah, Francis,' the mincing voice greeted me, 'you obviously got my little note. How very kind of you to telephone.' I told him it was my pleasure and trusted he was well. 'Well, I *am*,' he twittered, 'quite overwhelmed really!'

'Really? In what way?'

'You see, I have just received a telephone call from America . . . well, I say "just received" but in fact it was two in the morning, if you please! At first I thought it was a practical joke . . . I don't know about you, Francis, but I am unused to being rung up in the middle of the night – most unsettling. When I pointed this out in no uncertain terms to my caller, he said it was only nine o'clock on that side of the Atlantic and he hoped I wasn't too disturbed. Well, *of course* I was disturbed – extremely! However, he explained that he is some academic in the Greenholt Institute, an offshoot of Harvard, I gather. In fact I think he said he's the curator there – a Dr Hiram K. Flutzveldt.'

'What?'

'Yes, Flutzveldt – Hiram K.' He spelled it out for me.

An image of Groucho Marx instantly filled my mind, but I said nothing, and listened politely to what he had to say.

'I gather he is an avid collector of animal figurines, specifically British pigs and badgers of the eighteenth and nineteenth centuries. Rather an eclectic field, I grant. But you know what we connoisseurs are!' He gave a modest laugh. 'Apparently he edits a rather prestigious New York magazine dedicated to this kind of thing and is most eager to feature *my* Beano Pig, with several photographs and lengthy contributions from myself! Most flattering really. In fact he has already prepared the article's title: "Blenkinsop's Bone Idol Brings Home the Bacon!" What do you think of that, Francis ... international fame at last!' He gave an ironic titter but the underlying glee was obvious.

'Er ... but the thing isn't British exactly, is it? It was stolen from Ali's collection ...'

'Ah, but my dear chap, the Beano link and the addition of the gems have put the imperial stamp upon it: it's what you would call British by association – or accident as some might prefer.'

'I see ... But this Dr Flutzveldt, does he know your model is not the original? I mean –'

'Oh yes, of course. Apparently a mutual acquaintance made some reference to it, which is how he got my name. But that doesn't matter. It is enough that mine is quite likely to be the first reproduction of its kind and therefore of considerable interest and appeal to the *discerning*. I am sure you will appreciate that!' I assured him I did.

He prattled on fussily about the form the article would take and his central role in it, while I made the requisite responses. Given my own recent experience with both items, genuine and bogus, I cannot say that I was entirely smitten with the subject.

Claude continued. 'However,' he confided, 'apparently Flutzveldt has been on the trail of the original for years, indeed he told me the pursuit had become quite an obsession. He even wondered whether I had any ideas on the subject, and if so he would be "grovellingly" grateful if I could give him information. He certainly sounded eager – said he would give his eye teeth to buy it, his *eye teeth*! Anyway, I am afraid I had to tell him that, flattered though I might be to have such a distinguished academic grovelling with gratitude, I feared that I had simply no idea of its whereabouts and that the thing was probably lost for all time ... hence of course the special importance of *my* delightful little trinket!

'He agreed I was probably right, but said he lives in hopes, especially since some of his researches have suggested it might still be in England ... Personally I rather doubt that but I said I would apprise him of any "clues" should they come my way, as naturally I was always glad to accommodate a fellow scholar.' Down the line came the faintest sound of a self-satisfied sniff. 'Naturally he was exceedingly grateful, but assured me that in any event he would have great pleasure in compiling the proposed article and that I should be sent *several* copies of the issue the instant it is published.' Here Claude paused, cleared his throat and added magnanimously, 'And since you share similar interests, Francis, I think I could manage to spare one. The publication is doubtless not unknown to you: *Collections Privées* – highly exclusive of course.' He gave a discreet cough.

Strange to say, his assumption of my knowledge was unfounded, but I thanked him for his generosity and enquired whether by any chance he would also be sending a copy to his brother.

'I most certainly will,' he declared sharply. 'I fear Vernon has few cultural interests and it is high time he perused something a little more artistically elevated than diocesan accounts and *Picture Post*. It may also serve as a gentle reminder to him that distinction is not the exclusive preserve of the archdeaconry!' This last remark was delivered with the waspish petulance one had come to associate with both the Blenkinsops, Major and Minor, and it was with some relief that I heard him announce that he was *far* too busy to continue chattering and that he really must 'bustle' off to prepare vital notes on Beano and the precious pig.

Time, too, for me to bustle into the kitchen and retrieve my supper from the oven . . . But needless to say, despite the carefully lowered gas, the pie looked worn and leathery; and after one bite, and cursing Claude, I tossed it irritably into the dog's basket where it was received with noisy joy.

What with one thing and another it had been quite an eventful day, and wearied by Claude and smarting from the deprivation of my pie, I decided to have an early night.

It was only when I awoke much later and lay staring into the dark, that the relevance of his words began to impinge. Evidently this Hiram K. Flutzveldt was genuinely eager to get his hands on the original item, and according to Claude was prepared to pay big money to do so (assuming, of course, it was not merely his teeth that he was ready to trade). My own proximity to the creature had not exactly enlightened me as to its intrinsic appeal, but there was no accounting for tastes. And in any case, as both Claude and Ingaza had pointed out, it was largely its history that fascinated collectors and guaranteed a market – assuming it could be traced. But then, of course, it *had* been traced and was now firmly in Nicholas's grip awaiting a buyer.

I reflected upon this, wondering if he had already found such a person, and if so, what sort of smokescreen was being concocted to obscure how it had been obtained. However, I cannot say that aspect occupied me for long, as I knew from old that my persecutor's capacity for fabrication was prodigious. What did begin to occupy me was the idea of the sale itself. My role in the execution of the theft irked me considerably (though not perhaps to the degree of the other little matter), and I was loath to hear another word about the perishing creature ... Nevertheless, I mused guiltily, the whole affair had been so onerous and my part so crucial (and for once successful), that perhaps indeed some small recompense was due. When Nicholas had mentioned my receiving a 'cut' were a sale achieved, I had firmly spurned the suggestion; but in retrospect I began to resent that he should benefit so much at my expense. I was more than tired of being his exploited lackey. To use his own words, a little quid pro quo was surely in order!

The moment that term came to mind, I flinched, fearing that I was beginning to absorb not only my master's style of speech but possibly his mode of thought as well. However, it must be said in my own defence that I am not by nature mercenary (a fact that readers of earlier sections will perhaps recognize), but I did feel that something was owed nevertheless. The Custodians of the Church Roof were finding it increasingly difficult to afford builders of sufficient calibre to maintain its upkeep, and a little financial aid would be looked upon most favourably. Some of the older pews needed to be replaced as well, and a few pounds in that direction mightn't come amiss either ... Thus I brooded until, befuddled by grappling with the moral niceties, I shelved the matter; and drawing the blankets over my head lapsed into dreamless sleep.

I awoke to the sun beaming through the curtains and the repetitive rhythm of next door's lawn mower being given its first spring outing. The window was open and I could smell – or thought I could smell – the faintest whiff of freshly cut grass. A blackbird twittered busily to itself in the crab-apple by the tool shed. Somehow these harbingers of summer gave a reassuring prospect to the day, and I found myself alighting from bed in a mood almost bordering on pleasure.

Still in pyjamas I went downstairs to prepare breakfast (a hearty one in view of the previous night's meagre scrapings), and even spoke to the animals who seemed vaguely surprised by such overtures. I lingered over coffee, read the newspaper, puffed at the first cigarette of the day – and then without further ado went into the hall and lifted the receiver.

'Ah, Nicholas,' I began briskly, 'I've just been thinking about that Bone Idol, I rather –'

'Bit early in the day, isn't it, old cock?' was the sour reply. 'I've got one hell of a head!'

Only slightly put out, I said I was sorry to hear that but, having a taxing schedule to complete, thought I would grab the present chance to see if he had found a buyer for the pig.

This was greeted with a loud yawn, followed by the grumbling observation that, taxing schedule or not, it was still too damned early to talk business, and anyway it was not like me to show such concern for his affairs.

I reminded him lightly that I did have some small interest in proceedings, and asked again whether there was any sign of a client.

There was a silence. And then he said, 'Well, not at this precise moment, Francis, but then these things take time. It requires some careful planning – not something you would understand. These things are always complicated – wheels within wheels, you know . . . but I'm working on it all right, shouldn't take too long. Now if you don't mind, could you get off the effing line and let a chap have some sleep!'

'I've got you a buyer,' I announced. 'Bird right in the hand.'

It is remarkable how the smallest hint of monetary gain can have such a transforming effect on the human psyche.

Ingaza seized the titbit, toyed with it, and then proceeded to chew with merciless dedication. Headache apparently gone, yawning arrested, even language tempered, he subjected me to a probing catechism: who was the man? what was he worth? where did he live? what was his background? And anyway, how reliable was Blenkinsop for heaven's sake!

I told him as much as I knew, which admittedly wasn't very much, but he seemed confident that he could trace him by the name Claude had given (which I too had to spell out) and the institute to which he was attached. 'Right,' he said briskly. 'I'll get the reference books out, make a few discreet phone calls to New York, and we'll soon see if he's really kosher and not some figment of Blenkinsop's demented fancy. With a name like Shickelgrüber or whatever, it shouldn't be too difficult!' And with a crack of laughter, he rang off.

I returned to the kitchen, made some more toast, and continued quietly with my 'taxing schedule'.

35

The Vicar's Version

As I might have guessed, Ingaza moved speedily with his enquiries, and three days later telephoned to say that he was satisfied that Claude's American was who he claimed to be: a senior curator of the Greenholt Institute with a reputation as an exacting editor of the arts magazine Claude was so eager to feature in. Thus he had already established personal contact with Flutzveldt who seemed cautiously eager to do business.

'Naturally,' he said, 'the chap wanted to see all the relevant documentation and details of how it had been obtained. But I told him that I was afraid that was impossible as I was acting on behalf of the owner who was extremely reclusive and *always* had his transactions executed on trust, and that naturally I would abide by my client's wishes in the matter.'

'Huh,' I said, 'that must have reassured him, I don't think!'

Ingaza tutted. 'Now, now, don't be sarcastic, Francis, it doesn't suit you . . . As a matter of fact he had no choice. "Take it or leave it," I said, "it's entirely up to you. Personally I would prefer the convenience of a quick sale, but it's no skin off my nose to delay things for a year or so while *others* make overtures. I have no doubt the wait will be worth it."'

'So how did he react to that?'

'Slowly. Kept muttering that it sounded highly irregular and he would really need some proof of provenance. "My dear fellow," I said, "I could give you all the proof in the world if I chose – nothing could be easier! You do know, I imagine, that the English are renowned for their expertise in forgery: I could have the relevant papers done in a trice if required and you would be none the wiser. But being rather keen on upholding the standards of my profession, let alone the value of my own reputation, that is something I choose not to dabble in, simple though it would be."'

As he spoke, Nicholas instinctively assumed an air of casual indifference and moral rectitude, and I was reminded of how easily he had fooled the authorities at St Bede's all those years ago, and how presumably his shadowy pursuits in Brighton continued to thrive. I also thought of Primrose and the way she had been so smoothly seduced into supplying the Canadian art market with her fraudulent pictures . . . I thought too of myself and what a fool I had been ever to ask him to corroborate my tale of the binoculars in the Fotherington affair. It had all sprung from that moment, I mused bitterly. If I hadn't picked up the telephone and asked for his co-operation in providing that one small detail, none of this would have happened and I should be free from his blandishing clutches . . . Though on the other hand, I recalled ruefully, I suppose I could equally well be a hanged man by now, or at best banged up for life amidst ruffians and lunatics! I sighed, and returned my mind to his words.

'And the upshot?'

'Oh, the *upshot* is that he wants me to go over there as soon as possible, bring the pig for him to make an assessment and talk further. Plain sailing!'

'So I suppose you're about to rush off – booking plane tickets and all that?'

'Rush off? Certainly not, dear boy. We're not all impetuous idiots! No, he'll have to stew for a bit; told him I had a number of pressing engagements and couldn't possibly get away until the end of the month. These things need careful handling, Francis. Doesn't do to look too keen.' He giggled, and added, 'If you weren't such a liability I would take you with me; as it is you're far safer polishing candlesticks in St Botolph's or whatever you do. Can't afford the risk!'

I was stung by that, but also slightly regretful. I had never been to America (or anywhere very much) and my knowledge of the country was based largely on what I had seen in the cinema via the exploits of Humphrey Bogart, George Raft, Sydney Greenstreet, and other denizens of Manhattan with its ritzy bars and swish hotel suites. I experienced a pang of envy as I imagined Nicholas ensconced in the Algonquin, sipping stone dry martinis while cutting a lucrative deal with Hiram K. Flutzveldt to the elegant strains of Cole Porter . . .

My reverie was interrupted by his next words, 'In the meantime, Francis, I shall be coming up to Surrey next week to see my Cranleigh pal. Perhaps I could drop in on my way back – I've got a little something for your Primrose which you can pass on when you next see her, a small cheque actually. There's a postal strike down here and God knows when deliveries will be reliable again, otherwise I'd send it direct. Wouldn't mind a spot of grub if there was any going.'

Rather reluctantly I said there probably would be some going; and we set a date for his visit. Clearly in high spirits, and with fulsome praise for my cooking (!) he then rang off, leaving me to light a cigarette and brood.

I didn't brood long, for five minutes after his call there was another one, this time from my sister inviting herself to lunch on the same day. Apparently she would be passing near Molehill on the way back home from Derbyshire after addressing that county's Guild of Artists' Pastoral Circle. This group was an offshoot from the main body, dedicated to the depiction of rural pursuits and ancient churches.

'Just my pigeon,' she had said, 'I can prose on for hours about wool-spun flocks and lichened buttresses, and when it's all over rake in a nice fat fee *plus* supper, board and vast expenses. Very handy!'

I enquired what expenses other than petrol. 'Lunch of course,' she replied.

'But you will be lunching with me,' I pointed out. Apparently that was neither here nor there.

'Funny you've picked that date, ' I said, 'because as it happens, Nicholas Ingaza has threatened to drop by at the same time. He will have been seeing his contact in Cranleigh – some scam brewing presumably – and he did happen to mention that he had a small cheque to deliver which I could pass on to you. The Canadian business, I suppose.'

'Well, that's a stroke of luck,' she replied. 'Entrusting a cheque to your hands would be asking for trouble.'

'What do you mean?' I gasped indignantly. 'I am a model of probity!'

'That's as may be. But you are careless, Francis, *careless*!'

I let it go and confirmed details of her arrival. We decided this should be earlier rather than later as it would give us time to have a coffee and a natter before Nicholas arrived, and she would not be rushed getting back to Sussex to prepare the chinchillas' supper. 'Karloff is so particular,' she declared. 'If he doesn't get his carrot compôte on time he has the vapours and then throws all his bedding about cheered on by Boris. It's a nightmare!'

Not wishing to incommode Karloff I indicated that she would be welcome any time after ten o'clock.

She arrived bearing some pots of Sussex honey, a Spotted Dick pudding, and a large vegetable marrow in a paper bag. For some reason Bouncer took an excited interest in this and seemed eager to remove its wrapping. I pushed him away and put the marrow on the hall table but he kept circling and jumping up. 'I never knew a dog so greedy,' she exclaimed. 'I suppose he thinks it's a bone. I brought

216

him one once and he's never forgotten.' She removed the bag, and the dog took one sniff, gave a reproachful snort and mooched off.

I made some coffee and we settled in the sitting room and chatted about her talk to the Pastoral Circle and my inaugural Canonical Address.

'I'm rather dreading it,' I admitted. 'There's only a couple of months to go and I really haven't given it a thought, and as one of my colleagues so helpfully pointed out, it isn't like any ordinary sermon, it's supposed to have style, dignity and distinction – or be so obscure that people are impressed without understanding a word.'

'Well, why don't you impress them by departing from the norm?' she said encouragingly. 'I mean, you could start cracking jokes and have them rolling in the aisles. Why, you could even do an imitation of Arthur Askey pretending to be a clergyman. He did that at the Palladium, it was marvellous. They would probably love it!'

'What an absurd idea! . . . Besides, Arthur Askey is half my height.'

'All right, how about Max Miller?' This was followed by further suggestions in similar vein, none of which was remotely enlightening. We turned to other matters and gossiped at length, until glancing at the clock I realized it was high time I put on the stew. Primrose collected the coffee cups and followed me into the kitchen.

'Oh really, Francis,' she expostulated, 'this place is appalling. Look at the mess everywhere! Can't you get some of your female followers to lend a hand? I'm sure they would be only too delighted.'

'No fear!' I cried. 'Anyway, haven't got any *followers*, as you so sweetly put it.'

'What about that Mavis person? Surely she'd be happy to wield a bucket and mop.'

'The only thing Mavis can wield is a limp wrist and a volume of nauseating poems.'

'Oh well,' she grumbled, 'I suppose your poor sister will have to get down to things. Nicholas is arriving soon and

I do have my reputation as an international artist to think of. Seeing the squalor of your kitchen might turn him off giving me any more Canadian assignments!'

'Not if money is involved,' I retorted acidly. She ignored this, and donning a pair of rubber gloves began sweeping vigorously round the boiler. I sighed, and having put the casserole on to simmer, started to make my escape to the study; but as I crossed the hall I heard her exclaim, 'Oh, for goodness sake, you don't keep the cat litter tray here, do you! It'll have to go!'

I returned wearily and explained that the discreet corner by the back door was the only place for it and that since Maurice was impeccable in his ablutions there really wasn't a problem.

'Well, I am sure it can be pushed further out of sight anyway, it's bad enough being faced with the dog's basket!' And so saying, she gave the thing a sharp shove deeper into the corner. As she did so something fell out of the space between the tray and its base: a crumpled and dirty packet of papers tied in frayed blue ribbon.

'Whatever's that?' said Primrose, stooping to pick it up.

I had had enough of these domestic manoeuvres, and indicated that I really didn't care and was going into the study to make some phone calls before Ingaza arrived. Thus I made my escape, and collapsing into the armchair lit a cigarette and closed my eyes.

I was just wondering whether I had the courage to telephone Colonel Dawlish to explain that I had blundered with dates and could not after all attend his charity whist drive, when Primrose appeared at the door in a state of voluble excitement.

'Francis,' she babbled, waving the mangled packet at me, 'you'll never guess – these are the deeds to the Fotherington Folly! That place in France the old girl wanted you to have. They've even got your name on them and some sort of seal. Isn't it incredible!'

I gazed horror-struck. The last things I wanted were

those deeds and further connection with my victim Elizabeth Fotherington! Besides, how in living hell had they found their way into the cat's tray? It was impossible – grotesque! Then just as I had started to think that few nightmares could be more ghastly, there was the sound of the doorbell and I knew that Nicholas had arrived . . .

I arose zombie-like and let him in.

'Hello, hello, hello!' he breezed. 'Long time, no see! How's clerical life these days? I must say, you don't look too well on it, old boy – white as the proverbial sheet. Still, I expect we can fix that!' And he thrust a bottle of gin into my hands.

I mustered a smile of thanks and took him into the sitting room where Primrose was still drooling over her find.

After lavish overtures, he stuck a hand into his waistcoat pocket and drew out a slim envelope which he presented to her with a little bow. 'First remuneration,' he murmured. 'Courtesy of Canada: not too big – but not too small either, I think you'll find.' He smiled slyly.

Primrose tore open the envelope with an avidness of the kind displayed by Bouncer when thrown a new bone. The cheque inside evidently met with her approval, for grasping the bottle of gin she exclaimed gaily, 'We must drink a toast – to sheep and churches!'

'Long may they both flourish,' added Nicholas gravely.

I fetched the glasses and we tackled the gin: they in happy celebration, me in some need. I felt gloomy, knowing that it could only be a matter of minutes before Primrose apprised Ingaza of her remarkable find in the cat litter.

My fears were well grounded, for after a couple of gulps she turned to him and said, 'You know, something quite extraordinary has happened but we'll tell you about it at lunch. It's very exciting – isn't it, Francis?'

'Yes,' I said glumly.

* * *

219

Inevitably lunch was no picnic. It was taken up with endless speculation as to how the deeds got where they were ... Perhaps, for example, Mrs Fotherington had dropped them in the road, and Maurice, seeing the be-ribboned packet and thinking it a new kind of toy, had promptly hijacked it. Nicholas declared that he knew several cats given to just such magpie activities and it would be far from unusual.

We thought about that possibility. And then Primrose suggested that Elizabeth, engaged on one of her intrusive visits to the vicarage, had deliberately secreted the deeds in the receptacle hoping to persuade me to play a kind of hunt-the-parcel at a later date – 'You know, as a sort of playful prelude to her generosity!'

I shuddered at the thought, while Nicholas shrieked with laughter, spluttering, 'Oh yes, I can just see old Francis on hands and knees sniffing round the cat litter trying to pick up clues to a fortune!'

Primrose joined in the mirth, and the two hooted and gurgled merrily at my expense.

'Look,' I said stiffly, 'it is all very well, but I am the one who will be implicated if it is thought that I have gained from her death or even her romantic partiality. The more tenuous the link between myself and Elizabeth, or indeed the wretched daughter, the better. As far as I am concerned those deeds are a hot potato leading to God knows what. I do not want them!'

'Mixing your metaphors again, old boy,' observed Nicholas. 'Besides –' he coughed delicately – 'you might have given consideration to that when you were busy in the wood. I've told you before, you have no sense of foresight.'

'He's right,' chimed in Primrose. 'Daddy was always complaining. Don't you remember when you threw Amy Ponsonby's teddy bear in the duck pond and there was such a shamozzle? Pa kept asking why you couldn't have chosen a bear belonging to some lesser child, i.e. not the High Sheriff's brat. He said the whole thing would have been wrapped up in a day instead of dragged out for weeks!'

I glared at her. 'Amy Ponsonby had it coming! She had stolen my favourite lead soldier, and what's more –'

'Yes, yes,' broke in Nicholas, 'charming though these family reminiscences are, I think we should stick to the matter in hand: the deeds and how best we can utilize them.'

I laid down my knife and fork, and fixing him with a frosty stare, said in my best clerical tones: '*We* are not going to use them at all, Nicholas. Nor for that matter am I. In fact, I have every intention of disposing of them forthwith!' I began to get up from the table.

'Oh, don't be so melodramatic, Francis!' cried Primrose. 'Sit down and wait for pudding. It's your favourite, Spotted Dick and custard – and I've put extra currants in this time so it should be really good.'

'Rather, Francis!' agreed Nicholas. 'Definitely worth waiting for – plenty of time to throw away your key to a fortune afterwards.' He smiled encouragingly; and irritated though I was, I stayed in my seat lured by the Spotted Dick.

The rest of lunch moved in calmer fashion. And although I felt uneasy at their sprightly talk about the success of the art forgeries, my concern over the deeds grew less acute. Naturally, just to satisfy curiosity I would examine them more closely once my guests had departed; and then after due consideration would in all probability – and as had been my first intention – destroy them. Obviously fire would be the best method and I would light one that evening after Primrose had returned to Lewes. Yes, I had been panicking unnecessarily: the whole embarrassment could easily be resolved and I should soon be free both of the deeds themselves and of Ingaza's officious interest in the property and its absurdly alleged Nazi gold!

Thus I applied myself with relish to the pudding and cheese, and after lunch helped Primrose with the coffee while our guest read the newspaper and parleyed with the dog in the sitting room. Fortunately the question of the deeds was not resurrected, and, sooner rather than later, Nicholas announced that he really must be going as it was Eric's birthday and they would thus be spending the evening at the dog-track.

'Well, that all went very well, I think,' said Primrose after he had left. 'A nice little fee for the Canadian things – and I am sure he charged considerably less commission than he had originally said.'

'Huh!' I replied. 'That's just a sweetener to get you hooked – you'll see. It'll get steeper as it goes on.'

'Oh, don't be such a cynic, Francis! I do realize of course that there's an element of dodginess there, but clearly not nearly to the extent you seem to suggest. It doesn't do to be so negative about people.' She spoke with good-humoured authority, and I said nothing but thought the more.

We lit cigarettes and settled down to the crossword. But our efforts were not very successful, and after twenty minutes of frustrated pondering, she cast her pencil aside and said, 'I say, Francis, I do think you ought to look at those deeds. They're really quite interesting, you know. There's a plan of the property and it looks pretty big, with several outhouses and barns. Must have been intended as a farm or even a winery originally. The only snag is it seems to be miles from anywhere – I mean really in the depths . . . well, the heights actually, it's halfway up some mountain! So who knows, there may just be some truth in that gold rumour, it's conveniently remote all right. Don't you think we could go and have a peek at it?'

'No,' I said shortly. 'I am far too busy with the church, couldn't possibly get away. Clinker's due for the Confirmations soon, and after that, as I told you, I've got the Canonical Address to prepare.'

She raised her eyes to the ceiling. 'You could at least look at the damn things anyway . . . Where are they – in the kitchen?'

'No, here. They should be on the piano. You put them there when Nicholas arrived.'

'I don't think so – or at least they're not there now. They must be in the kitchen. I'll go and have a look.' She got up with a determined air, while I vaguely scanned the sitting room.

A minute or so later she was back looking perplexed. 'There's no sign of them out there.'

'What about the hall table?'

She shook her head.

'Well, they must be somewhere. This is ridiculous!' I sighed. 'You take another look in here and I'll do the kitchen again.' I searched everywhere – even in Bouncer's basket where Nicholas had once dropped his car keys. There was nothing.

'Well, where the hell are they?' she cried.

I was silent. And then I said quietly, 'I can tell you exactly where they are.'

'Where?'

'In that bastard's wallet . . .'

I was enraged. How could he do that! Silly question: quite easily – typical in fact. However, I certainly wasn't going to let it go. And once I had got rid of Primrose and spent an hour in much-needed rest, I went downstairs and seized the telephone.

'I think you've got something of mine, Nicholas,' I began coolly, 'and I should be glad if you returned it.'

'Don't know what you are talking about, dear boy. Getting confused with someone else.'

'Nonsense, you know perfectly well I am referring to those Fotherington deeds which you appropriated when lunching at my house today. Kindly return them!'

There was a pause. And then he said, 'Ah *those*! Yes, I was going to mention them to you . . . Do you know, when you and Primrose were in the kitchen after lunch I started a quick perusal of the things – fascinating! In fact so fascinating that quite without thinking I must have slipped them in my pocket. Silly me! It's amazing how absent-minded one gets!'

'Nothing absent about your mind,' I replied angrily. 'Just hand them over!'

His voice became conspiratorial. 'Well, actually, Francis, if it's all the same with you, think I might hang on to them for a while, you see –'

'It is not all the same with me, I want them back immediately!'

'As I was saying – you see, I was rather thinking of popping over there at some point to take a look around, a sort of reconnaissance. After all, one might as well see what's what. And that tale of Nazi gold is *very* intriguing . . . could make all our fortunes. Think of that, Francis! Mind you, it'll have to wait till the pig transaction is all wound up, mustn't lose sight of Mr Shickelgrüber!' He gave a nasal titter.

Making a fortune from my victim's gift was the last thing I needed. Benefiting from her will had been bad enough. Fortunately I had been able to wriggle out of that by disposing of the funds before anyone could accuse me of having had sinister motives. But at least then *I* had been in control and could organize matters as seemed appropriate. Now, however, I was in thrall to Ingaza and his wiles, and God knew where that might lead! Having her property thrust upon me was an awful embarrassment, and my own instinct was to destroy the deeds and get on with my life as if the thing did not exist. I need never know anything about it, and for all I cared it could rot in the ground – or better still, go to blazes! Simple really. But Ingaza's intrusion naturally put paid to that. I closed my eyes. What *had* I done to deserve him! There was, of course, an answer to that . . .

Anyway, I told him I thought the whole idea totally preposterous, and that even if he were to go over and start snooping around, there was sure to be some sort of concierge or local official who would doubtless want to know who he was and what he was doing there. It could all be rather awkward.

'Not awkward at all, old cock,' was the reply, 'I shall just say I am the Reverend Francis Oughterard from Molehill come to inspect my property.'

I replaced the receiver, took three aspirin and retired to bed.

36

The Vicar's Version

There was nothing for it but to grit my teeth, mentally close my eyes and hope it would all somehow go away. After all, I did have a parish to run . . . And in any case, with luck Nicholas just might break a leg or contract typhus.

Such hopes buoyed me up briefly, but the rosy picture was dispelled by the arrival of a postcard from Brighton thanking me in glowing terms for the lunch and saying he was due to fly off to New York for a few days' vacation prior to entering upon negotiations with Flutzveldt. He would be back shortly having concluded, he was sure, 'a most gratifying little piece of business'.

My feelings were ambivalent: if he was successful it would perhaps put me in a stronger position to deter him from pursuing the Folly escapade, gratitude for my suggestion making him more amenable to dropping the idea. I also gave thought to those roofing costs . . . On the other hand, were he to return flushed with cash and triumph I should be even further compromised. Not only would I be accessory before, during and after the fact of the Idol's theft, I would also be implicated in its lucrative disposal! Such considerations were all too much for me, and calling Bouncer and briskly shooting my cuffs, I settled at the piano for a display of stupendous virtuosity.

* * *

A few days later I was due to attend the Sunday school prize-giving, but with half an hour to spare was busily putting my feet up with the *Telegraph*. I had just flipped over the third page, when my eye was caught by a vaguely familiar name – Greenholt. It was part of a headline attached to a small item at the foot of the page: 'Greenholt Institute Seeks New Curator'. The article that followed was thus:

Harvard's prestigious Greenholt Institute is without a curator having just bade an embarrassing farewell to its long-serving custodian Dr Hiram K. Flutzveldt. A distinguished name among collecting circles, Dr Flutzveldt is currently being investigated by the CIA for tax evasion and other questionable activities. His lawyer, Sebastian Rothmann of Rothmann, Carfax & Swindley, says he is the victim of a highly orchestrated conspiracy, and is confident that he will soon resume his desk at the Institute, and indeed be reinstated as editor of the exclusive arts magazine *Collections Privées*. When interviewed, a colleague said he was surprised at such confidence as in his opinion the bastard had had it coming to him for a long time.

I stared open-mouthed. With names like that there could be no mistake: obviously Claude's contact and Ingaza's buyer! Whether this might jeopardize Claude's chances of appearing in the magazine I could not have cared less. What *was* crucial was how it would affect Ingaza and the sale of the wretched Idol!

Time was pushing on, and grabbing my cassock and prayer book, I left the house and strode swiftly to the church, my mind in a whirl of confusion and questions. Did Ingaza already know about it? Would the whole deal be scuppered? Would he see his visit to America as an expensive fool's errand and blame me? (Without doubt.) Had Flutzveldt already bought the pig, and if so had he quietly disposed of it or would it form part of those 'other questionable activities' which the CIA was so keen to investigate?

Might Nicholas himself be questioned? It could be any or all of these! He was due back the following evening, and until then I would know nothing. Perhaps I should phone Eric and tactfully enquire the lie of the land . . .

Immersed in these thoughts I did not see Mavis Briggs until it was too late and I had already cannon-balled into her. She lay strewn beneath the lychgate looking martyred and reproachful, surrounded by sheets of paper evidently fallen from her bag.

The last time I had hauled Mavis to her feet was when she had been knocked flying by the setter O'Shaughnessy on the dreadful night I had been aiding Maud Tubbly Pole and her bulldog in their flight up to London. She had been in the way then just as she was now; and late already I was none too pleased by the delay. However, I set her on her feet, made apologetic noises, and rather cursorily asked if she was all right.

She nodded vaguely, and then just as I was about to hasten on up the path, exclaimed, 'Oh dear! Do you think you could help me collect my gems?'

'Your what?' I said impatiently.

'My poems, my *Little Gems of Uplift* – the new manuscripts, they've gone everywhere!'

I surveyed the scattered pages and, cursing inwardly, stooped to gather them up.

'Er, if you don't mind my asking, Mavis, what are you doing with them here? Off to the printers?'

She beamed brightly. 'Oh no, Canon. I am on my way to the church, the prize-giving, you know! I thought that since it was such an *important* occasion it would be most suitable if at the end I gave a little recitation of my latest offerings. I am sure the children would enjoy them, especially the older ones. I think it would be a fitting conclusion to it all!' And she beamed again.

'But, Mavis,' I protested, 'the conclusion is to be the mammoth cream tea in the parish hall. It's the *grande finale*. Edith has gone to great trouble to get it organized, and she won't want things delayed.'

Mavis's eyes, normally pale and vacant, took on a dark and steely hue. She tossed her head. 'Edith Hopgarden will just have to wait!' she snapped.

We walked in silence up the path and entered the church.

That evening, safely back at the vicarage, I telephoned Eric.

'I say, Eric,' I began tentatively, 'I gather there's been a little hiccup with Nicholas's contact in New York. Apparently he has been –'

There was a snort of mirth. 'Yeah, silly git. Ballsed things up there all right!'

'But, er, what about the deal – has it gone through?'

'Why, getting worried about your cut, are you?'

'No, of course not,' I protested (some degree of truth there), 'I just wondered how things were and whether Nicholas was all right.'

'Oh yes,' he replied airily. 'He's all right. Coming back tomorrow night with a 'tachy case of dosh. No flies on old Nick!'

'Good gracious!' I exclaimed. 'An attaché case of dosh – is that so?'

'That is so, my ol' son. That is so.'

'But, uhm, well – what about Customs? I gather they're rather hot on that sort of thing.'

'Nah,' he replied, 'got it down to a fine art, has Nick, been doin' it for years. Don't you worry, Frankie.'

'*What!*' I cried, unused to being thus addressed.

'Like I said, he's done it too often to get caught. Mind you, it takes its toll, always does. Sort of delayed whatsit, I suppose. He won't speak to no one for at least a week, never does. He's what you might call delicate.'

I cannot say that I had ever witnessed that aspect of Ingaza and was far from convinced. However, if, as Eric seemed to think, the whole affair had been successfully completed, then with a bit of luck Ingaza might be so glad of my tip-off and its financial yield that he would be content to drop the Folly nonsense. After all, there were now two things I had achieved for him – purloining the pig and finding a productive buyer. Surely that merited some peace!

I was just reflecting on this when I heard Eric say, 'And after that he's taking his auntie to Bournemouth, a little celebration you might say.'

'Taking Aunt Lil to Bournemouth!' I exclaimed. 'What ever for? What's wrong with Eastbourne? I thought she liked the bandstand there.'

'Yes, but she likes the casino better.'

'The *casino*?' I cried. 'But surely Bournemouth doesn't have a casino, it's a most respectable resort!'

There was a chuckle. 'For them what's in the know there's a very good casino, but not what you'd call open to the general public. A bit 'ush 'ush if you get my meaning, Frankie.' This was followed by a further dark chortle.

I stared at the opposite wall where danced unsettling images of Aunt Lil ensconced in some dimly lit gambling den shouting the odds and haranguing the hapless croupier. I flinched. Rather Nicholas than me!

'Well, Eric,' I said politely, 'most kind of you to fill me in on things. Er, glad to hear that all is well despite Dr Flutzveldt's misadventure . . .'

'Silly sod,' was the scathing response. 'You wonder about some of these Yanks, not as bright as they think they are!'

'No, perhaps not . . . Anyway, nice to talk to you.'

I was about to replace the receiver when he said, 'I'll tell His Nibs you was asking after him, but like I said, what with him goin' into purdah and then gadding off with Lil, you may not hear from him for a bit. But he'll make contact sometime, don't you worry, ol' son.'

'That's quite all right,' I replied eagerly. 'Absolutely no hurry, no hurry at all!'

We concluded our conversation, and I lit a cigarette and sat for some time on the hall chair, brooding. Frankie indeed!

37

The Vicar's Version

The next day I was scheduled to attend the gathering of a newly formed sorority – the Guild of Christian Ladies. Actually the organization itself was not new, but it was the first time that a branch had been established in Molehill and they were eager to get things off to a good start by throwing an inaugural soirée. Despite the worthiness of the event, my current pressures put me in no mood for jollification, and I set off that evening feeling far from sociable.

However, to my surprise the Christian Ladies came up trumps. My gloomy mood was partially dispelled, and I found myself staying longer than I had expected. They had put on a magnificent spread which knocked the Mothers' Union's customary fare into a cocked hat. There were spectacular sandwiches, some peculiarly delicious corned beef and cucumber fritters, and the most inventive dessert concoctions which I had ever tasted: wonderful fabrications of nuts, nougat, British sherry and mock cream, all topped with pyramids of meringue and flakes of sticky toffee. The Ladies had also contrived to produce gallons of Blue Nun Riesling which, although very quaff-able at first, did tend to pall after my fourth glass. In fact, quite a lot had started to pall by that stage and I was rapidly becoming in need of a soft pillow. Thus making tactful excuses and pleading copious paperwork, I slipped away into the dark and made my slightly uncertain way home.

To my irritation I noticed the front gate was flapping open. This was not the first time the evening paper-boy had been remiss, and I guessed that Bouncer would have seized the opportunity to stretch his legs and seek romantic adventure.

Clearly he had done just that for, so used was I to his excited barks of welcome, the house seemed strangely silent when I turned the key in the lock. Without bothering to switch on the hall light I took off my coat, visited the downstairs cloakroom and then went into the sitting room. I put on the reading lamp and was about to draw the curtains when I saw that they were already in place. This startled me as I was pretty sure that I had not bothered to pull them on my way out. Still, memory plays odd tricks and perhaps for once I had had a rush of busy blood to the head! I reached for the decanter . . . but my arm stopped midway. There was someone in the room – sitting in my chair in fact. I gaped thunderstruck at the fat face of Victor Crumpelmeyer . . .

He returned my horrified gaze with a deadpan look. And then his features slowly formed a sardonic smile and he raised a podgy hand in mock salute. I don't know how I managed to stay calm: I was furious, and also deeply shocked. But there must have been some instinct at work which warned me not to vent my feelings. Instead I heard myself saying (with only the mildest sarcasm), 'Ah . . . another visit, Victor. Can I offer you a drink?'

He nodded silently, and I poured a small glass of whisky and set it on the table in front of him, having no wish to place it directly in his outstretched hand.

He took a sip and then said conversationally, 'I expect you wonder why I am here . . .'

'I do rather,' I replied with equal calm, 'and I also wonder how you gained entry. I tend to lock my doors at night – unlike in the afternoons.'

'Makes no difference,' he said blandly, 'there are always ways and means – skeleton keys specifically.' And reaching into his waistcoat pocket he produced what certainly looked like a replica of my own.

Naturally this angered me further but I was determined to appear unruffled ... though what I really wanted to do was knock his block off. In fact it was the prospect of doing just that which enabled me to retain a semblance of poise. It would, I thought, be quite easy: I was considerably taller than him and, judging from the pasty complexion, probably much fitter. Yes, if he started to be too impossible I would land him a swift upper-cut to the jaw (as Bulldog Drummond might have said). I contemplated the idea with some relish, imagining the impact of knuckle on flab, and trying to recall the bawled instructions of our boxing coach at school. But the only clear direction that came to mind was, 'Idiot, Oughterard! Not that way, boy, the other!' The reverie promptly vanished; and thinking that sympathetic tact might be the better course, I murmured a few words of condolence about the loss of Violet.

It was not a good course at all. He grimaced, gave a bitter laugh and then said petulantly, 'No loss at all. An error of judgement: I slipped up there all right! She was supposed to have pots of money, the cow, but thanks to the grasping fingers of the Church the pots were fewer than they should have been. It was all a *singular* disappointment!' He twitched with suppressed rage.

'The Church?' I said faintly. 'Why the Church?'

'Not it – *you*, you fool! I know your sort: righteous do-gooders with an eye to the main chance. Prissy, smarmy, wheedling swindlers, that's what you all are. You think you're clever, but not half as clever as Victor Crumpelmeyer, oh no!' And with another mordant laugh, he downed half the tumbler in front of him

I was incensed that my whisky should lend confidence to one so crude, and felt affronted at the insults being poured upon myself and the institution I represented ... He would have to be told!

'Now look here, Crumpelmeyer –' I began.

'Oh no, *Reverend*, you just listen to me,' he sneered. 'First you sweet-talked the mother, then robbed the daughter. Legacy, bracelet, deeds – you've snaffled the lot. I suppose you think you can get your hands on that château and its buried gold. Well, you can think again! Except that the old girl was too addled to know what she was doing, those deeds should have gone to my wife – so they're mine by rights. I've come for them and the rest of what's owed me. If it hadn't been for your interference Violet would have had at least a million. So you'd better pay up if you've got any sense!'

The idea of my 'sweet-talking' Elizabeth was preposterous, not to say distasteful; but I was even more indignant at the allegation of having appropriated the daughter's wealth. I had never asked to be involved with the Fotheringtons, merely wanting a quiet parish and an untroubled life. Instead here I was in my own vicarage being accused of greed and duplicity by one of their demented in-laws eager to get his hooter in the family coffers. It was appalling! But what on earth was I going to do? Clearly nothing constructive, for when I took a deep breath and began to explain that I had never considered the Fotherington riches let alone had access to the deeds of the French estate, my guest crashed his fist on the table and launched into a rant of monumental egotism and mania.

In the course of this he made it clear that marrying Violet had been an act of great faith and substantial sacrifice, neither of which, thanks to me, had borne fruit. 'You cannot imagine,' he whined, 'how awful it was being her consort!' (I could actually, but had no intention of showing fellow feeling with that little crook.) In one of his few pauses I observed mildly that surely he was exaggerating his deprivation, and that most people would be more than content with the large Godalming property and the doubtless perfectly adequate capital that went with it.

He glowered at me. 'I was not born for adequacy.

Neither was I born to be pipped at the post by some slick-handed sodding vicar. You won't get away with it!'

This was really too much, and I was just thinking that despite my youthful blunders in the boxing ring, I might after all try clocking him one, when he said in a suddenly casual tone, 'Got my letters all right, did you?'

I froze. Such had been my shock at finding Crumpelmeyer stuffed into my own armchair that the question of the anonymous notes had been driven from my mind. But now of course it all made sense. Yet even as I recoiled from his increasingly patent lunacy – and thus the very real implications of 'You are next' – I also experienced an immense surge of relief: evidently the 'Nemesis' of the second letter referred *not* to the mother's murder, but the daughter's assets and Crumpelmeyer's crazed belief that I had stripped them bare.

'Yes,' I replied, 'I got your letters. And now would you kindly leave my house or I shall be forced to call the police.'

'How?'

'What do you mean, "how"?'

'How will you call them?'

'By telephoning of course!' And I started to move towards the hall.

'Oh, I don't think so, Reverend,' he said softly. 'You see, I've cut the wires with this.' And from down the side of the chair he drew a knife whose long and lethal blade glinted malevolently in the lamplight.

My mouth was suddenly sand-dry and I could feel sweat in my hair and on my neck. As a young soldier in the war one had been under dreadful bombardments from enemy shell-fire and aircraft. But those had been collective threats, and unlike some of my companions I had never experienced hand-to-hand fighting. Thus I found the close intimacy of this personal, solitary encounter terrifying. However, as from a distance, I heard my voice saying sternly, 'For God's sake, pull yourself together, man! You'll kill us both!'

235

He leaped up, knocking the table over and brandishing the steel wildly. 'Not me, Oughterard – only you!' he rasped. It would have been madness to try to wrest the thing from him, and I realized that my only hope was flight. I made a rush for the door, tripped over one of Bouncer's bones, and fell headlong. He loomed over me, eyes and knife flashing, and fat cheeks explosive with fury.

'You thieving bastard!' he shrieked. 'I'll rip your guts, I will!' And he made a lumbering lunge which, had he been more adroit, would have got me square in the stomach. As it was, he missed by about a foot and fell against the wall, while I was able to roll myself to the scant protection of the upturned table. I had watched such scenes in the films and recalled that invariably the intrepid victim would get the upper hand by reasoning, even wisecracking, with his assailant. Wisecracking has never been my forte – besides I wasn't in the mood. But I might try a little light conversation . . .

'For Christ's sake back off, you raving maniac!' I gasped. 'What the hell are you up to, you effing oaf!'

On reflection I think my words could have been better chosen for they seemed to inflame him further; and screaming, 'I did for her and I'll do for you!', and pointing the knife like a bayonet while emitting the statutory yell, he rushed at me and plunged the weapon into my shoulder.

At such times, I discovered, shock takes precedence over pain, and it is the brain rather than the body which is the more sensitive. Thus as I lay paralysed less by agony than by amazement, my mind filled up with images of Elizabeth's dead face framed by her rakish hat and Violet's rearing jack-knifed legs. The two corpses and their contexts – the sunlit glade and the darkened creosoted shed – mingled and danced before my eyes, and I wondered what specific features of my own demise would haunt the demented memory of Victor Crumpelmeyer. In blurred confusion I awaited the fatal thrust that would surely come.

He bent down, and there was a rushing in my ears, excruciating noise – thudding, roaring, screaming – and his face came nearer and nearer . . . so near that I could feel my own face enveloped by his gulping breath. I shut my eyes. And then as I opened them for the last time saw that the flaccid white skin had been replaced by thick, shaggy grey fur and an enormous drooling tongue. Oh my God, a werewolf to carry me off . . .

38

The Cat's Memoir

What it is to be a cat in this madhouse! Really, one is subjected to the most vexatious indignities! Take that evening, for instance, when I returned from the graveyard eager for my milk and supper: instead of F.O. crashing about on the piano or smoking idly in his chair, what did I find sitting in his place but that whey-faced scoundrel whom Bouncer had once tried to devour! Not content with rifling the vicar's desk, he now had the effrontery to sprawl himself in the sitting room! I can tell you, seeing him there gave me a very nasty shock. Indeed, such was my surprise that I marched straight up to the creature and with a loud hiss delivered a brisk claw to the ankle. The rasp of talon on unsavoury flesh is always agreeable . . .

Alas, such valour did me little good – for with a violent oath the intruder kicked me right across the room – from chair to door! Not since the outrageous attack by the Veasey twins have I been so affronted or discomposed.* But naturally, once recovered, my instinct was to retaliate with all claws firing. Then as I prepared for precisely that, it occurred to me that it would be more prudent to summon reinforcements. So I gallantly limped out into the front garden and set up a loud caterwauling. Within moments Bouncer had appeared from the potting shed

* See *A Load of Old Bones*

followed by the gigantic shadow of Florence. I told them what was afoot and said that a three-pronged assault was required. And then just as we were racing towards the house, to my amazement I suddenly saw the weedy Samson crawling on all fours in the flower bed under the sitting-room window! I called the other two to heel and, pointing him out to Bouncer, asked what he thought he was up to. The reply of course was typical – 'Bones, Maurice. He is burying bones.'

I was about to tell the dog exactly what he could do with his stupid ideas, when fortunately the wolfhound interrupted and said gently to Bouncer that in Samson's case osseous pursuits of that particular kind were extremely unlikely, and that our best course of action was to sit quietly and assess the situation. So we sat and assessed . . .

And then suddenly F.O. appeared, walking up the path (a trifle unsteadily, I recall) and whistling under his breath. Huddled behind the garden roller, we watched intently as he went into the vicarage, and then listened to the ensuing silence. This went on for some time. And then glancing in the direction of the flower bed, I realized that the crouching Samson had disappeared. I was just wondering where he had gone, when there was a great commotion from within accompanied by a maniacal yelling. Florence bounded to the open window, and standing on her long hind legs peered in. 'Well, I never!' she exclaimed. 'Just look at that!'

'What?' cried Bouncer.

'It's the loon,' she barked, 'he's attacking the vicar!'

Before I had a chance to collect my wits, Bouncer had shot past me and was thrusting himself through the pet flap. As I followed I noticed Florence clambering over the sill, and then in the distance the hoot of a police whistle and the wail of an approaching siren.

I slipped through the flap and into the sitting room, and despite my poor bruised hip, sprang adroitly to the top of the bookcase. The scene that met my eyes was absurd and distasteful: the loon being mauled by Bouncer, Florence slobbering over a recumbent F.O., and Samson and his cohorts rushing around like flies in a jam-jar. The noise was insufferable. But not to be outdone I naturally added my own subtly orchestrated yowls.

Eventually things calmed down, and the Crumplehorn was handcuffed and hauled off, and the vicar bundled into an ambulance. As I later observed to Bouncer – all it needed was for Mavis Briggs to come drooping in spouting her verses! But fortunately we were spared that . . . Still, I suppose such theatricals all add to life's rich cabaret! Other cats, I have noticed, lead less eventful lives than my own.

39

The Dog's Diary

'Which bit did you like best, Maurice?' I asked the cat. 'The bit where I rushed in and savaged his bum AGAIN, or when Florence sat on his head and then went and woke up F.O. with big kisses?'

'To tell you the truth, Bouncer,' he said, 'I think it was the first part really – your *redoubtable* attack!' (I've been practising that word, you know. It's given me a lot of trouble, but the cat doesn't often give praise so I wanted to get it just right.) 'You see,' he went on, 'well meaning though Florence is, I think she frightened the life out of the vicar and if she had continued much longer we might have lost him for good.'

'You're right,' I agreed. 'If the weedy Samson hadn't squirted him with the soda siphon he'd have been a gonner.'

'Yes,' grumbled the cat, 'but you do realize that half of that went on *me*. I was soaked to the skin all along my left flank! Co-ordination of hand and eye is not within Samson's compass.' (I think he meant he couldn't aim straight.)

'Oh well,' I replied, 'what's a bit of wet if it meant F.O. was all right!' There was a long pause while Maurice stared at me blankly. He opened his mouth a couple of times as if he was going to speak but seemed to think better of it. And then he started to groom his ears while I had a go at my rubber ring.

We chewed and groomed for a while, and then he said, 'I daresay the Samson person will get a medal – or promotion at any rate. He actually seemed to know what he was doing – an achievement, I fear, which has generally escaped our master.'

'But he is kind, isn't he, Maurice?'

'Oh yes, *kind* – just incompetent.' I wasn't quite sure what that last word meant, so kept quiet and went on chewing.

And then I said, 'But I tell you what: though that Samson was quick off the mark and put two and two together and followed the fat thug to the house with those other cops, it was us that got there first and buggered things up. I mean, if we hadn't made OUR PRESENCE FELT – as you would say, Maurice – he might have been too late and we would have been left with a third corpse on our paws and that mad chump rampaging all over the shop. And then what!'

I think I may have been making a teeny bit of noise because the cat just nodded and kept his eyes tightly shut. He does that sometimes if I get excited. But you know, it's difficult not to make a noise living in the vicarage, there are so many things going on – which is what I like really. No point if nothing happens. BORING! I told O'Shaughnessy once about the cat saying I spoke too loudly, and *he* said why wouldn't a fellow want to air his lungs now and again, it was the most natural thing in the world, and to tell the mog he was an eejit, so he was! I tried to explain to the setter that you didn't say things like that to Maurice, not if you valued your snout you didn't. But he just laughed and went leaping down the road. Mind you, he won't laugh when I tell him about this latest thing – it's the second time he's missed out on a bit of craic. He won't like it at all!

Well, it's been a pretty long day what with one thing and another and I'm feeling a bit snoozy. So I'm going down to the crypt now to get some kip, and when I wake up I'll listen to the ghosts and tell the spiders everything . . . but they won't believe me, they never do.

40

The Vicar's Version

When I regained consciousness it was to find myself lying damp and blood-soaked on the sitting-room floor, in the midst of what I can only describe as a scene of spectacular unreality. Lights, noise, people, animals, the strident wailing of a police siren – I seemed caught in a vortex of chaos and cacophony. But despite the muddle, what was very clear was the kneeling figure of Victor Crumpelmeyer, head down and arms pinioned behind his back, howling obscenities while a cherubic-faced constable struggled to apply handcuffs. The youth's difficulty seemed to lie less with his captive than with Bouncer (emerged from goodness knows where) who, whooping frenetically, was intent on assisting the process. Another uniformed shape was shouting loudly down a walkie-talkie; and up on the bookcase, miaowing the odds with fur *en brosse* and furious tail, crouched Maurice. The din of course was appalling; but it was not so much the mayhem which made me think I had been shifted from vicarage to circus ring, but the fact that only a few feet away there seemed to be a couple dancing!

I assumed I was delirious and the dancing couple a figment of waning senses. Dazed from loss of blood and the pain in my shoulder, I strained to stay conscious, focusing my hazy eyes on the close-knit pair holding centre floor. One of them seemed to be enjoying the dance rather more than the other – indeed was full of affectionate delight, pawing and snuffling at the neck of their partner with unconcealed pleasure. The other, I suddenly realized, was struggling frantically to get free. There was a burst of laughter from somewhere in the room and a voice rang out: 'She *likes* you, sir!' And immediately all was clear: the dancing vision was no less than the wolfhound Florence of Fermanagh, immense on her hind legs, and embracing for all she was worth the diminutive form of DS Sidney Samson.

I must have passed out again but they evidently patched me up and carted me off to hospital for tests and rest: a brief sojourn, but in the circumstances quite welcome.

While there I was visited by March and Samson, the latter bearing a bunch of grapes which he placed morosely on the bedside table. They had come, March explained, to 'put me in the picture' and to confirm that I would stand witness in the police prosecution of Crumpelmeyer. I wasn't entirely happy about that, feeling that the less I had to do with such matters, the better. After all, who knew what skeletons might emerge! However, it would have looked odd if I had declined, and so smiling benignly I reluctantly agreed.

March seemed pleased but said ruefully, 'He'll get off of course – plead insanity and be sent to Broadmoor, you mark my words. A pity really because apart from that poor Ruth Ellis, we've not had a hanging for some time. The public expect it, you know.' He stretched for a grape, while under the bedclothes I clenched my knees in terror.

'Anyway,' he continued, 'on the whole it's all worked out very well. The culprit's caught, Slowcome's preening himself, *and* it's obvious to anyone with a ha'porth of sense that he did for the mother too! Oh yes, no doubt about it: he knocked her off knowing she was loaded, and then married the daughter expecting to get the lot. But then of course, as I'm sure you tell your congregation, sir, "the best laid plans of mice and men" and all that . . . Yes, a good bag, a left and a right as it were!' He took another grape and

244

turned for confirmation to Samson who was staring out of the window and seemed not to have heard.

'Extraordinary,' I murmured. 'But what put you on to Crumpelmeyer? And how did the police arrive so quickly?'

'Ah well, that was the sergeant – no flies on our Sidney,' said March. 'He'd had that Crumpelmeyer in his sights for some time, ever since the two of them started making such a fuss about that buried diamond bracelet. "There's something wrong there," he said to me, "very wrong indeed, and I'm going to get to the bottom of it, you see if I don't. I can always spot 'em."' He turned to the Whippet. 'That's what you said, isn't it?' The latter nodded expressionlessly. 'Like a leech, Sidney is,' March continued with pride. 'He put a tail on him some time back, been watching his every movement. Mind you,' he added, 'he's had good training from yours truly, even if I do say it myself – isn't that so, my lad? Best mentor in the Force is old March!' His gave a rumbling laugh while his colleague remained silent.

I coughed quickly, and turning to Samson said, 'Well, I have much to thank you for, Sergeant ... why, without your sleuthing skills and exemplary speed and courage I might not be here today – dead as the proverbial doornail no doubt!' I spoke with genuine gratitude, but as usual in Samson's presence felt a twinge of nervous unease – and, as always, it was justified.

'Ah well, sir, you know how it is – win one, lose one,' he replied carelessly. 'There's always one that gets away ... leastways, so they *think*.' He looked at me thoughtfully and only the thin mouth smiled.

They took their leave and I settled down thankfully for a much-needed doze. When I awoke it was tea-time. A nurse looked in and announced that I had another visitor. I held my breath, fearful it might be Mavis Briggs ...

Savage appeared bearing flowers, fruit, magazines, and the ubiquitous but always welcome fairy cakes. He

245

plonked them down on the bed and, manoeuvring with his stick, found the chair and sat down next to me.

'Cor,' he exclaimed, 'you have to walk miles in these places. No wonder everyone's in bed – exhaustion, I should think! ... Anyway, Rev, how are you keeping? Quite a little dust-up, that was! Got yourself knifed in the shoulder, I hear. You do lead a busy life! Still, as I told Mrs S., that'll rope 'em in on a Sunday all right. There's nothing like a bit of blood and guts to fill the aisles ... and the collection plates too, I shouldn't wonder.' He grinned slyly and commiserated again about my shoulder.

'As a matter of fact,' I grumbled, 'it's not so much the shoulder as the knee.'

'What's wrong with the knee then?' he asked. 'Took a pick-axe to it, did he?'

'No,' I laughed, 'Bouncer's bone. I fell over it trying to escape that maniac. Practically crippled me, it has!'

'Ah, well,' he observed sagely, 'they say it's always the little things that trip you up and bring you down. I remember in Normandy when that mine got me. If I hadn't stopped to tie my bootlace I'd probably have my sight today ... Still, that's life, isn't it: all in the detail, as you might say. Just goes to show, can't afford to overlook anything – not even the dog's bones!' He smiled cheerfully and fumbled for the fairy cakes. We munched in brief silence, he possibly recalling the perils of Normandy, and me anxiously racking my brains to think what disregarded detail would play its lethal part in my own downfall ...

He stayed a little longer and we mulled over the Crumpelmeyer business.

'Well, there's certainly one thing I'm thankful for,' he said. 'At least it wasn't *done* in my shed. Mrs Savage is very particular about that sort of thing, she wouldn't have liked it at all and I'd never have heard the end of it. In fact,' he went on, 'a lucky escape really – I mean, if it had been where the deed actually happened and not just the dumping place, she'd have probably made me pull the whole lot down. I took a heap of trouble over that shed – getting it painted and properly kitted out; it would have been a blinking waste to have had to get rid of it – a real waste.'

'Frightful!' I agreed.

'Mind you,' he mused thoughtfully, 'I expect I could have thought of something to bring her round – I generally do. There's usually a way if you don't get panicked . . . like those tiddlywinks counters and the coppers for example.'

'What counters?' I exclaimed sharply.

'The ones found in the shed that the police were interested in.'

'I didn't know about those!'

'I told you, didn't I?' he said vaguely.

'No, you did not.'

'It was when they interviewed me the second time – after I first reported finding the body. "Mr Savage," they said, "can you account for these here three plastic counters we found on the floor by the potatoes? Because if you can't it's our belief that they may be a crucial lead to the murderer. He may well have dropped them in his haste to get away. Follow these up and I think we've got our man!"'

'Good Lord!' I gasped. 'Whatever did you say?'

'I said they were mine.'

'Yours?'

'Well, the nipper's really; said I had given him a set of tiddlywinks for his birthday and the little tike would never put the things back in the box but insisted on keeping them in his pockets.' He chuckled. 'Anyway, they seemed to swallow it all right . . . Just as well really, otherwise your friend would have had a bit of explaining to do, wouldn't he? '

'Yes,' I agreed grimly, 'he certainly would. Thanks, Savage, you're a brick.'

After he had gone I lay back on my pillows, closed my eyes, and meditated upon bishops and their quirks and carelessness . . . Where would they have come from, for God's sake! His trouser turn-up?

* * *

Fortunately I was kept in only briefly, though in a way it had been a pleasant interlude – hospital life, even in passing, inducing a liberating sense of aimless coma.

Once home, I was greeted by both animals with attentive approval, Maurice going so far as to present me with his woollen mouse. However, I was just getting used to the gift when it was briskly retrieved. Bouncer's offering – a freshly chewed bedroom slipper filled with macerated Bonio – was of longer duration for unlike the mouse it seemed on indefinite loan. My shoulder was still painful but fairly bearable, and my knee considerably helped by my father's old walking stick. I recalled ruefully – and perhaps a little nostalgically – that the last time I had had recourse to that particular prop was after the belfry expedition with Mrs Tubbly Pole and her impossible bulldog.

What did unsettle me, initially at any rate, was confronting the chair in the sitting room where Crumpelmeyer had fatly sat on that dreadful evening. It was where I would normally sit myself, and the idea of resuming my usual place was distinctly unnerving. I toyed with having it re-covered, or better still, thrown out; but I quite liked it, and the combination of habit and idleness ensured it remained, and eventually we became reacquainted.

As to Crumpelmeyer himself, March's prediction of his being unfit to stand trial proved correct, and, as I learnt from the police officer who came to interview me, moves were afoot to send him to Broadmoor for an unspecified period. That was certainly a relief – both his fate and the fact that I should not be required to give evidence in a public court of law. In my situation a low profile has much to commend itself.

Less welcome was the confirmation that, handy though Savage's shed had been as a place of concealment (and possibly a means of implicating some random allotment owner), the victim's end had indeed been elsewhere: Foxford Wood to be exact – a few yards distant from the spot where Elizabeth had lost her own life. Much was made of this fact, and the *Clarion* wrote excitedly about the 'mother-daughter scenario' and the 'dramatic properties' of the crime. However, it was not a subject that I personally cared to pursue.

Thus, after the general hue and cry and the topic of 'The Canon's Ordeal' finally exhausted, life in Molehill and at St Botolph's reverted to its placid norm, and I was able to resume my parish duties with a modicum of ease.

Primrose had shown great solicitude, and while not actually inviting me down to stay (the damaged shoulder being clearly unsuited to grass cutting), she had generously sent a case of her excoriating sherry. Eric had telephoned with renewed invitations to avail myself of the sea front at Brighton. However, feeling insufficiently strong to face the full brunt of his raucous good cheer, not to mention the fearful prospect of encountering Aunt Lil, I thanked him warmly and made my excuses. Still, it was nice to be asked. Of Ingaza nothing was said and, deeming myself too fragile, I refrained from enquiring. Presumably he was either still languishing from the nervous strain of foiling the Customs as Eric had hinted, or (the more likely) living it up with his smuggled funds in the Bournemouth casino.

In fact I was just reflecting upon that as I passed the Swan and Goose one evening on my way back from a parish meeting. Coming out from the pub's doorway was the lumbering figure of Inspector March – this time not only minus the Whippet but also divested of his customary fawn raincoat. Without the po-faced Samson and wearing what might be termed his mufti outfit, he looked quite human.

He greeted me warmly. 'Good evening, Canon! Nice to see you out and about again. Shoulder getting on all right, is it?' I told him it was behaving admirably and I would soon be as good as new. 'That's the ticket, doesn't do to let the criminal fraternity get us down, does it! Up and at 'em, I say!'

'Absolutely,' I murmured.

'Yes, sir, you handled that little business very well. Not the sort of thing a clergyman can expect every day, I shouldn't think – a real credit to the Church *Militant*, one could say!' And he chortled, amused by his own pleasantry.

'Oh, I am afraid I wasn't much use,' I coughed, 'it was Sergeant Samson who came to the rescue and –'

'Ah, Samson. I was coming to him,' he intoned with a note of pride. 'He's got promotion, you know . . . yes, our Sidney has gone to higher things. Up at the Yard, he is now. Just the place for him – doesn't miss a trick, you know, sir, not a trick!'

'Is that so?' I asked.

'Oh yes. Molehill doesn't realize how lucky it's been having Sidney in its midst. Sidney Samson has what you might call *acumen* – mind like a razor, nose like a ferret. Not much escaped him, I can tell you!'

'No . . . not very much,' I agreed. 'And, er, what about you, Inspector? I suppose you'll have to train up another assistant now.'

'Oh no. Pension time for me, and a good thing too. I've done my bit for law and order, thank you very much. Time to hang up the handcuffs and attend to the dahlias. I'll get that first prize if it kills me!' He chuckled, and then added, 'Tell you what though, with Samson and me out of the way, Molehill's villains can rest easy in their beds at nights . . . Very easy, because I don't think our Mr Slowcome is going to be much cop, if you'll excuse the pun! Too fond of all these new-fangled courses and *psychology* seminars. Doesn't like to get his hands dirty!' He laughed wryly and we bade goodnight, he returning home to dwell on dahlias and glittering prizes, and me to sleep easy in my bed.

In fact I didn't go to bed immediately as I was waylaid by Maurice and Bouncer, both of whom seemed in matey mood and eager for my attention. The cat was showing rare good humour by wrapping himself around my ankles and toying daintily with my shoelaces, while Bouncer, determined to share one of his Bonios, lay sprawled on my lap chewing rhythmically. I settled myself further into the sofa, lit a cigarette and reached out an arm to switch on the nine o'clock news . . . It was good to be home. With Crumpelmeyer en route for Broadmoor, Samson stalking on the rarefied heights of Scotland Yard and March out to grass, possibly, just possibly, all would be well. I stretched contentedly and lent a languid ear to the reassuring voice of the Home Service.

The voice was rudely interrupted by the jangling of the telephone. I winced: probably the verger. He had caught me earlier in the day, for some reason hell-bent on re-arranging the pews in the side chapel. I had managed to fob him off but knew it was only a matter of time . . . Reluctantly I turned off the wireless and ambled into the hall.

It wasn't the verger. It was Ingaza – incandescent.

Recovering from the torrent of blasphemy, which seemed to involve myself in some large measure, I asked him what the problem was.

'The problem, Francis,' he said in grating tones, 'is that the American joker whom you so kindly introduced me to has turned out to be an unscrupulous thieving bastard who has cost me not only a hell of a lot of money but also a great deal of time and ingenuity. And it's all your fault!'

I was bewildered. 'But surely you got the money, didn't you? Eric told me you had clinched the deal before he was arrested. Flutzveldt had already paid up and you were returning with an attaché case full of dollar bills. What went wrong?'

'What went wrong was that the sod short-changed me: the top two layers of notes were kosher, the rest frigging counterfeits, and I've only just discovered. I used some in America to begin with, and then when I was back here started to exchange them for sterling in batches and at intervals. Everything was fine. But *yesterday* when I took a small wad from the lower layer into the Eastbourne post office, the snivelling little clerk had the nerve to tell me they were fake. Naturally I evinced shock and horror (came quite naturally, I can tell you!), spun some yarn about my grandmother's footsteps and got out sharpish before he could gather his wits. When I consulted with a colleague in the business he confirmed they were all as fake as a tart's kiss.'

'Oh dear!' I said.

'I should think it is "oh dear"! My total profit from the whole project is about two hundred quid, and if you think for one moment that you're going to get a percentage of that you can think again. In fact, if anything, it's you who should be paying me – it cost me a fortune taking Lil to Bournemouth, and now the old bat's saying she can't wait to go again. If you hadn't been such a smart-arse none of this would have happened!' He paused, presumably collecting his breath for a further onslaught.

I tried to divert things by asking about Claude, and whether his hopes of appearing in Flutzveldt's publication had also been dashed.

'No such luck,' Nicholas said bitterly. 'Bought a copy of that magazine to read on the plane, and there was his smug face simpering out from the centre page along with a load of bilge about that bloody pig. I'm fed up with it all!' He sounded deeply troubled.

'Well,' I said gently, 'after all, you have made *some* profit – and I daresay something else will turn up in due course.'

'Oh, it will, Francis, it will. In fact –' and here his voice reverted to its familiar silken suavity – 'that's really what I am telephoning about. Those deeds which you were so kind as to lend me – I think it is time we put them to some use.'

I had feared as much, and with sinking heart asked what he proposed.

'What I propose, dear boy, is that you and I – and of course your delightful sister whom I've already approached – should embark on a little jaunt to the Auvergne, make an assessment of La Folie de Fotherington

252

and then, all being well, stake our claim – that is to say, of course, *your* claim . . .' (At least he had the grace to make the correction.)

'But I thought you were going under your own steam anyway,' I replied dully.

'Yes, a passing thought; but on reflection and in view of recent events, I think it would be *so* much nicer if the three of us went together. After all, although the deeds are in my temporary possession *you* are the title holder; and were there to be any tiresome local difficulties it would be helpful to have the actual owner to hand. You know how bureaucratic the Frogs are. Besides, I could do with a little Gallic gaiety after all I've been put through.'

'Hmm,' I grunted, wondering ruefully what he imagined I had been enduring for the last eighteen months.

'And I tell you what, while we're there I can get old Henri Martineau to come down from Taupinière. Being both of the cloth you'll have so much in common.'

'Martineau!' I yelped. 'You surely don't mean that maleficent French priest who hid your rotten paintings in his bell tower!'

He coughed delicately. 'Well, one of the two . . . the English counterpart made rather a mess of things . . .'

It was a blow beneath the belt but I let it go, and instead demanded why on earth he thought that unsavoury cleric from the Pas de Calais would be remotely relevant to his scheme.

'How's your French, old man?'

'What? Er . . . not too good really.'

'Exactly. Doubtless mine is better than yours, but nevertheless it lacks refinement. Hence Henri. He could be very useful.'

I very much doubted whether any use, let alone refinement, could come from that particular quarter; but it was obvious that Ingaza had the bit between the teeth and there would be no stopping him. Images of Foxford Wood on that fateful June morning came to mind: the bluebells, the rabbits – Elizabeth's lolling corpse. And with a weight of resignation I knew then that I would be forever in his grasp . . .

'At the moment,' he continued blandly, 'I am rather deluged with other considerations, but give me a month or so and I'll be in touch – be assured, you can count on it!'

'Wonderful,' I murmured.

41

The Cat's Memoir

Needless to say, there were irritating repercussions to the Crumplehorn business, not least the vicar's sister finding those Fotherington deeds which I had so carefully secreted in my litter tray. At first I did not think this would amount to anything very much: the sister would create a drama and F.O. curse and bluster – and that would be it. Foolishly I had overlooked the Type from Brighton. His interference has since caused the vicar endless perturbation, and I fear more is to come. From what I could make out the Ingaza person is intent on going to France to investigate the property to which the deeds belong. For some reason this induced in our master a state of pallid inertia, a condition which did not prevent the house reverberating to the sound of loud groanings and expostulations over the damaged shoulder. Anyone would think he was the only one to be so afflicted! After all, I too was a martyr to the gross one's fury, as after the disgraceful episode of my being kicked the length of F.O.'s sitting room it has taken me considerable time to regain my usual agility. Naturally, unlike the vicar, I have borne this with reticent fortitude. So reticent, in fact, that Bouncer seemed unable to grasp why I was in no condition to play leap-frog with him in Mavis Briggs's cabbage patch. However, I grow stronger daily and if that dog imagines for one minute that I have lost my skill *sportif* then he is in for a nasty shock!

My convalescence had given me time to mull over the question of the Fotherington deeds and the French property – although I like to think that my own cogitations upon the matter were conducted in a vein rather calmer than the vicar's. When I told Bouncer that I thought we might be faced with some sort of Gallic fracas, he launched into a disgusting rhyme which began, 'Le chat crept into la crypte, shat et . . .' It was of course one of his puerile variations on an old theme, and I told him that though doubtless that was the sort of low obscenity which O'Shaughnessy might appreciate, cats had superior tastes. He then had the nerve to reply that, given my propensities, perhaps I would prefer a ditty involving a 'pauvre petty souris'. (Obviously Pierre the Ponce's influence.) I retorted that if he did not curb his crude inanities I would sing him a ditty he would be unlikely to forget! However, my words had little effect, and he wandered into the shrubbery snuffling at the awful bell-jangling ball.

Left alone I harried the hedgehog, unravelled the string securing a hollyhock to its cane, and scratched up a few shallowly planted bulbs in next door's garden. I would have stayed longer but the baby was giving tongue and I cannot abide its caterwaulings. So returning to the vicarage I decided to indulge myself in a warming patch of sun, and thus jumped up on to the wide ledge beneath the study window and stretched my length. I was just beginning to melt into a doze when I was startled to hear thunderous snoring from within. Annoyed by the din, I glared through the glass and then poked my head round the frame.

Lolling on their backs on the sofa, legs akimbo and eyes tightly shut, lay dog and vicar dead to the world. I stared irritably – bone idle the pair of them! And then as I watched, unaccountably my mood began to mellow and I had to concede that on the whole I could do far worse than suffer a buffoon for a companion and a murderer for a master. After all, if it had not been for F.O. I should still be enduring the incessant cooings of Mrs Fotherington! And thus as I gazed, and perhaps mesmerized by their rhythm, I once more felt sleep coming upon me; and alighting from my perch joined the snorers on the sofa.

42

The Vicar's Version

Ingaza's proposal had been the last straw, and I tentatively wondered about invoking St Jude, saint of hopeless cases; but feeling he had probably more than enough on his plate thought it unfair to add my woes to his burden. Instead I sought temporary refuge by trying to bury myself in the busy normality of parish life. Compared with Ingaza and his machinations even Edith Hopgarden seemed a welcome relief (initially at any rate). Indeed, so eager was I to resume the norm, that seeing her emerging from the vestry I seized the chance to pay fulsome compliments about the brilliance of the gilded eagle on the lectern. 'Amazing what a good dose of Brasso does!' I exclaimed jovially.

She looked surprised. And then giving me a withering scowl, replied that it had nothing to do with Brasso and all to do with elbow grease. Duly admonished I smiled weakly, said it was jolly good anyway, and scuttled on.

I didn't get far, as at the south door I was waylaid by Miss Dalrymple evidently arrived to pursue her foraging for the choirboys' chewing-gum deposits. She wore that avid expression which I rather imagine is seen on the faces of truffle hounds in the Dordogne.

'Ah, Canon,' she boomed, 'I was just thinking about you!'

'Oh yes?' I said nervously.

'Yes. I mean to say, your inaugural address isn't far off, is it?' She grinned wolfishly.

'Er, no,' I replied vaguely, 'no, it isn't . . .'

'We are so looking forward to it!' she brayed.

'Good,' I said shortly.

'Indeed we are,' she enthused. 'After all, it can only be better than the last one . . . Can't remember the man's name now, but it was awful. All about turning the other cheek to those that smite you. Well,' and she lowered her voice grimly, 'I can tell you, Canon, were anyone to smite *me* they certainly wouldn't get away with it. There is something known as righteous anger, you know!'

'Ye-es,' I conceded uneasily, 'but –'

'Anyway, there will be no such tosh from you, I'll be bound. Why, I was saying to Colonel Dawlish only the other day – "Oughterard will have something useful up his sleeve, you mark my words!"'

I thanked her for her faith and enquired diffidently what Colonel Dawlish had had to say on the subject.

'Oh, you know him,' she said dismissively, 'sucked on that foul pipe and said nothing. But *I* know that something good is brewing!' And with a conspiratorial leer she stomped off towards the choir stalls.

I gazed after her flattered and despondent . . . A theme, a theme, my parish for a theme! If nothing emerged soon, and as a last resort, I should be forced into asking Clinker for an idea. Presumably he would at least come up with something a little more helpful than the Max Miller suggestion from Primrose! I sighed, and wandered out to inspect a damaged drainpipe.

On my way home I did something which I don't normally do – stopped at the Swan and Goose for a pre-prandial. It's not that I have anything against public houses, and in my Bermondsey days such visits by the clergy were considered de rigueur (all part of the democratizing process, we were earnestly told), but I am not one who is instinctively matey and I suspect that the sight of a dog-collared figure downing shorts on his own would do little to enhance the spirits of the Molehill regulars. However, that evening for some reason the inclination came upon me, and I slipped into the saloon bar and ordered a whisky and a bag of crisps.

I sat on one of the wooden settles and was just about to open the packet, when a voice cried, 'Ooh, I could do with a couple of those, Reverend. Just what I fancy!' I looked up startled. It was Mrs Carruthers.

She detached herself from the bar stool and, rather carefully I thought, made her way to where I was sitting. Placing a large sweet Martini on the table, she sat down beside me grinning broadly. 'Well, dear, this is a happy surprise and no mistake! Haven't seen you for *ages*. Where have you been hiding yourself these days?'

I murmured something about being terribly busy with meetings and funerals, and then offering her the crisps asked how she was.

'In the pink, dear, in the pink! Do you know what – I've just won fifty nice ones on the three-thirty at Newbury. A real outsider, came in at fifty to one. And you'll never guess its name, not in a million years you won't!'

I took a gulp of my whisky and regarded her soberly. 'I think I can.'

'Course not – you're having me on!'

'Want a bet?'

She cackled with laughter. 'We'll settle for a drink. I'll buy you another of those if you get it right, but you won't!'

I had in fact glanced at the list of the Newbury runners earlier in the day. At the time they had meant little to me, but talking now to Mrs Carruthers one in particular came back into my mind.

'Gnomic,' I said. 'You bet on Gnomic.'

There was a pause, followed by a scream of mirth so loud that I thought the glass in the lamp might break. 'You are a one,' she gasped, 'trust you to know that! Really stolen my thunder, you have!' She turned to the barman. 'Did you hear that, Harry? The vicar's guessed the horse I backed – what do you think of that! We'd better have another couple!'

'Well, it was hardly difficult,' I said. 'I mean, owning a place positively rampant with garden gnomes what else could you have chosen?' This was met by further gusts of delighted mirth as she scrabbled in her handbag for her purse. I told her I had no intention of accepting a drink from such a charming lady and that naturally the second round was to be mine. I ordered a small Scotch and another large Martini for her, making sure it came richly embellished with a double cherry stick.

'Well, here's to gnomes, dear!' she cried gaily.

'To gnomes,' I said, raising my glass.

She sipped with pleasure. And then leaning towards me and lowering her voice, said, 'You know, I am rather worried about our Mr Clinker. He's missed the last two sessions. It's not like him at all, specially as he hasn't sent a message. After you telephoned that time to say he was ill and couldn't keep his appointment for the practice I got quite anxious. In fact I did call the Palace once, but there was a very hoity-toity voice on the other end who said he was in the peak of health – his wife, I suppose!' And she giggled.

'I think he's been lying low rather . . . er, that is to say,' I added hastily, 'I think he's been pretty occupied. Synod, Lambeth and things . . .'

'Sounds awfully bleak to me. He'd do far better to come back to the Wednesday sessions. Buck him up, they would. Besides,' she added wistfully, 'we miss him, you know, things just aren't the same when he's not there. He's ever such fun when he really gets going!'

I had often witnessed the bishop 'get going', but in my experience fun was rarely the outcome. However, it is amazing how limited one's knowledge of people is . . . But then I recalled Ingaza's extraordinary revelation about his pre-episcopal days at Oxford; and indeed, nearer the present time, the spectacular dancing display on my sitting-room carpet fired by drink and absence from Gladys . . .

I smiled. 'Yes, I expect he has his moments.'

'Oh, doesn't he just!' she crowed. 'But I tell you what, why don't *you* have a word with him? Tell him his partners are pining and that we'll never win the Bracknell Cup without him!'

'Me?' I said, startled.

'Oh yes, he'd take it from you all right.'

'I rather doubt that –' I began.

'Oh yes, dear,' she exclaimed. 'If he's said it once, he's said it a dozen times: "Ah, Oughterard – a safe pair of hands there, very safe."' She intoned throatily in a voice not dissimilar to Clinker's. And giving me a playful slap on the knuckles, she added, 'Well, I wouldn't know about safe of course, but they're very nice!' I blushed to the roots while she lapsed into the usual cachinnations. And then recovering herself briefly, she added, 'No, seriously, it would be ever so helpful if you could put in a word, it's not half as nice without him.'

She looked quite pensive, and I heard myself saying that I would certainly do my best. She brightened immediately, and I think that, had I not stood up making noises about getting the animals' supper, she would have invited me to share in a third Martini.

As I reached the door she waved a voluble and lavish farewell before turning back to engage the barman in garrulous banter.

I reached home curiously invigorated; and then, with the gales of her laughter ringing in my ears, took the bull by the horns and dialled the bishop's number . . .

Instantly my buoyed spirits sank. It was Gladys. 'What do you want?' she rasped.

The combination of two whiskies and the gaiety of Annie Carruthers had rather blunted my mind to the possibility that the recipient might not be Clinker. Thus when she declared curtly that he was very busy and couldn't it wait, I was at first nonplussed as to how to answer. Clearly a covert message of encouragement from his erstwhile tiddlywinks partner could not be delivered. Something else was needed.

'Ah ... His Lordship may recall that my inaugural address to the diocese is in the offing and I was rather hoping he might be able to give me a little guidance ... There are one or two things that I just need to straighten out –'

'Oh, if that's all,' she said impatiently, 'I expect he can spare a few minutes. But kindly don't keep him long; we have my sister staying again next week and it is essential that I go over the arrangements with him.' There was a clatter followed by a silence, and then in the distance I caught the tail end of a shouted delivery, '. . . Oughterard, rambling on about some sermon. Don't let him take all night . . .'

I heard the sound of footsteps and the receiver was picked up. 'Ah, Francis,' said the familiar voice, 'glad you've phoned, dear fellow.' ('Dear fellow' – was he abstracted?) 'Now what can I do for you? Something about your address, I gather.' The tone was unusually emollient, avuncular even, and I guessed she had been giving him a hard time.

I wanted to launch straight into Mrs Carruthers but felt some tactful prelude was required. 'Er, yes actually. Sounds ridiculous, sir, but I'm a bit stuck for a theme – I mean one that would be both appropriate and topical. It seems a little feeble relying on the safe and tried, but on the other hand one doesn't want to be *too* radical! I suppose for this sort of thing it's a question of finding just the right balance, and I'm not sure that I've –'

'You're *so* right, Oughterard,' he broke in, 'all a case of fine tuning, as I used to tell my students. Fine tuning! Sensible of you to appreciate that.' The voice of confident patronage held an almost genial note, relief presumably at dealing with one more tractable than his spouse.

I told him I would be grateful for any tips. Unfortunately such deference was only too well appreciated, for the next ten minutes were taken up with a barrage of recommended topics including one which he entitled 'spiritual homicide'. I was tempted to say that I was better acquainted with the physical kind – but refrained. However, he then got on to matters sexual and declared that in view of the current lamentable lapse into sensuality doubtless a subject along those lines would fit the bill. I said I did not think so.

'In that case,' he opined, 'a good general topic on which you can put your own top spin . . . Sin and Sloth, that's the one! There's far too much bone idleness around these days – and I think somebody like you could convey that very well, and what's more . . .' And thus on he prosed, temporarily freed from Gladys and in his element. It had to stop.

'I say, sir,' I cut in brightly, 'I was talking to Mrs Carruthers the other day and she was very worried that your tiddlywinks might be getting a little rusty. Seems to think that without you the Bracknell Cup is a lost cause – quite upset she was.'

There was a long pause. And then he said *sotto voce*, 'Look here, Oughterard, to tell you the truth, since that ghastly business in Savage's shed I've rather lost my nerve. Every time I think of counters and dice all I can see are those frightful legs! It's beginning to get me down.'

I felt scant sympathy. Got him down? He wanted to try being knifed by a paranoid lunatic! However, assuming my most cajoling tone, I said, 'Ah, but that's probably what's needed – what I believe our Freudian friends call aversion therapy. Apparently when you confront what most unsettles you there's a sort of relief, and all the tension just drains away and . . .'

'Hmm,' he muttered. 'Drains away, does it?'

'Oh yes,' I said authoritatively, 'completely.'

Somewhere from the far distance there sounded a muted bellow. 'Right!' said Clinker hastily. 'Tell her I'll be in touch – soon!' And with a peremptory clearing of throat he rang off.

I returned to the study feeling vaguely pleased that by effecting a rapprochement between the bishop and Mrs C. I had made modest contribution to the cause of tiddlywinks and the securing of the Bracknell Cup. It was gratifying too to think that each would once more be enjoying the other's company and benefiting from the pleasure. For a short while I sat immersed in these rosy speculations.

And then of course I thought of Ingaza and the rosiness promptly withered. Bloody man – was he really serious about our visit to France? Foolish question, it was virtually a fait accompli! I sighed, got up and went to the bookcase. My old school atlas was on the top shelf. I took it down and searched for the Auvergne. Always as well to know where you are going, I thought gloomily.

For half an hour or so I immersed myself in the contours and place names of that mountainous region. 'Wild, volcanic, mist-ridden . . .' ran the accompanying text, 'a land of tumbling waterfalls, brooding cliffs, forested ravines and primitive legend. Indeed, rumour has it that wolves still roam its perilous crags – but such tales are unlikely to daunt the modern wayfarer . . .' Oh no? I thought grimly. Trust Nicholas to drag us into this Shangri-la!

I remembered the diary March had shown me with Elizabeth's scathing allusion to the Folie and its 'dark and sinister' setting, and my gloom deepened. One bleak thought invariably leads to another: and the lowering face of the Curé of Taupinière came into my mind. Just the companion needed for such a venture! I cursed Ingaza again and, pouring a small restorative nightcap, reflected wryly, and not for the first time, that it was something I had brought entirely upon myself . . . Yes, the Fotherington Folly was aptly named! I closed the atlas, stretched, and prepared for an early night.

I was halfway up the stairs, relishing the prospect of a long bath and a good book, when the telephone rang. At first I was tempted to ignore it but the sound persisted, and reluctantly I returned to the hall. The dog pottered out from the kitchen and watched me quizzically. 'My lord bishop presumably,' I grumbled to Bouncer, 'with more prattle on sin and sloth no doubt!'

In fact it was a woman's tone, though due to an impossibly crackling line barely audible. I strained my ears and caught dislocated phrases – 'my father', 'bone idle', 'tiny green eyes', 'several reproductions', 'pig in Poona'. I listened bemused by the words. But from what I could make out she seemed to be alleging that her parent was some indolent swine from Poona with mean green eyes and a penchant for procreation . . . Surely not! However, one of the hazards of clerical life is sudden ambush by the woolly and unhinged; and I was beginning to think that the caller was just one such, when the line became horribly clear.

'Oh yes,' continued the voice of Mrs Pindar, my recent luncheon companion at the Bishop's Palace, 'as mentioned, Daddy was very *big* in Poona and so knows quite a lot about those Indian bone idol things, and it was just wonderful to hear your expert views on the Beano replica – such an intriguing subject! A few of us are meeting after church on Sunday . . . Daddy of course, with two or three other eager beavers, and dear Claude Blenkinsop smothered in laurels from that recent magazine article! And I am rather hoping that Professor Purbright will grace us with his illustrious presence. But *such* a treat for everyone if the renowned specialist could attend as well!' She paused expectantly.

I stared at Bouncer, who vigorously wagged his tail. Then resting the receiver on the table, I lit a cigarette, expelled a perfectly formed smoke ring, and with a degree of pride followed its spiralling progress as it wafted upwards into the vacant air.

'Are you there, Canon?' the voice anxiously enquired.

'Yes,' I replied, 'but not for much longer. You see, unfortunately I shall be absent on that date. Out of the country actually . . . I may be gone for some time. In fact I am about to depart at this very moment . . . the taxi awaits!'